To a good f[riend]

Be[...] [...]ows

Hermann Kauders

Hermann Kauders

This is a work of fiction. Resemblance to actual persons, living or dead or events is entirely coincidental.
Copyright © Hermann Kauders 2015. All rights reserved.
Published by Lulu.com. UK bookshops £6.99. Amazon.co.uk. ISBN 978-1-326-19133-7
Cover images: Front cover: Riversmead, courtesy Pye's of Clitheroe. Back cover: The author.
This book is sold subject to the condition that it shall not, by way of trade or otherwise, be lent, re-sold, hired out, or otherwise circulated without the author's permission.

Author's Note

It has taken me the best part of a generation to see this to completion. How things have changed since I started writing this! I'd like to acknowledge my thanks to my family and friends who have supported me, also to express my appreciation to the Rayleigh Writing Group and others, especially Clive, who have assisted with the editing and have helped me along this long road and got me over the finishing line.

FOREWORD

The countryside of Austria and the city of Vienna were places of contrast between the Two World Wars. The rural districts were mostly peopled by peasants: conservative, Roman Catholic and traditional in outlook. Vienna was more developed, a melting pot of people and cultures from across Eastern Europe and the Middle East. The City had become one of the largest settlements in the Jewish Diaspora.

In Vienna the Social Democrats were in overall control and strove to make the City an example of socialist politics. In the mid nineteen twenties the *Gemeindebau* (Municipal Housing Block) project was developed, consisting of the construction of monolithic blocks, often housing more than 60,000 people. Most of the buildings, which are still standing today, incorporated large courtyards. Construction costs were raised from so called *"Breitner Taxes"* – a tax on luxuries. The rents were subsidized, making them affordable to workers.

From 1925 to 1939 Vienna was a city at the forefront of development and innovation in music, science, philosophy and the arts. Arnold Schoenberg was writing compositions using the twelve-tone system and establishing the Second Viennese School with students Alban Berg and Anton Webern. Sigmund Freud was developing his controversial theories and ideas in psychology. Although not a member, Oscar Kokoschka was probably the most influential artist on the German Expressionism movement.

Contrasting this, the Viennese people tended to take refuge in easy-going sentimentality between the two World Wars, often typified by the Blue Danube Waltz, café houses, kitsch and cream cakes. Austria, like the rest of Europe, was unable to foresee what was to come.

The Social Democrat Party and the Conservative Christian Social Party incorporated paramilitary units: the Social Democrat *Schutzbund*, and the Christian Social *Heimwehr*. Skirmishes between the two opposing factions and the dissolution of parliament by Chancellor Dollfuss lead to Civil War in March 1934. Members of the *Schutzbund* barricaded themselves into the Municipal Housing Blocks including the showpieces Karl Marx and Engels Hof. Chancellor Dollfuss ordered shelling of the buildings. Nazis exploited the conflict. They assassinated Dollfuss in the summer of 1934.

Many Social Democrats turned to Hitler and joined the banned Nazi Party. They were known as *Illegaler*.

The novel, drawing on the author's own experiences, explores the innocence of childhood set against the sophistication and intrigues of the adult world; people whose lives were affected and changed by the tumultuos events occurring in Vienna and Europe at the time.

Into this world comes Alexander Anzendrech, little Xandi, the third and youngest son of Brigitte and her tram conductor husband Rudolf. Xandi's early childhood was covered in *And God Created Bedbugs Too*. It is 1936, and the family are now living in a light-coloured housing block known as the Milk Block. Xandi is 11 years old and attending his first day at the First Technical Grammar School of the City of Vienna...

Robert Kauders

Characters in *And God Created Bedbugs Too*

ANZENDRECH, Alexander or Xandi. Youngest son of Brigitte and Rudolf.
ANZENDRECH, Brigitte, Frau. Wife of Rudolf, Mother of Alexander (Xandi), Pauli and Rudi.
ANZENDRECH, Pauli. Middle son of Brigitte and Rudolf.
ANZENDRECH, Rudi. Eldest son of Brigitte and Rudolf.
ANZENDRECH, Rudolph, Herr. Tram Conductor, Father of Xandi, Pauli, Rudi.

BADER, Herr. Supplier of transport for Nazi activities.
BERGMEISTER, Herr. Milk Block tenant, Socialist.
BERTI. Poldi's half-brother.
BITMANN, Frau. Martha's grandmother, tenant in Milk Block.
BITMANN, Martha. Girl living in Milk Block, Xandi's friend.
BREITWINKEL. Policeman, Sessl's deputy.
BRUNNER. Supervisor of the Municipal Milk Block laundry, Nazi.
BUDAPEST, Herr. Alias Herr Spagola.

CZARNIKOW, Frau. Tenant of Milk Block, Manni's mother.
CZARNIKOW, Manni. Bully boy living in Milk Block.

DUFFT, Frau or Mama. Richard's mother.
DUFFT, Richard, Herr. Jewish satirical journalist.

FANNI. Freiherr's fiancée.
FLEURIE, Madam or Vikki Huber. Half-Gypsy fortune teller.
FREIHERR, Antonius, Herr. Dufft's fellow Officer in First World War.
FRITZER, Lutschi. Teenage assistant in Morgenthau's shop.

GINA. Prater artiste in the shimmering green costume.

HILDEBRANDT, Heinrich, Herr. German Nazi.
HUBER, Vikki or Madam Fleurie. Half-Gypsy fortune teller.
JARABEK, Aunt Anna. Brigitte's sister.
JARABEK, Big Alexander. Youngest son of Anna and Hans Jarabek, Alexander's cousin.

JARABEK, Uncle Hans. Husband of Aunt Anna.
JARABEK, Robert. Son of Anna and Hans Jarabek, Alexander's cousin.

KRANITSCHEK, Herr. Milk Block tenant, Socialist.
KRISTOPP, Frau. Neighbour to the Anzendrech family in the Milk Block.
KRISTOPP, Herr. Neighbour to the Anzendrech family in the Milk Block, Painter, Nazi.

LISL. Balloon seller in Prater.

MARSCHALEK, Herr. Co-owner of the refreshment hut on the Danube Meadow.
MARSCHALEK, Frau. Co-owner of the refreshment hut on the Danube Meadow.
MORGENTHAU, Herr. Jewish owner of toy-come-jewellery shop.
OTTAKRINK, Herr. Alias Herr Spagola.

PETERSENGEL, Frau. Purple Pimpernel activist.
POLDI. Illegitimate daughter of Gusti.
QUELLE, Herr. Fugitive.

REIBEISEN, Herr. Jewish manager of the Danube Coke Company.
ROSA, Aunt. Brigitte's sister.
ROSENFINGER, Frau. Neighbour to the Anzendrech family in the Milk Block, Socialist.
ROSENFINGER, Herr. Neighbour to the Anzendrech family in the Milk Block, Socialist.
SESSL, Herr. Chief of Police, Brigittenau District, Vienna.
SKELETON. Policeman patrolling the Danube Meadow.
SMALIZ. Hildebrandt's mentor, Nazi.
SPAGOLA, Gusti, Frau. Common Law wife of Karl Spagola, Mother of Berti and Poldi.
SPAGOLA, Karl, Herr, also known as Ottakrink and Budapest. Father of Berti.
STEFFI. Balloon seller in Prater

VIVIAN. Smaliz's companion.

PART 1

WAHNSINN (LUNACY)

CHAPTER ONE (1936)

Stubenegke

Alexander's aunt Rosa habitually burdened the number three with misadventure. Other people showered it with good fortune. Many held the belief that besides good or bad luck, special significance spun around it.

The tradition is probably as old as the hills, or at least as old as the abacus. Or it dates from the genesis of homo sapiens, when, like in early childhood, numbers consisted of one, two, *three* and many. The notion that calamity comes marching in ranks of three, or conversely luck dances in on us in waltz time rhythm, may induce smiles in folk gifted with logic; it is however a fact that a *three*-legged support assures stability, and that Christendom is based on the concept of trinity. One event is an occurrence, two similar events are a coincidence, three or more related happenings draw the attention of science, or of fanatics.

Three weighty incidents at short intervals beset Alexander Anzendrech on school opening day in the autumn of 1936.

Alexander, his two brothers, and two hundred and forty seven pupils of male gender between the ages of eleven and eighteen, entered the building. He, for the first time, encountered the legendary Herr Pflaume standing firm as a rock, legs astride, hands clasped behind his back, facing the incoming tide of boys; unsmiling, disseminating the message that attending the First Technical Grammar School of the City of Vienna was a serious business. The sight of Herr Pflaume stopped the scramble up the staircase turning into a stampede.

Herr Pflaume, school warden, observed the progression of boys to higher grades year by year. He mentally catalogued new, anxious faces on opening day, and when diffidently approached, directed them to Alpha Premier on the third floor without waiting to hear their enquiries. Alexander followed his instructions, searched for the Greek inscription but nothing resembling it met his eyes. When he saw youngsters of his own size pushing through a door marked Class 1A, he followed, hoping he was entering the right place.

The classroom abounded with boys, a few shouting and jumping, the majority sitting quietly, awaiting doom. Three rows of seven desks filled the room. The rowdy crowd congregated at the rear. Alexander noticed that each desk held space for two pupils, and that the only one which had remained wholly vacant was situated within smiting distance from the podium. He approached a seat next to a robust youth in the middle of the middle row.

"Is this free?" he asked politely.

The accosted nodded, and Alexander, claiming his territory, saw that his neighbour possessed a large, round, ruddy face topped by short, cropped hair, and big, red ears giving extra width to his head. Alexander wondered whether he had chosen wisely.

The boy extended a large, red paw with rotund, red fingers on it, and said, "I am Herbert Stubenegke, spelt with gk. I am a Protestant according to the Lutheran Creed of Augsburg."

"I am Alexander Anzendrech, Xandi for short. I am a Protestant according to the Lutheran Creed of Augsburg." He shook his companion's hand, which felt like jiggling a bunch of *Knackwursts*, of large pork sausages. He smiled because Protestants were rare in predominantly Catholic Austria. It constituted the first in the triad of significant events.

A bell sounded, loud and shrill. It quietened even the noisy element at the rear. The tension of the unknown welded the boys into a clot of homogeneous apprehension. A man in a black gown entered and Alexander's heart sank. Professor Treibwasser, learned in the unusual combination of Mathematics and Biology, known fleetingly to Alexander through personal confrontation at the entrance examination. He was also portrayed by his older brother Rudi as a dispenser of mountains of equations, meted out to anyone caught ignorant of Pythagoras, his theorem and the proof of it, or of pages of written aphorisms like 'I may be as stupid as an Aborigine but I do not have to behave like one,' assigned to pupils guilty of more than average student nescience. He carried a bright yellow wooden ruler for whacking the knuckles of offenders against his code of conduct.

Professor Treibwasser, as he mounted the rostrum, began, "I am your Class Master. This means that I am in charge of all matters pertaining to Class Alpha Premier. It also means that any misdemeanor committed by you inside or outside school will be reported to me to be dealt with by me. Professors in general, and I in particular, do not hold with fairy tales, so there will be no purpose served by anyone concocting one. I may also tell you I am not known for shedding tears in sympathy with the pains of correction, and I believe in the motto: *mitgegangen, mitgefangen, mitgehangen,* gone with, caught with, hanged with."

Professor Treibwasser was in control. His heavy frame, and his square face in which two dimples below his eyes and in line with his chin lent it the likeness of a 5 on a dice, created the impression that any antic devised by eleven year olds, or for that matter by eighteen year olds, would founder like a caper dreamt up by tadpoles against an alligator.

Alexander's heart stayed at low ebb. He expected the circular eyes to single him out, and the thin-lipped mouth to question what he was doing here. He had stumbled over words in the oral test because the question had contained verbiage unknown to him, and Professor Treibwasser had wiggled outstretched fingers under his nose and had said, "not so my boy." Alexander had then remembered hearing brothers Rudi and Pauli using similar language when doing their homework, and he had guessed the meaning and had answered, but had thought it had been too late. He felt dubious whether he had passed the examination, and whether his eventual admission was an error.

Professor Treibwasser stepped down from the podium, and walking up and down between the benches, striking his own hand with the yellow ruler at protracted intervals, harangued, "Mathematics is an exact science. Mathematics is based on logic. You cannot argue with logic. If A is equal to B, and B is equal to C, it follows that A is equal to ...?"

He pointed his measuring stick at the Alpha Premier student nearest to him, who, having come across the designation of the unknown quantity, said, "X."

"Idiot! Anyone too slothful to think cannot count on my friendship!" He bellowed and singled out another quarry who gave the correct answer.

"You can, if you use your brain, work out mathematical theorems entirely by yourself. But you cannot establish by reason that the human body is seventy per cent water, a compound of hydrogen and oxygen in the ratio of two to one. You determine this by experiment and learn it. Colossal discoveries emerge when combining scientific observation with mathematical proof. The Teutonic explorer Darwin, using this process, demonstrated that evolution depends on natural selection, on the biology of the strong achieving supremacy over the biology of the weak. This process is still going on. Today we find that people stemming from the Aryan race are superior to all other races."

The class had hoped to detect the semblance of a smile between the square-set cheekbones. The search for humour in the professor's utterances, as the foundation of building a pupil-teacher rapport, had so far yielded no fruit. Moreover the seven Jewish boys sat up, alerted. They knew, from past experience, and through hearing news filtering through from neighbouring Germany, that non-Aryan citizenship can lead to unpleasantness.

"Eminent men of science are confirming, through measurement and analysis, that the shape of head, the colour of hair and skin, facial features, have developed in Aryans which set them above peoples of inferior cultures."

The seven Jewish boys shifted uncomfortably on their seats.

"The biology of the Aryan man ..." the professor continued relentlessly when a monstrous fart ripped through the classroom. It began as a mellow, sonorous tremble, crescendoed into a roar, and faded by breaking into pulsating mini bursts of lesser intensity. Alexander knew that the product originated from his neighbour because he felt the shared seat's vibrations. The class, after a moment of stunned disbelief, broke into uncontrolled laughter; Professor Treibwasser or no Professor Treibwasser, nothing could divert it. Even the seven Jewish boys heaved.

Alexander's face went bright red, partly from efforts to suppress his mirth whilst eying the approaching professor, partly from his knowledge of who the culprit was. Treibwasser took measured steps towards the middle of the middle row. As he came nearer evidence of the presence of H_2S became overwhelming. He looked at Anzendrech's crimson cheeks.

"Stand!" he commanded.

Anzendrech rose, expecting Herbert Stubenegke to speak up.

But his fellow Protestant According to Lutheran Creed of Augsburg did not move a muscle.

"What is your name?"

"Alexander Anzendrech."

"What have you to say for yourself?"

Alexander trembled that he would wet himself with the struggle to keep a straight face. His brain formulated the sentence, *It wasn't me, it was Stubenegke spelt with gk, sitting next to me; I know because I felt the bench quiver,* but he guessed that vociferation would induce irrepressible convulsions, especially when it came to the word *quiver*. And in any case Stubenegke himself should own up.

"Well?" thundered Professor Treibwasser.

"It wasn't ... it wasn't done on purpose. It happened because I ate a bad egg at breakfast," Alexander heard himself saying, and was surprised at his ability of fast thinking in a crisis.

"So. You ate a bad egg for breakfast." Professor Treibwasser's owl-like face betrayed no emotion. "You will report to me in the Staff Room at three pm, today. Understood?"

"Yes, sir. Please may I be excused?"

"Go."

Outside Alexander caved in. He slouched away fearing his guffaws would pierce the walls. He delayed going back until after the bell had signalled end of lessons, and he had seen Professor Treibwasser march away.

He received a hero's return. His fellow pupils crowded round him, hailed him, heaped upon him tributes of titanic proportions. They emulated sound effects, plunged into fresh outbursts of merriment. Herbert Stubenegke, totally unaware that the glory would have been his had he admitted guilt, joined in.

So ended the second event of special significance.

The third took shape soon afterwards, when the subject on the timetable spelt Religion. The mainstream received instruction in Catholic Catechism, the Jewish boys were shepherded into another classroom by a Rabbi, but no one bothered about the Protestants. Alexander and Herbert found themselves wandering along the stone floors of the high corridors. Alexander had brought pieces of coconut with him. He divided the white, nutty chunks into two equal portions, and gave one to his companion and with it indestructible friendship.

The coconut had been a present from Martha Bitmann, who, like Xandi, resided in the municipal Milk Block. The gift, in celebration of his entry to the sought-after school, had been handed over in the presence of his brothers, the occasion a source of anguish for Alexander, as he was loathe to admit that he cherished a female admirer. He liked Martha well enough, had indeed fulfilled a promise of earlier years to introduce her to the thrills of watching the shunting of goods trains from the footway of the Northwestrailway Bridge. She, in turn, liked him more than well enough, as had been confirmed when, again to Alexander's consternation, in reply to Frau Kristopp's query whether there was anything which Martha liked better than a mill'n shill'n, she had retorted: "Marrying Xandi."

Stubenegke's father owned a small stationery business, and was, in Alexander's eyes, rich. Proof of the wealth lay in his son's consistent supply of ten or twenty groschens. During subsequent Religion Hours he and Alexander explored the streets of the neighbourhood, and a ritual arose consisting in the purchase of cakes, chocolate, ice-cream, and *Wurstsemmels*, sausage filled bread rolls. And since Alexander had introduced a precedent by sharing his coconut, the flood from Stubenegke's inexhaustible well ended in both bellies.

Purple

One day, well into term, the two Protestants sneaked stealthily down the last flight of stairs. They moved softly because they harboured the feeling that if confronted by staff, they would be directed to waste their free hour in the school library, a fear originating from observation of Alexander's brother Pauli frequently bringing home half-read books on days when his time tables featured Religious Instructions. But since nobody had ever told Alexander Anzendrech and Herbert Stubenegke what to do or where to go, they contended they were breaking no rules when escaping through the entrance door. On this occasion this same door opened before they reached it, and in struggled Herr Pflaume, hobbling on one leg.

"What are you doing?" queried the school warden sternly, his formidable body blocking their way.

"We are Protestants," replied Herbert.

"According to the Lutheran Creed of Augsburg," augmented Alexander.

"We can't stay in the classroom when it's religion."

"What's your name, boy?" Pflaume looked severely at Herbert.

"Stubenegke, spelt with gk."

"To my knowledge roaming the streets is not a subject in the school's time tables. Do you contend otherwise, GK?"

"We visit the Augarten," Stubenegke replied. "We pick up thrown-away paper. We like lending a helping hand keeping things tidy."

"May we help you up the stairs?" queried Anzendrech.

"You may help me up the stairs." And muttering more to himself than to the boys, he elucidated, "Standing on a chair reaching for a bedbug, I lost my balance, jumped off and twisted my ankle." He scrutinised Alexander with fixed eyes and said, "The Rossigasse is on your way."

"Yes," said Alexander who had never heard of it.

"It's the street near the main entrance to the Augarten."

Arriving at the first floor, Herr Pflaume disengaged himself from his youthful aides, said, "Wait," dragged himself into his office and emerged a minute later holding a white, sealed envelope. "Take this to Rossigasse twenty-seven A, Staircase five, Door three. It's an important note to a parent. See that the parent, Frau Petersengel, personally receives it."

On the way to the Rossigasse Herbert held the thin envelope against the sun, and strained to discern the few words scribbled on the single scrap of paper. "I can't read it."

"Shall we steam it open?"

"There isn't time."

They handed the note to the parent, Frau Petersengel, an elegant lady endowed with slender proportions and a very smooth face. They told her Herr Pflaume had sent it.

A male voice came from a room inside called out, "What is it?"

She tore open the envelope, read the few words. "Purple," she replied and closed the door upon the boys.

Left by themselves, Herbert observed, "Miserable bitch."

"Was worth twenty groschen," Alexander nodded in agreement. "Not even a cake."

"At least we'll have Pflaume eating out of our hands."

"Purple's their password, whatever they're up to," said Alexander.

"He's screwing her. He can't do nothing to us now. He can't do nothing if he catches us."

"He's already caught us. He knows we go out on the street," said Alexander.

"I mean catching us smoking. Or eyeballing *Die Nackte Frau*."

"Where do we find a naked woman?"

"It's a magazine, Stupid."

"My brother Pauli got in a rumpus with Pflaume over a magazine."

"Your brother should have told him Frau Petersengel's feeling purple."

"Somebody in his class brought *Der Ewige Jude,* 'the Everlasting Jew' into school," explained Alexander. "You know pictures of dribbling noses and *Hakenkeuze,* Swastikas, everywhere. They were looking at it in the corridor during break. Pflaume strolls up, everybody scarpers, except my brother. Pflaume takes his name for gawping at it because it's illegal. Says he'll pass on particulars to Director Weicholz. Treibwasser appears. He shoves the paper into his pocket, sends Pflaume packing. Pauli's left standing. He hasn't a clue what's going to happen."

"Nothing. Treibwasser is a brown-shirt man, a Nazi," said Herbert.

"And Pflaume?"

"A purple-shirt man. Race you to the kiosk."

Herbert Stubenegke sped off. At the snack booth in front of the entrance to the Augarten, he bought a *Wurstsemmel* and broke it into two halves.

In time the one-directional flow of gifts pressed on receiver and donor alike, and Alexander resorted to acts of appreciation like presenting his friend with drawings of Vienna trams for which he had earned admiration in his class, or handing him algebra homework for copying. Since Stubenegke wrote into his exercise book everything Anzendrech had written into his including mistakes, and since they were sitting next to each other, Professor Treibwasser, without inquiring who copied from whom, suggested Alexander Anzendrech should put to use one hour every week in instructing Herbert Stubenegke to master examples where X=?

$$X = ?$$

Professor's Treibwasser's suggestion reached Frau Stubenegke's ear. She pledged to pay Alexander Anzendrech thirty groschen after each lesson, and the boy felt like stepping onto the first rang of the ladder to millionaire status. He strolled confidently to Stubenegke's door with the algebra book under his arm.

Confronted by an elderly woman, he said, "I've come to help GK."

The lady led him into a sombre hallway and disappeared.

A moment later the windowless chamber was illuminated by the entry of a heavenly creature emitting a radiance prone to pierce the heart of any youth exposed to it. Her enquiring look suggested unawareness of her prowess, or if conscious of it, she chose to feign innocence. She would be fifteen years of age. Alexander's eyes devoured smooth waves of glowing red hair exquisitely harmonising with a serene forehead, hazel eyes, delicately chiselled nose, inviting lips, slender neck, half concealed pair of dainty ears. She wore a light orange coloured dress which clashed against her hair, but which nestled to her young body, and revealed just a hint of a burgeoning bosom.

"You wish to see me?"

Alexander grappled with confusion on hearing the angel's voice.

He gulped, "I've come to help GK."

"I am Greti Katherine. GK are my initials. I wonder what it can be you wish to help me with?"

Alexander blushed, thinking, *she must believe I am a dimwit.* Then in faltering haste, he explained, "Herbert Stubenegke. He always says his name is spelt with gk. That's why we call him GK. At school."

"Herbert is my brother. You wish to help Herbert. Not me. That's a shame."

Alexander had no reply to her teasing other than letting his cheeks advance into a hue competing with her hair.

"Actually my name is Greti Katherine Hilde, I don't use Hilde because it stands for battle, and I like to get what I want without a fight. I rely on my good looks."

Alexander's mouth opened, stayed open, delivering no sound.

"I just told you a piece of useless information, don't you think? But I'm a collector of useless things."

"It might come in useful." Alexander felt more foolish than ever. "One day."

GK, the Angel, grasped his hand and led him into a room furnished with desk, chairs and waste paper basket, where GK, the round-faced, red-necked Herbert sat, his mother standing by his side, fingering through an exercise book.

"Best let you get on with it," said Frau Stubenegke after she had laughed at Alexander's faux pas which her daughter related, not once but twice, the second time in the presence of the elderly woman, the Granny.

The boys got on with it. Alexander stressed again and again that whatever is equal, like the two sides of an equation, stays equal if you do the same thing to both sides. To Herbert, X was not only the unknown, but remained the unknowable. They accepted the hopelessness of the situation. So it was that when the clattering of crockery penetrated through the wall from the adjoining room, signalling the pending arrival of coffee and biscuits, they buried their heads into the pages of the text book purporting to teach the ABC of the mathematician's XYZ. At other times they occupied themselves with tin soldiers, or with screws and nuts of a Meccano set, or with gloating over a pack of picture cards, which Herbert normally kept hidden in a locked casket inside a locked drawer.

A second, less venerated set of picture cards lay loosely scattered in an unlocked drawer and revealed colourful images of Karl Mai's Wild West Red Indians in full-feathered headdress. These enjoyed widespread popularity among adolescent males, and featured extensively in schoolboys' barter. Herbert's prize possession consisted of two identical cards of the Apache Chief's son, Winnetou. One day Alexander, fingering through the celebrities of America's native tribes, saw that the head of Winnetou was blackened out on one portrait, and that his moccasins on the twin picture looked as if he had pranced through a sea of tar.

"My stupid sister did this," grumbled Herbert. "She got wind of my other pictures. I told her there was nothing for *her* to see in them. She made a dive for my drawer, and spilled a bottle of ink over my Winnetou cards. They are absolutely worthless now." He threw the blemished prints into the waste paper basket.

"Hold on," cried Alexander, retrieving them.

He laid the identical cards on top of one another and cut through their middle. He selected the two unspoiled halves, lined them up and stuck adhesive tape across their backs. "There," he said. "Restored to health and vigour."

They also played with a pair of scales, survivors from a chemistry box, which had contained powders that set water fuming, but which had been quickly used up. The game consisted of guessing how many one groschen pieces would balance articles such as pencils, pens, erasers, pieces of cake, tin soldiers, a screw, a depleted roll of adhesive tape, nuts, a swastika badge, orange peels, coffee spoons, nails, keys, sweets, buttons. The boy nearest to the correct number of groschen won one groschen.

Herbert's grip on things algebraical remained at zero point in spite of Frau Stubenegke's investments. She enquired how they were getting on when she carried in the refreshments, and Herbert always replied: "Beginning to grasp it."

One afternoon sugar-sprinkled, diminutive chocolate biscuits artistically arrayed in a star pattern came in on a tray supported by delectable hands. These connected to two magnificent arms, these to enchanting shoulders, on to the angelic neck, face and glowing hair of Greti Katherine.

"You managed to get another one?" she said when her eyes fell on the salvaged Winnetou. She picked the card up and examined the handy work closely.

"Thank Anzendrech for that," snapped Herbert.

Greti Katherine turned to Alexander: "Well done. Can the great professor *help me* with a mathematical problem?"

Her deliberate emphasis of the phrase "*help me,*" which had sparked off the embarrassment at their first encounter, did not escape Alexander, and he reddened accordingly.

"If one brick weighs one kilo and half a brick, what do a brick and a half weigh?" She bent slightly forward as if to bow in deference to the intellectual challenge.

Alexander's heart pounded. He reached for one tiny chocolate biscuit, broke it in half, and found to his extreme satisfaction that by coincidence one half balanced one groschen on Herbert's chemistry scales. He would demonstrate the solution.

He cleared his throat. "Let one chocolate biscuit represent one brick, let one groschen represent one kilogram."

His eyes focused on the black pupils of the greenish-brown circles looking back at him. "I repeat: one groschen is equal to one kilogram, one biscuit is equal to one brick." He paused. When just looking into her eyes ceased to be an option, he said: "Half a biscuit is equal to half a brick. Now, as the puzzle stipulates, I place one biscuit, or two halves, on this saucer. Like so. They represent one whole brick." Ruefully he diverted his gaze to execute the task. "Now I place one groschen and half of a biscuit on the other saucer. Like so. They represent one kilogram and half a brick"

The scales balanced. Alexander returned to the hazel eyes: "One brick weighs one kilo and half a brick, as the question states. See?"

The large, ruddy head of GK Herbert nodded. The hazel eyes of the Angel stayed still.

Alexander removed half a biscuit from each saucer, leaving half a biscuit against one groschen. The scales remained balanced. "Half of a brick weighs one kilo."

Again GK Herbert signalled agreement. The hazel eyes merely observed.

Alexander added two half biscuits to one saucer, and two groschen coins to the other. The scales remained balanced. "One and a half bricks weigh three kilos."

GK Herbert struck the desk with his fist.

GK, the Angel said: "You clever dick. Thank you for your help. Are you good at other things?"

Alexander could only blush in reply, so Herbert answered for him: "He's clever at drawing trams."

"Is he?" Voiced the Angel, "he must show me." Then turning again to Alexander. "Have you got stamps?"

"Stamps?"

"Stamps. You know, the little, coloured, serrated paper squares or rectangles which people of all countries stick to the top right hand corner of their letters before pushing them into posting boxes."

Alexander's brow, heated during the demonstration, remained hot. He shook his head.

"Stamps: quite useless pieces of paper. I said I collect useless things." She walked out of the room.

"Don't mind the silly cow," said her brother. "She badgers anyone and everyone for stamps."

Herbert reached for the algebra book, pencil and paper. He flicked through the pages and tackled, first hesitatingly, then with rapidly increasing confidence, example after example. The proverbial groschen had dropped. He understood. X had ceased to be an unsolvable mystery. He danced Winnetou style ceremonials. He grasped Alexander's hands and dragged him around the chairs and desk. He placed his forefinger into his mouth, oscillated it to produce the trill of a Red Indian battle cry. He brought out his other cards from their secret hiding place, kissed the bare breasted images thereon, and handed them to Alexander to do likewise.

The bedlam drew Frau Stubenegke, the Granny and Greti Katherine back into the lecture quarters. They caught Herbert fondling one card and Alexander holding the rest. Frau Stubenegke slapped her son's cheek, and told Anzendrech to leave instantly and never to set foot in the apartment again.

As Alexander walked past the angel, he heard her delicate tongue produce *ts, ts, ts* sounds against her pristine teeth.

Herbert Stubenegke obtained a Very Good mark against Mathematics in his school reports henceforth.

" # CHAPTER TWO (1937)

A Debt of Seventeen Groschen

The Austrian Post Office, like that of most civilised countries, transported letters of given weight, irrespective of contents or gloss, from anywhere to everywhere within the country's borders, for one set stamp charge. The Vienna Tramway Authority, aspiring to a similar egalitarian principle, conveyed the populace from here to there within the city boundary, regardless of status or length of trip, for one set ticket price.

However there were difficulties. Whereas a postage stamp is franked during its travels from A to B to prevent further posting from B to C, a Vienna tram ticket could not be cancelled in the same manner without penalising passengers whose destinations could only be reached by availing themselves of more than one tramline. It became necessary to implant upon tickets intelligence as to location of boarding, direction of travel, time of day, day of week, month, year in order to prevent passengers, having reached their legitimate journey's ends, embarking on further trips. The mechanics to attain this feat led to tickets printed with a multitude of small, coded squares plus manufacturing special pliers for punching holes through the squares.

Straightforward enough as long as you were not a tram conductor. Rudolf Anzendrech, Alexander's father, was.

"Look," he said to his youngest son, "the punch rod is hollow. Peep through it and you can just see a few squares. Now line up the square you want, squeeze the pliers and make a hole. Try it."

Alexander tried.

"That's no good. Your hole cuts across a line. You got to have eagle eyes and elephant feet. The tramcars shake you like the Crazy Walk in the Prater Ghost House. And you got to use both hands when you punch, so you can't hold on anywhere, not even when the driver breaks suddenly because *Rotkäppchen*, Red Riding Hood, wants to catch the tram."

"Rotkäppchen?" Brigitte chipped in.

"Everything stops for her," explained Rudolf shifting his eyes from son to wife: "She wears a red beret over her scarlet hair. A proper Little Madam she is. Got the better of the Tramway Authority. But she didn't fool me."

"Who's she then, may I ask?" his wife wanted to know,

"And I tell you this: To know just by looking at three holes in a ticket where someone got on and when, or whether the ticket is valid or not, needs a brain bigger than a bedbug's. You go to a special school and you pass a special examination before they allow you alone on a tram."

"What happened with this Rotkäppchen? Tell me."

"Well, you see, the tramway bosses aren't as smart as they think they are. I've worked out long ago how to get a tram ticket for free. All you need to do is to find two discarded tickets, one with all the holes above a certain line, the other with all its holes below the same line. You lay the tickets on top each other, you tear both apart along that line, you throw away the holed bits, and you keep the two hole-less portions. And they match. Torn tickets are acceptable. Well, evidently Fräulein Rotkäppchen made the same discovery. She often comes on my tram, more than once she hands me two halves of a torn ticket."

"That's cheating," said Brigitte.

"I say nothing, it's not my problem if the Tramway can't figure out a better way. Until the other day. There she is and we have an inspector on board. And by devil's luck, she's been careless, she's laid the two tickets on top each other haphazardly before tearing them, and there's a discrepancy between the two halves. I didn't want to get her into trouble, after all she's only a *Spatzerl*, a wee-little sparrow, of a girl, and they make you pay a heavy fine if you're caught swindling."

"You are too soft," remonstrated Brigitte, "especially with young girls."

"I couldn't say anything to her, because the inspector's within earshot. So when I see the two halves don't match, I crumple them up and put them into my pocket, and hand her a new ticket from my block. Of course I expect her to pay for it."

"Well, didn't she?"

"She didn't have any money. She says she gave me a ticket. A passenger backs her up. The inspector hears all that and wants to see the ticket. I says it must have dropped to the floor. I couldn't very well fish out the torn halves from my pocket. I would have had to explain why I hadn't challenged the girl in the first place. My chivalry would have counted for nothing."

"Your chivalry towards a charlatan, just like you," retorted Brigitte.

"We looked for it under the seats and everywhere. Of course we didn't find it. The inspector looks grim and gives me a reprimand. I said I didn't feel too well, had a bit of a headache. The inspector asks her if she wants to lodge a complaint."

"I'd lodge a boot up her backside."

"She said she knew what it was like when you're afflicted with headaches. She said she got them frequently herself and she'd let me off this time. Cheeky little minx. But I told her, when the inspector had gone. I said to her: 'Fräulein, you can't hoodwink me. No more torn tickets in future. You didn't do a proper job on the last one. You owe me seventeen groschen.'"

Tram conducting, in spite of galling inspectors, irreverent passengers, lacerated tickets, the rigour of manipulating optical pliers on erratic foothold, and a host of irritations which Rudolf rattled off at the slightest motivation, not always to the edification of the listener, nevertheless offered one compensation: you met people, sometimes folk you hadn't seen for a while, who fell into chatting and filled you in with events that had happened to them during their absence.

"You know, Briggi," Rudolf said to his wife, "today they put me on the number 71 because half their conductors had gone down with stomach ache in consequence of a *Leberkäs,* a heated meatloaf, they ate when they celebrated Albert Dreissigblätter's retirement. Dreissigblätter's been on the trams since steam time. The 71 line's a popular route, it runs to the Municipal Cemetery, so they had to find replacements. I don't like the new line much, I've to remember to punch holes in different places. It's easy to make mistakes."

Brigitte, herself conducting trams when he had proposed in 1919, still retained sufficient grasp of the whole complexities to understand his irritation. She expected more to come and shot him an enquiring glance.

"Guess who I saw on the number 71?" He voiced in a ceremonial air.

"Gusti Spagola."

Rudolf's ego deflated. The pleasure of extended speculation ruined.

"How did you know?"

"It's not difficult," Brigitte said nonchalantly. "She visits Poldi's grave."

"But she went off to America with Frau Hannick, the singer."

"They're back on a visit before touring Holland. We must call her by her proper name, Schattzburger. She and Richard Dufft. You know."

"Know what?"

"Herr Dufft says when Hitler comes it'll be the end of Jews and anyone having an independent mind. I am worried about the boys. They want to get married."

"Rudi's seventeen, Pauli' fifteen, and Xandi's twelve!" Remonstrated Rudolf.

"So?"

"Boys don't get married in their teens! You're beside yourself."

"Gusti and Richard Dufft."

"What about them?"

"Haven't I been telling you she's here to see Richard Dufft?"

"How do you know that?"

"She told me."

"You've seen her?"

"Of course I've seen her. She knocked on our door first thing after she'd been to her fiancé. She talked of nothing else but the wedding."

"You didn't tell me that."

Brigitte assumed astonishment; since when were men interested in weddings. She said, "You don't tell me everything."

"We've known Frau Spagola twenty years."

"Schattzburger."

"We've known her when she lived next door to us before we moved here. Her child Poldi was Xandi's friend. Xandi went to eat meals with them, her kids had dinners with us. Poldi drowned and it upset us all. Gusti lived with Karl Spagola who ran off with the girl from the shop over the road. We've known Dufft for how long? He calls every week. There was always something between Gusti and

Dufft. Three years ago Gusti left for America. And you say I wouldn't be curious to hear what's going on?"

"Didn't she say what was going on? When you saw her on the tram?"

"She moaned about the strain moving from one place to another with her singing companion. From Chicago to St Louis to San Francisco to Memphis."

"You didn't tell me that."

"I was going to. Just now."

"You didn't tell me about Rotkäppchen. Until I had to drag it out of you."

"What d'you mean? You think I'm after her?" He laughed "You know my motto: happiness lies in enjoying second best."

He put his arms around her. She responded and her pouting lips gave way to a smile.

She said: "They're in this predicament because Herr Dufft looks after his ailing mother. This stops them from emigrating. Staying on means waiting for Hitler, and as he says, Hitler doesn't take kindly to Jews."

Unravelling his wife's thought processes as well as coping with the drift of international politics produced horizontal furrows on Rudolf's forehead. "On the streets I'm pestered with the nonsense of The Everlasting Jew, here at home I'm confronted with the gloom of the everlasting pessimist! You never say anything cheerful. Nothing will happen. England and France won't allow Hitler to march in." Then, as his wrinkles disappeared, he continued, "That redhead. You know what she said? She said she'll pay her debt of seventeen groschen next time she sees me, but I shall have to give her some stamps. She must be a stamp collector."

"You're going to humour her?"

"She's only a Spatzerl of a girl." He called out, "Rudi."

"What is it?" The reply came from the family bedroom into which the eldest son, also a keen philatelist, had withdrawn, actually to pursue this very hobby.

"Can you spare a few stamps?"

Alexander had been in the room with his parents, drawing a picture of a tram, and had listened to the conversation. He knew who Rotkäppchen was.

He went into the bedroom and addressed his brother: *"Rüdilein,* dear little Rudi, give me some stamps."

"What's the matter? First father, now you? What do you want stamps for?"

"I want to give them to somebody."

"Who?"

"Somebody who collects stamps."

"Well, I'm always looking out for people to swap with," said Rudi. "Has your friend got a decent collection?"

"Yes. I'm sure she has."

"She?"

"She's the sister of Herbert Stubenegke. He sits next to me in school. He calls for me every morning."

"A girl? I am not trading with a girl."

Kristopp, the Painter

The outlawed National Socialist Movement needed martyrs.

So when the illegal members of the illegal Brigittenau Branch stood rigidly to attention, right arms stretched out in the Heil Hitler salute, and gave vent to the forbidden words of the Horst Wessel song,

> *Kameraden, die, Rotfront und Reaktion erschossen*
> *Marschier'n im Geist in uns'ren Reihen mit,*
> Comrades, shot by the Red Front and Reaction,
> Are marching with us in spirit in our ranks,

Everybody, from the firmly established Herr Kristopp down to the newest recruit and one time Socialist Herr Bergmeister, both residents in the Milk Block, focussed their eyes upon the painting depicting the fallen hero Brunner. The picture showed his brawny arms lifting high the sacred swastika emblem, whilst Jewish Bolsheviks were creeping upon him from behind and firing from a multitude of gun barrels into the back of his Aryan head. At the same time the Jewish bandits peered voluptuously at the blue-eyed, golden-haired, through-and-through Teutonic features of a Nordic maiden. The picture, encircled by flowers, was Herr Kristopp's creation.

Of course Herr Kristopp knew the real history of his close associate, laundry supervisor Brunner, who had blown himself up handling letter bombs shortly prior to his planned wedding to Augustine Schattzburger. She, in turn, had been woven into the myth as the golden-haired damsel in the picture to win the hearts and minds of the compassionate masses for the Movement.

That the same Augustine Schattzburger was engaged to the Jewish journalist Richard Dufft, and was accompanying a singer of Jewish faith in the United States of America at the time of the painting's inauguration, was not touched upon.

It was a well-executed work, for Herr Kristopp was an accomplished artist. His regular paintings, like the scenes in oil of the Kahlenberg and Leopoldsberg hills as seen from the dam of the Danube Meadow near the Floridsdorf Bridge, where he set up his easel, and where tall elm trees produced a sterling foreground and the horizontal line of the Northwestrailway Bridge a subtle middle theme, found ready appeal. It induced Frau Kristopp to postulate that they were worth a mill'n shill'n although her man got only a pittance for them.

The three Anzendrech boys, themselves showing signs of artistic bent, frequently crowded round the master's outdoor work place. Herr Kristopp relished their presence. Alexander's countenance of awed adoration cajoled his ego, and he welcomed the opportunity to instil in the boys the essentials of the decade's burgeoning political ideology.

"Herr Dufft is a thoroughly nasty Jew," he ranted, "you know the other day I saw him snatch a ten schilling note from the hand of an old lady."

"Herr Dufft gives me presents," Alexander sprang to his benefactor's defence. "He gave me a telescope, an umbrella and chess men and lots of eucalyptus sweets and when I cut my finger on Manni Czarnikow's pen knife because he was fooling with it at Martha Bitmann, and my hand filled with blood, Herr Dufft cleaned it with his handkerchief and bought a big plaster from Morgenthau's shop."

Herr Kristopp graced the youngster with a smile. "The Jew is nice to children, so they become easy targets for his filthy appetite. The Jew is like a bedbug, sucking our blood, set on destruction of Aryan culture." Turning to the eldest, he went on: "The Jew exalts in decadence. You only have to look at Surrealism and Dadaism."

Rudi had been initiated to Modern Art at school. "The works of Max Ernst and George Gross ..."

"They're *Scheisse,* shit," interrupted Herr Kristopp.

"Of Picasso ..."

"He paints Scheisse."

Rudi enjoyed debate. "Picasso's works of Scheisse haven't been shown to us, so I can't comment on them. Perhaps Picasso painted shit to demonstrate the symbolic significance of the substance. All mankind produce it. The beautiful, the ugly; the rich, the poor; the strong, the weak; the kind, the ruthless; the powerful, the helpless; the Aryan, the Jew. Hitler's shitheap looks pretty much the same as Herr Dufft's."

"Looks pretty much the same, stinks pretty much the same," added Pauli.

Alexander's laughter was a joy to hear. But Herr Kristopp was not amused. Poking fun at the Great Leader had no place in the National Socialist rulebook. Here was proof of Jewish degeneration, pumped into wholesome, Germanic minds. All the Anzendrechs suffered from the malaise. Hadn't Parteigenosse Brunner always singled them out as Jew lovers? But Herr Kristopp considered himself a forbearing man. There was a long way to go. He planned to rescue the boys and prepare them for the coming of the Third Reich.

"Deeds," he said, "heroic deeds, like Herr Brunner sacrificing himself for the Führer. That's the stuff that'll make the world kneel at our feet."

In addition to painting, Herr Kristopp practised artisanship of Aryan significance. He constructed a crossbow following an ancient Rhenish design. The Danube equalled the Rhine in status, and the Danube Meadow was an ideal place to inspire the boys with the great exploits of their Valhalla Hero forefathers. They tugged along when he went to try out his formidable weapon.

The Arrow that Missed the Heart

Shooting from a distance of ten meters at a rotting timber notice board bearing the message that the pursuit of ball games on

Inundation Land was prohibited, the arrow went straight through, leaving a neat, circular hole. This stirred Rudi's inquisitive mind, and he asked, "Would the arrow go through a board made of tin?"

"Yes," answered Herr Kristopp.

"Of glass?"

"It would go straight through."

"I think the glass would shatter," said Rudi.

"Never," said Herr Kristopp.

The boys ran in search of a suitable test piece on the nearby Mistgstettn, the city's rubbish dump. They found a small window frame holding a grimy but unbroken pane in crumbling putty. Plenty of torn and frayed sacking lay about. They wrapped it around the frame to collect any glass splinters if smashed, and tied the thing to the post.

Herr Kristopp handed the taut crossbow to Rudi. "Imagine the window is a Jew."

The arrow flew past the target, and all eyes followed its flight until it disappeared into a depression. The boys set off to retrieve the missile, but were impeded by a strikingly alluring face topped by glowing scarlet hair underneath a red cap, rising from the hollow.

"Who shot this?" demanded the face, which turned out to be attached to a most enchanting body.

She carried the arrow by its feathers at arm's length, as if any nearer, the shaft might decide of its own volition to perforate her skin. She held her other hand behind her back as if nursing a sore spot. Alexander recognised the angelic figure of Greti Katherine Hilde Stubenegke. She wore the same light orange coloured dress she had on when he first saw her.

"What in the name of all the blasphemies in the underworld are you trying to do? Kill us?" She asked exquisitely.

"I missed," said Rudi.

"You *were* aiming at us?" cried the outraged girl.

"I missed the legitimate target."

Alexander felt instinctively that, if properly managed, here lay a chance of Greti Katherine and Rudi agreeing on a get-together for the purpose of stamp exchange, which meant that the Angel would come to the Anzendrech household and that he, Alexander, would cherish her nearness in his own territory.

He pointed to the notice board, "Rudi was aiming at the glass in the sack."

"Oh, the legitimate target was glass," retorted the Angel, "he was not, after all, aiming at my heart. In that case I shall confiscate the arrow for presentation to the officers at the Engerthstrasse Police Station. The notice board reads ball games are forbidden. I shall petition the law makers to impose penalties on arrow shooters as are levelled on ball kickers."

Rudi perceived himself facing interrogation by Chief Police Officer Sessl, or worse, by the mounted policeman, the Skeleton, and he rattled on, "We were conducting a scientific experiment. The investigation revolved around the reaction of an amorphous, isotropic supercooled liquid consisting of a mixture of silica, soda and lime, commonly known as glass, to high velocity impact of a pointed object. The absence of a crystalline structure should cause the glass to split into a multitude of fragments. On the other hand the high resistance between projectile and glass could give rise to sudden increase in temperature, creating plasticity along the edge of penetration, thus ending up in a hole."

"Well," said Greti Katherine," we have two professors. One who helps me with mathematical problems, the other who talks about penetration ending up in a hole! Preposterous. There is I, giving Helmut a treat in the hollow where the grass is thicker and greener, and we are bombarded by murderous missiles!"

Herr Kristopp's silence reflected his worry that as maker and owner of the weapon he could be taken to account for the transgression. He waited for an opportunity to turn defence into attack.

But Rudi carried on, "The trajectory of an arrow in flight traces a parabola and this means its course can dip into a trench. Propagation of light follows a straight line so that nothing is observed lying outside its path, for instance below the edge of a hollow. Hence this unfortunate incident, because we didn't see you."

"Now he is ranting about propagation! What next? You'll be able to out-prattle Adolf Hitler with your tongue. But it won't do. You should have made sure there were no living creatures within the range of your lethal toys. You should have looked. This arrow is going to the Police Station."

Herr Kristopp saw his chance, "What, if you please, were you doing down there?"

"Minding my own business," replied the redhead.

"We'd have seen an interesting spectacle if we had looked."

"Why?"

"You and Helmut. In your own words, 'giving Helmut a treat'."

"And that is?"

"The police and your parents might consider it as something unpalatable."

"Why?"

"Shall we ask Helmut? Where is he? Where's he hiding?"

"He's right here." Greti Katherine swung her hidden hand into sight. In her palm sat a cute, little tortoise, its tiny head on the longish neck swaying to and fro.

Pauli aimed at conciliation: "We didn't mean to hurt anybody. Is there something we can do for you?"

And Alexander, quicker as the shot over which the dispute raged, chirped in, "My brother collects stamps."

The Angel rested her hazel eyes on Alexander's. "Spoken like a true professor. Maybe something can be arranged. Maybe I shall keep the arrow that missed my heart as a souvenir."

Herr Kristopp raised his voice: "You are very lucky young woman. If this was Germany, you would be under arrest."

"Me?"

"You'll regret slandering Adolf Hitler. He doesn't prattle. Some of us have long memories."

But Greti and the boys devoted all their attention to Helmut who had waddled off her hand and dropped into the grass. He lay upside down on his shell, and in the scramble to turn him over, Rudi's and Greti's arms touched.

CHAPTER THREE (1937)

Disillusion

Alexander Anzendrech washed behind the ears, brushed his teeth twice, and asked for a clean shirt. He polished his shoes without having been prompted to do so by his mother.

This was the Sunday when Greti Katherine Hilde Stubenegke would come with her stamp album. Rudi had already commandeered the soft, wooden table in his father's bedroom, had laid out envelopes from which the Anzendrech addresses had been obliterated and titles like: Duplicates, Madagascar, China, Rare, Very Rare, had been substituted. Brigitte had bought twenty dekagrams of chocolate wafers.

The bell rang and Alexander opened the door. There she stood, wearing, as was her wont, a reddish coloured dress which clashed with the radiance of her hair. Alexander, having rehearsed his welcoming speech all morning, stood speechless.

"Is the great professor working on another mathematical problem?" she teased, "or will he come back to earth and show me in?"

"Yes." Alexander's blush added a further shade to the colour dissonance. "Yes. Rudi has got his stamps. Have you brought yours?" He cringed at the stupidity of his remark.

"I come equipped with all my accessories." Her hand held the handle of a bulging briefcase, and she tapped its shiny leather surface with an extended, superbly formed middle finger. She smiled at him, lifted her locks with a delicate thumb and nudged a strand of pure red gold over her hazel eye whilst inclining her head to one side. She took a prolonged breath which pushed out the contours of her budding chest.

Alexander realised that once the angelic creature crossed the threshold he would lose her. What could he do to delay that painful, inevitable moment? What else was there to say?

"How is Helmut?"

"He's fine. He's a great thinker, and like other great thinkers and professors, rather slow in getting to the point. He lets me stand in doorways for an eternity before asking me in."

Brigitte walked up, shoved Alexander to one side and led the visitor into the living quarters. "Rudi's waiting for you."

Alexander busied himself arranging his tram drawings into a neat pile, stationed himself near the closed door to his father's bedroom. He listened to any sounds filtering through: muffled voices, the occasional shriek of surprise, giggles.

"I think they'd like coffee and the chocolate wafers," he said to his mother.

"That's thoughtful of you, Xandi. You take them in."

Brigitte brought a tray, but Alexander chose to carry in the refreshment item by item so he could make three journeys. Barging in with the first coffee mug, he saw them bent over the table, their heads close together, their temples grazing against each other.

"There's a chip on the handle" exclaimed Rudi, "I'll have that. Make sure you bring Greti a wholesome cup."

Alexander returned with the Angel's coffee. His hand jerked as he placed it in front of her. The turbulence caused a spatter of the dark brown liquid to moisten the wooden tabletop.

"Careful!" shouted his brother. "Careful, you're swamping everything!"

It was a small spillage, away from the array of colourful stamps. Alexander shot a glance at the Angel to see whether she would come to his aid and say "no harm done", but she picked up the coffee mug and held it at arm's length, as if leaving it on the table would precipitate serious flooding. He came back with a plate of chocolate wafers and the tram pictures. Hadn't Greti Katherine said he must show them to her? Perhaps she would query what was on the papers, look at them, admire them, even ask one for keeps. Indeed she reached for a sheet.

She wiped the coffee stain with it, laid it on the table in the manner of a napkin and planted her coffee mug on top. Rudi took one likewise and treated it in similar fashion.

Alexander waited. Maybe his brother would point out the pictures.

"Well," said the big boy, "you've done *your* job. Credit earned for good intention: one hundred per cent, the execution has a lower grading. Nevertheless we thank you. Now let us get on with *our* job. Why don't you shut the door behind you, and play with your railway set."

Alexander heard the Angel's voice. "He plays with railways? How cute."

He fled down the stairs taking two steps at a time to deceive himself that the way things had turned out had *not* swallowed his high spirits. Nevertheless he reached the conclusion that girls, even endowed with flaming red hair, angelic voice, delicate fingers, exquisite ears, sweet demeanour, belonged to a species foreign to human understanding and, like an overdose of sweet syrup, led to pain. His hand clutched the remaining tramway drawings, and eying them now, found them bland.

"What you throwing away?" asked Martha Bitmann, and she fished out the pictures from the Milk Block rubbish bin. "Aren't they good! Aren't they good! You're throwing them away? Why are you throwing them away, Xandi?"

"They're awful."

"They are good. They are ever so good. Can I have them?"

Why not, if they pleased little minds.

"Manni Czarnikow jabbed me with his fishing rod," said Martha, raising her pale blue frock and displaying a reddish discolouration on her thigh.

Oh no. Was his role in life for evermore protecting Martha Bitmann from the excesses of the court yard bully? Martha pointed in the direction of the yard's Stone, the base to a monument on which the Municipality had forgotten to erect a testimonial, where Manni stood astride his bicycle. A thick, wooden stick with string wound round it, was strapped to the crossbar. Herr Kristopp was talking to him and handed him a package, which Manni pushed into his pocket.

Herr Kristopp walked off to check the progress of a tarot game on a nearby card table. Manni, spying the two youngsters near the dustbins, mounted his bicycle, accelerated towards them to brake sharply with a screech, and came to rest with the front wheel a few centimetres from Martha's tender spot on her thigh.

"Play with people your own size," scolded Alexander.

Manni said, "I am watching *your* play all right. I'm watching you don't overreach yourself playing with *her*."

"Go away. Go away fishing."

"That's what I intend to do," said Manni, snatching the tramway drawings from Martha's hand. "Aren't they cute," he sneered, "Trams. Bim, bim. Anything to please little minds."

The word *cute*, Greti Katherine's last shot, and his own appraisal of *pleasing little mind*s reverberated on Alexander's eardrums. In a spurt of ire he pushed against the bicycle, and the instability of the big boy's pose with the crossbar between his legs, caused it and him to keel over. Alexander retrieved the drawings from Manni's befuddled fingers.

"I gave you a bloody nose once," Alexander shouted, "I don't mind giving you another."

Manni scrambled to his feet. "Yeah?"

He disengaged himself from his bicycle and threatened to advance upon his challenger, when the tall, robust figure of Herr Dufft towered over them.

"Xandi," said the journalist, unaware that he had stalled a conflagration, "is your mother at home?"

"Yes."

"Good." He noticed the sketches in the boy's hand. "May I see? Did you draw them?"

Alexander nodded.

Herr Dufft examined them one by one, hailed Herr Kristopp who, having diagnosed the distribution of tarot cards as uninspiring, was returning to his studio abode. "Look. What do you make of these? What do you say of Alexander Anzendrech, the up and coming artist?"

Herr Kristopp stopped reluctantly. He would not, under normal circumstances, engage in chit-chat with a Jew, but faced with the enquiring looks of the children, he scanned through the drawings.

He spoke at last, "As an artist myself, I say young Anzendrech has talent. As an Aryan, I say he should avoid contact with Jews who'll push him into decadence. As a German-speaking citizen, I look forward to the days when the depraving influence of Jews upon aspiring artists will be abolished by law."

He thrust the sheets back into Dufft's hand, turned and vanished through the door of the staircase from which Alexander had previously emerged.

The boy looked up into Dufft's eyes, the middle aged man looked down into the child's. Empathy surged between them, a similar feeling of affinity they had shared four years earlier when sitting on a bench in the Cemetery, mourning the death of Gusti Schatzburger's child, Poldi. Herr Dufft laid a gentle hand on Alexander's head.

"Can I borrow your pictures?" He asked.

"I gave them to Martha Bitmann."

"May I select one, Martha?"

Martha nodded. Herr Dufft took his choice and left.

Manni climbed onto his bicycle and chanted: "The Anzendrechs are Jew lovers! The Anzendrechs are Jew lovers!"

"Push off!" snapped Alexander. "Ride your bike to the Danube Meadow, to the Zinkerbacherl. The lake's full of tiddlers. Just the right size for you. Rev up when you see the bank and don't brake."

Manni said to Martha, "You coming with me? I'm going to the Engels Block. You can ride on the crossbar."

Martha made no sign of acquiescence, and Alexander said: "The Engels Block? There are no ponds in the Engels Block. You won't catch nothing there, not even tiddlers."

Manni said, "There's fish there all right. And I have the bait right here." He patted the pocket into which he had stowed away Herr Kristopp's package. He hoisted himself into the saddle and sped off through the passageway into the Engerthstrasse.

"He's nuts," said Alexander. "What does he mean there's fish in the Engels Block?"

"He means Jews." Martha nudged up to her chosen peer. "He asked me to go with him before, but I never did. Are you glad I never did?"

Alexander shrugged his shoulders.

"He told me his parcels are full of worms and maggots crawling in and out of rotting *quorgel,* smelly cheese."

"He's barmy."

"He shoves the worms and maggots into envelopes and pushes them into letter boxes of Jews."

"He's mad."

"Sometimes the letters move about with the wriggling going on inside."

"He's insane."

"He does it all the while, only to Jews though. Let's go watching the shunting of goods train from the Northwest Railway Bridge."

"Can't. I've promised to see my friend Stubenegke," replied Alexander and feeling uneasy because he had given no such pledge, he added, "Another time. We'll go another time."

Favours

Herr Dufft climbed the stairs to the Anzendrech flat, where Brigitte was pleased to be able to offer him chocolate wafers with his coffee.

"Your boys are artists," he opened the conversation. "This is young Alexander's effort." He placed the picture on the table.

"He's always drawing trams," replied Brigitte.

"Herr Anzendrech may have told you: the Municipality are campaigning to boost transport, they're launching a revamped tramway coach. My newspaper's contribution is Herr Anzendrech's story *Americans on a Vienna Tram*. I reckon Alexander's drawing would make a fitting supplement. A rhyming caption like:
> Attention quick, two craftsmen:
> The father a writer, the son a draftsman,

would go down well with the readers."

Brigitte was delighted.

"The other reason I called," said Herr Dufft, picking up the thread, "is to ask a favour."

"Of course, Herr Dufft."

"You're friendly with Gusti. Frau Gusti Spagola, or rather Fräulein Schattzburger."

"Yes."

"She and Frau Hannick are off again, to Amsterdam, next week. Today the two have gone to finalise legal matters concerning her boy Bertram with the father, you know Karl Spagola. I wanted to go with them to Tulln, that's where he lives, but Gusti said Karl might create trouble seeing us together. And if he finds out we're getting married..."

"Herr Dufft, once again congratulations. I'm so happy for you. It's been coming a long time."

"We got engaged over a year ago, just before she set off on her first trip with singer Fanni Hannick. She was still in a trauma then with one tragedy after another: her partner, Spagola, disappearing before running off with that shop girl; Poldi drowning; Brunner's dreadful death; the aborted wedding; her miscarriage. Staying with Frau Hannick's doing her good. They nurture one another, Fanni having lost her daughter as well,"

"When's the happy day?"

"We were going to thrash things out tomorrow. The three of us: Gusti, Mama and me. Mama's better, she'll cope with the journey and living abroad. But I need to find a job first; otherwise they won't let us in. And now an opportunity has suddenly come up for work in London. An English newspaper consortium wants someone with knowledge of our politics and history to vet their articles on current affairs. I heard today. I've to leave early tomorrow to beat the deadline for the interview. I hope my English is good enough. I practice with your Rudolf ..."

"I thought you said America."

"Eventually. America or England or anywhere away from this seething cesspool. Hitler's primed to pounce. The Jews here have no future. Nobody here has a future. The only way out is to get out. That goes for your family too."

Brigitte sighed, "Oh Herr Dufft. Leaving the Danube Meadow, leaving the Vienna Woods, leaving everything we know and love. I know you're right. I can see it coming, the cataclysm. But we can't just pack up and wave good-bye. Where would we go? Where's the money?"

"Our problem too. But look, you sniff half a chance, grasp it. Waiting for the Nazis is no good. They don't lay down the red carpet for emigrating Jews either. They steal their last groschen. There's even space for non-Jews in Hitler's concentration camps, if they are too free with their opinions. Socialists and men like Quentin Quelle for instance."

"Quentin Quelle?"

"I met him on my travels to Berlin in 1933. A highly intelligent man, spoke English, French, Spanish. Of Mediterranean extraction I should have guessed. He was on the run then. He was heading for a safe house here in Vienna, gave me the address in case I ever have a need. The PP People he called it, because the first letters of the organisers begin with a P. Very enigmatic! Or the Purple Pimpernel. Borrowed from Dickens, the English writer, Tale of Two Cities. I'm going to one of the cities, for the London job. Gusti's in Tulln today and I won't be here tomorrow to tell her. She might be gone when I come back."

"I'll tell her."

Herr Dufft nodded. "Say to her I'll take the train to Amsterdam at the earliest and we'll arrange everything for the wedding then."

A few meters away, in Rudolf's room, Greti Katherine nodded also when Rudi asked her the favour of meeting again, for the purpose of repeating the exercise of looking at each other's...stamps.

Once More - Purple

"Know what? Let's write a note to Frau Petersengel. *I feel purple. Meet me by the Riesenrad at seven.* We'll say it's from Pflaume."

"Are you crazy? We'll get expelled," said Alexander.

"We'll give Pflaume a message from her. *I feel purple. Meet me at the Hochschaubahn, the Helter Skelter, at seven.* They'll be waiting for hours, twenty meters apart until they'll get proper purple. Maybe they'll see each other, maybe not. What a laugh!"

"Not much of a laugh for us when we face Treibwasser."

"I'm only kidding," said Herbert Stubenegke. "Anyway, Pflaume can't make it to the Riesenrad. He's twisted his ankle again. Like last year, remember?"

"He walks around with his head in purple clouds. He can't see where he's going."

A few days later, the limping Herr Pflaume intercepted the two on their way to the street. "You visiting the Augarten?" he queried.

"We might," replied Alexander.

"Will you take another message to Frau Petersengel in the Rossigasse?"

The two boys grinned as they took possession of the note. Outside, Alexander fingered the envelope. "We can eke out the love epistle," he cried. "Look, it's only been stuck down half way along."

Herbert opened his penknife and lifting the envelope flap, he inserted the thin blade and titillated the paper inside until a corner of it appeared. He gripped it between his fingers. The boy's eyes hung on the script in capital letters:

QU ORGEL 1210.10

They looked at each other. Certainly not a love epistle. Could it be something with ... *quargel*, the cheese?

"They're trading in purple quargel, or as we say *quorgel,* the flat, round smelly cheese," Herbert ventured a guess as he pushed the note back and sealed the envelope properly. "When it matures, it goes purple and pongs like the Floridsdorf Sewer. One thousand two hundred and ten shillings ten groschen worth of purple quorgel."

Frau Petersengel was not alone. Next to her stood a man, tanned as if coming from southern sunshine, wearing a nondescript suit underneath a chequered cap. She opened the envelope, read the note and handed it to him. He looked at it, removed his cap, kissed her on the cheek and said "That's it then."

The boys were struck by his baldness.

"Good luck," said Frau Petersengel.

"Shall we tell Pflaume he's got a rival?" asked Alexander when he and his friend jaunted towards the entrance to the Augarten.

"That man? Could be a *quorgel* merchant from Greece. They eat weird things down south. Like they do in China. Caterpillars, and eggs which they bury in the earth for months."

"He's got to wear a cap all the while because the globe on his neck dazzles you like a searchlight."

Naked on the Pier

Around that time, in the autumn of 1937, the First Technical Grammar School of the City of Vienna succumbed to an outbreak of gastro-enteritis. Professor Treibwasser blustered that the illness drifted over from the bent noses of the *quorgel*-smelling Jews living in the neighbouring Leopoldstadt.

"You know that's odd," said Rudi to his family, "Treibwasser spouts about the curvature of noses. He lectures us on the importance of proof when it comes to the congruency of triangles dating from ancient Greece, but he completely ignores evidence on matters touching the geometry of noses, dating from Modern Germany."

"Do purple *quorgels* come from Greece?" asked his brother, Alexander.

"Do pink icicles come from Spain?" replied Rudi insinuating that a stupid question warrants a stupid rejoinder. He added: "More likely red-hot bullets. Hickendorff in my class says he'll sign up with the International Brigade. He adores the Communists. He thinks he'll do them a favour if he gets killed. It's enough to make anyone fall ill and spew up yesterday's dinner."

"Civil War." Brigitte sighed. "It'll come to us. Herr Dufft's doing the right thing, getting out."

The epidemic in the school spread. Director Hofrat Weicholz fell victim, not to vomiting, but to headaches when battling with the task of operating the regular timetables whilst a quarter of professors pressed hot water bottles upon their abdomens in the privacy of their beds. In the reshuffle he allocated Double Religious Studies to Class 2A.

"We've got two hours," Herbert Stubenegke chirped at his fellow Protestant. "Have you ever climbed a Northrailway Bridge pier?"

"Yes."

"Let's go to the Danube Meadow and climb a pier. We can lie on the ledge there in the sun."

"I don't mind climbing up a pier, but it isn't very comfortable lying on it." Alexander knew from experience this was so.

The portion of the piers facing the Danube current were shaped like horizontal Gothic arches for streamline effect. About one metre above flood level the structures changed to flat fronts, but instead of level ledges, the designers had provided spherical domes. You could sit on such a round surface for a short period until the opposing curvatures of hard granite and soft anatomy gave rise to unbearable pressure. Shifting to an adjacent spot proved of no avail, as the shape of the stone remained the same wherever you sat. You could lie on your belly a little longer. Reclining on your back might have been sound practice for achieving the Reverse Arch in Physical Training, but otherwise related to an exercise unworthy of commendation.

"We can take our pants off. We can sunbathe without our pants on."

"What for?" asked Alexander.

"No one can see us up there."

"With the stone digging into our arses? No thanks."

"Go on. Do us a favour. It'll be fun."

Alexander could see no pleasure in the proposition. His groin had already absorbed a life time's dose of ultra-violet radiation when an infant on his mother's knitted blanket; also recurrences of his naked pursuit of fire engines at the age of three occupied his dreams several nights a year.

"I'd rather go swimming in the Zinkerbacherl," he said.

"You off your mind? It's freezing in October."

"The Danube is, Zinkerbacherl's not. Had the summer sun on it."

"I haven't brought my swimming trunks."

"Don't need them," said Alexander, "we can swim without."

"And have somebody steal our clothes! We'd be in a right fix then. Let's climb the pier."

"All right. But I won't take my pants off."

"Go on."

"No."

"You'd take them off if we went swimming."

"That's different."

Stubenegke sulked. "You're supposed to be my friend. I always give you things: chocolate, and ice cream, fig clusters and Wurstsemmels. You never do nothing for me."

"I helped you with algebra."

"You got paid for that."

They walked on in silence, and Alexander experienced the unease of obligation. Herbert had not yet spent his thirty groschen and Alexander wondered what would happen when he did. Would he divide the Semmels as always? It would be an unthinkable blot on their friendship if he didn't.

"Two minutes then."

"Two minutes what? "asked Herbert, knowing full well the meaning, but wanting to hear it.

"I'll take my pants off for two minutes. But you buy two Semmels with *quorgels* in them."

It seemed a fair compromise. "All right. A good idea. We'll have a picnic sunbathing on the piers. And nobody'll come near us because of the stink. Have you got a floozy?"

Herbert's sister, Angel GK Rotkäppchen sprang immediately into Alexander's mind.

"One who lets you," Herbert added.

Alexander conjured up the more realistic Martha Bittman, remembering when he had gone to pick lilac blossoms in the Allerheiligen Park for Mother's Day, Martha had been there too. Hidden in the bushes she had pulled her knickers down for him to see and grabbed his shorts and hung on them, but he had run off with his lilacs.

"I've got a girl," Herbert drew himself up big pushing two freshly bought *quorgelsemmels* onto his chest, "and I tell you she's got them. Here." He indicated his semmels. "Maria. I see her when I go out with Frederika."

"You go out with two girls?"

"Frederika's the name of my boat. I see Maria when I go rowing. Her udders are phenomenal."

The image of Greti Katherine's deft little roundnesses loomed up. Martha's chest was still flat. Alexander mentally shrugged his shoulders and wondered about the wisdom of the pending exercise for the sake of an aromatic cheese roll.

The ledge of the Northrailway Bridge pier could accommodate the length of one boy lying on the crest of the stony bend. To fit in two boys meant moving off the centre circle onto the side slopes, where anchorage of one elbow and one heel was necessary to prevent rolling off. A more uncomfortable, painful pose could not be imagined. But chubby Herbert Stubenegke said it approached perfection. He put his free arm under his head and shot discreet glances across to see whether his friend noticed the crop of newly sprouting hair on his groin. Alexander struggled to stack his shoes and socks in such a way that neither they nor he would drop into the smelly ditch between the pier and the meadow, where winds had deposited all manner of rubbish, and dogs and children their excrement.

"Your socks smell foul," observed Herbert.

"We're getting a noseful of the *quorgels*," replied Alexander.

"We'll tuck into them as soon as you got your pants off."

"All right, all right."

Just then they heard a train coming, and Alexander decided to wait for its passing, lest his unclothed body would be visible from the windows of the coaches. Herbert lunged for his tee shirt. Fifty metres off, the engine suddenly emitted a blast of steam from its belly. The jet impinged on the girders, turned into a dense white mass swooping from under the bridge. It sped towards the boys with the speed of a rocket.

"Jump!" yelled Alexander.

He rolled over in the grass. Where was Herbert? He saw pink flesh in the shape of toes above ground level; the rest of his friend was hidden from view. He crept to the ditch and looked down into it.

"GK. Are you alive?"

Herbert's bare thighs twitched in response.

"Watch out, someone's coming! Put something on. Do something with the shirt."

Herbert retrieved the singlet which had escaped from his grasp on impact. He scrambled to a kneeling position and surveyed the approaching couple. He pulled the tee shirt apart, stepped into it with one foot, then with the other. He dragged the thing up by its short sleeves, until the neck opening reached his navel. Made decent by this improbable, tight fitting skirt, he awaited the arrival of ... the bald-headed *quorgel* merchant, accompanied by a smartly dressed woman.

"What are you up to?" The lady spoke to Alexander who, still clad in his shorts, appeared more likely to retort with an intelligent reply.

"Nothing."

"We saw you. You were committing gross indecency."

"We were sunbathing."

"Why aren't you at school?"

"The class is taking Religion."

"Are you Jews?"

"We're Protestants."

"What an awful smell." The woman flared her nostrils towards the spot where the boys' picnic, split wide open, lay in the grass. "Which school do you go to?"

"The Wesergasse Gymnasium."

It was a lie, but Alexander felt relieved that GK had told it.

"Oh yes. I know the director."

"Director Hinterzweig," said Herbert Stubenegke.

"What are your names?"

"Willberg. Manfred Willberg and his name is Fritz Wassermann."

The woman took from her oversize handbag a pencil and a sheet of crimson paper and scribbled on it. Alexander marvelled at his friend's quick inventive brain.

"Where are your clothes?" She continued with the interrogation.

"Up there."

"Well now. Suppose I take you, as you are, to Herr Director Hinterzweig?"

The boys trembled at the thought.

"Have you been painting the slogans on the piers?"

They looked at swastikas and also at a rhyming scrawl in large, red letters:

FREIDENKER UND CHRISTEN
KÄMPFEN GEGEN FASCHISTEN
FÜR FREIHEIT UND BROT
IN SPANIEN'S GRÖSSTER NOT

Freethinkers and Christians
Fight against Fascists
For freedom and bread
In Spain's greatest troubles

"You know it's illegal to dab outlawed graffiti on walls?" asked the woman.

"We've done none of that."

"Well now. I suspect your sort wouldn't consider doing something illegal to be let off. Would you?" The woman extracted a fistful of the crimson sheets from her bag. "Red stands for Socialism, the brotherhood of men. Next week, when your class meditates on godly works, instead of committing gross indecency, you scatter these fliers about the corridors of your school. Failing that, I shall inform Director Hinterzweig of what took place here. He's a good friend of mine."

Stubenegke reached for the handbills and asked, "What if we get caught?"

"Don't get caught."

All this time the *quorgel* merchant had stood still, not speaking a word. Now he turned as a voice from the nearby riverbank rang out: "Come on, Qu Qu."

"Go, Quentin," said the woman. "Au revoir."

The man hurried towards the Danube. The woman watched for a moment before walking to the stairs of the bridge. Herbert climbed the pier to retrieve the rest of the clothes. Alexander followed the man after he had disappeared down the embankment.

Coming back he said to Stubenegke, "He got into a boat."

"Here's your shoes and socks."

Alexander sat down to put on his footwear. "The name on the boat was *Orgel*, you know like an organ in church."

"So? All boats have names. Mine's called Frederika. I told you."

"That message on Pflaume's note. His name is Quentin. Begins with Qu. QU and Orgel make Qu orgel. And the number one two one nothing one nothing."

"You remember the number?"

"I remember their colours. It's easy that way."

"What colours?"

"The colours of the numbers. Don't your numbers and letters have colours?"

"No."

"Mine have," said Alexander.

Neither of the boys being acquainted with the phenomenon of synesthesia, spoke any more of it, and Alexander continued, "It's today's date and time. What's the time now?"

"Ten?"

"He's on the run. He's doing a bunk. Over the border to Budapest. He's a fugitive. What's on the leaflet?"

Herbert handed him one. Alexander read the same slogan as was scrawled on the pier.

"What's all that about? "asked Herbert.

"Civil war in Spain." Alexander explained. "My brother told me Communists go there to fight. And die. Old Grecko's going bang-bang in Spain."

"We'll have Pflaume licking our arses when we tell him what we know."

"Don't be a buffoon. Not a whisper to no one. Chancellor Schuschnigg's twisting the necks of Communists, or anybody seen with them, just like the Nazis."

"I've seen Treibwasser wearing the Nazi brown shirt."

"He gets away with it. Same as Herr Kristopp on our staircase. Always on about Jews. Scheessig's the strongest in our class, don't we laugh when he tells us what goes on in his synagogue."

"I'm stronger than Scheessig," said Herbert. "I can lick him."

Alexander crumpled the leaflet into a ball: "Best we dump them."

Herbert shook his head, "We'll have to do as the woman said."

"What for? We don't go to the Wesergasse."

"Willberg and Wassermann do. They're my cousins."

"You idiot. Couldn't you think up other names?"

"What should I've said: Stubenegke and Anzendrech? She'll find out if we don't do her bidding. Director Hinterzweig's her friend."

"She won't do nothing."

"She wrote their names down on a leaflet," argued Stubenegke.

"She did that to frighten us. She's a Communist. She'd be committing suicide if she talks."

"I'll do it on my own if you're scared."

"How come you knew Hinterzweig's running the Wesergasse dump?"

"Greti Katherine goes there as well. She's playing *Völkerball* in the Augarten this afternoon. The entire gaggle of gardeners will be trimming the grass on the edge of the field, gawping at her. Beyond me what they see in the silly goat."

Alexander calculated, mentally, if he sprinted to the Augarten after lessons, he could be in time before the last whistle blew to terminate the ball game in which one side scores when an opposing player is hit by a ball having failed to move aside or catch it.

Courtship

It was a chilly November afternoon, but neither Rudi Anzendrech nor Greti Katherine Hilde Stubenegke felt cold sitting on a bench in an unfrequented alleyway of the Augarten.

"Do you like me?" asked Greti.

"Yes." Rudi squeezed the hand which nestled in his.

"Because I have a good stamp collection?"

"For that and other reasons."

"For other reasons as well? You like me because I have glowing red hair?"

"Yes."

"Because I have delicate skin?"

"Yes."

"Because I have captivating ears?"

"Yes."

"Because I have bewitching lips, enchanting eyes and a sweet nose?"

"Yes. But should not I be saying all this?"

"If you did you would be like all my other admirers."

Rudi let go of her hand: "You have other admirers?"

"Dozens and dozens."

"Who for instance?"

"For instance all the male students in the Wesergasse Gymnasium, and all the professors in the Wesergasse Gymnasium, including Director Hinterzweig, and your little brother."

"I can handle my little brother."

"I can handle the Wesergasse Gymnasium." She searched for his hand, and finding it, squeezed it in turn. "But you are different. You don't warble the tunes everybody else twitters. So I am curious to hear why *you* like me."

Rudi looked into her hazel eyes and smiled. "Our learned Professor Treibwasser would analyse it thus. the human body is made up of water and an assortment of substances in various degrees of combination. And this mix, its proportion and its distribution, is the key to a person's behaviour, likes and dislikes, strength and weakness. Over time, he says, those blessed with a strong mixture overpower those encumbered with a weak. This gives rise to races, and produces heroic Aryans versus heinous Jews. Treibwasser is our teacher in biology. He's a nasty fool. The reason why I like you? Because I am I, and you are you. The fact that you are stunningly beautiful, and that everyone else says so, is no deterrent."

She snuggled up closer. She asked, "Would you like me if I was ugly?"

"The point is: you are not ugly. If you were fat, if you were half a meter high, if you smelled of quargels, you would not be you. The fact is you are beautiful. So beautiful that, I reckon, it drives many of your admirers in the Wesergasse Gymnasium away for fear of losing out to ruthless rivals. It scares me to bits, but I can't do anything about it other than scratch your face to make it ugly. But that I will not do, rather I will scratch the face of any villain who sets out to harm you."

She leant her fresh cheek against his. "How you talk. And I thought I was a master at putting words together. But tell me: would you like me if I was Jewish?"

"Again borrowing from Professor Treibwasser's analysis: the human body consists of a lot of water plus a conglomeration of substances. This applies to all human bodies. To test the truth of this, peer at any Jew and you will see two legs, two arms, ten fingers, two eyes, a nose, a mouth, etcetera. You cannot tell just by looking whether the Jew undergoing study is good or bad, no more than if another person under examination believes in Christianity, Islam, Judaism or comes from Burgenland. Herr Dufft is a Jew and has been a friend of our family ever since I remember. He's never done us any hurt, in fact he has been rather kind to us. To quote the latest of his good deeds: he selected a humorous story my father wrote, and a picture of a tram my young brother drew, and presented them to his newspaper for publication. As a result, not only has our household become richer by twelve copies of the Neues Wiener Journal, our wealth has increased by one hundred and thirty shillings."

"You haven't answered my question."

"I like you, because, right now, I want to sit here beside you until the end of time, because you are you, because you have glowing red hair, delicate skin, captivating ears, bewitching lips, enchanting eyes and sweet nose, plus a fine stamp collection. I like you irrespective whether you were born of parents from Timbuktu, Shanghai, Palestine or Burgenland."

"I like you too, irrespective whether you are a philologist or philatelist or toxophilite. I too, right now, want to sit here beside you until the end of time." She brushed her middle finger against his nose. "Would you like me if I was a National Socialist?"

"Yes. Because it would make me sit here beside you, for a lifetime if necessary, explaining to you why you should not be so persuaded."

"If I was a Communist?"

"Yes. Because it would make you sit here beside me, for a lifetime if necessary, explaining to me why I should be so persuaded."

She laughed. She opened her little embroidered purse and brought forth a red object, which, when unfolded turned into a piece of crimson paper. "Our school was strewn with them." She handed the leaflet to Rudi. "Promise you won't join the International Brigade."

"My heart's not in Spain, my heart's right here next to yours on this bench."

"Director Hinterzweig had us all assembled in the hall. He asked who'd brought them in. Of course nobody owned up. We think Hinterzweig did it himself. He's a bit of a red himself. He waved the leaflet about like this, so we could all see it."

"Be careful with it," Rudi clutched her arm and steadied it. "If Schuschnigg's men see us with it, they'll transport us, against all our planning for the end of time, from this bench in the open air to one confined within narrow walls."

"As long as we'll be sitting on the same bench. But the politicians won't allow that, will they? And I'll never become a doctor."

"You'll be studying medicine?"

"Since all of mankind strive to heap their altruism upon me, I aim to reciprocate in kind. Is your future career based on such charity?"

"I'll be going to the Technical High School to study Chemistry. I aim to discover a substance which shall save humanity. Imagine an ointment curing a far-gone megalomaniac imbued with idiocy like Hitler. Charitable?"

"You be careful. He has spies here in Austria. With long memories. I hink of that man on the Danube Meadow with the bow and arrows."

"Herr Kristopp? Lives on our staircase. He's a painter, a Nazi and a nincompoop. What have you done with the arrow?" asked Rudi.

"The one that missed my heart? I keep it under my pillow."

"When we go, if we ever go, we'll walk through the rose garden. There may still be blossoms on show for picking."

"For me?"

"A token of my feelings for you. Push them under your pillow also. You'll be lying on a bed of roses all the time through the trials of your studies."

"Me: a quack for a person's headache. You: the curer of the world's headache. Sounds like a busy time for both of us. Sounds like this bench won't be occupied until the end of time."

"In that case, because we can't make hay as the sun's not shining, let's make ..." he hesitated.

"Love?"

He bent over to kiss her lips.

She placed her palm on his thigh.

He brushed his hand lightly over her tiny protrusions.

She pushed his wrist away. "We mustn't."

"Why? Because we're too young?" he asked.

"Because the professor's watching us."

"Who?"

"Your little brother."

Rudi jumped up, his head circled round like a spinning top. "Come here," he shouted. "You're asking for the biggest thrashing of your life."

Alexander stopped in his trek. "I'm only going for a walk."

"You're spying on us. Since when have you taken to walking on your own? Where's your friend?"

"GK's got the stomach humps."

"That's right," confirmed the Angel, "Herbert's gone down with the bug. Come and sit with us, professor."

Alexander complied speedily, and Rudi submitted to the vagrancy of fate.

"Are you two getting married?" asked Alexander.

He asked with pangs of jealousy, but also in the hope they would reply in the affirmative. He knew that there was no chance for him winning the heart of his Angel, so he aimed to keep her in the family. And, having absorbed much of his father's philosophy, he conceded that lifelong contentment springs from the ability to make do with second best if best lay beyond your grasp.

CHAPTER FOUR (1938)

Calm before the Storm

Brigitte ran her fingers over the shirt, which, having split across Rudi's ribs and later failed to close across Pauli's neck, now exhibited thin patches below Alexander's elbows. She cut off the buttons and placed them in husband Rudolf's spent tobacco tin. Then she shaped the material into squares to service the family's noses during future colds. Richard Dufft's eyes rested on the boys who pretended to do homework but hung on every word of the conversation.

"He already knows English better than I," observed Rudolf.

"Londoners will think I'm from America," responded Herr Dufft. "You said yourself, you're teaching me how they speak in New York."

"You're definitely leaving us?" queried Brigitte.

"Imagine to be standing on Westminster Bridge, London, and reciting: *Erde kann nichts schön'res zeigen,* Earth has not anything to show more fair. Wordsworth, an English poet."

"So it's all fixed."

"My cousin's taking the furniture. But Mama drives me round the bend: Pack it, leave it, pack it, leave it. I'm starting my new job in April. Frau Hannick has engagements in Holland and she's taken Gusti with her. It's not far from Amsterdam to London. You'll be there too, won't you? All of you, in July. Don't worry about the cost. We'll see to the expenses of my very-own-wee marriage."

An urge to perform a medley of somersaults of excitement flooded the three boys.

Brigitte said: "Herr Dufft. Thank you. It would be wonderful. But we can't accept you paying for us."

"Of course you can. This is what you do: You get a visa for attending a wedding in London. After it's over, simply don't return here. Whatever the consequences, you stay in England. Chancellor Schuschnigg won't hold out much longer."

"Against Hitler?" sighed Brigitte.

A vision of glowing red hair, lost for good, triggered a plummeting of the euphoria in Rudi and in Alexander. But their father's optimism rekindled the ecstasy.

"Herr Dufft," he said, "you and Briggi are incorrigible prophets of doom. Vienna folk aren't like the Germans. Hitler won't get away with it here. Things aren't so bad. I've had good news today. News that'll enable us to pay our own expenses. You know the fuss they're making about the revised tram car?"

"Rudolf's story and Xandi's picture in the newspaper," boasted Brigitte.

"Briggi knows about the inauguration already," Rudolf continued addressing Dufft and his boys. "They brought out this super tramway coach: quieter, more comfortable. They chose the end of line 39 as the launching pad. That's Sievering. Why they selected Sievering on the edge of the Vienna Woods remains a mystery, unless they wanted to promote the tourist trade at the same time."

"In the depth of winter," commented Brigitte. "It's to show how the all enclosed car keeps the cold out."

"Piles of snow everywhere. Now terminus 39 isn't a loop. The incoming tram which consists of the motor coach pulling one bye-coach has to perform a manoeuvre. The driver stops the tram, the conductor in the motor-coach uncouples the bye-coach, the motor-coach moves forward onto a single track, reverses over points onto a second track so it goes past the bye-coach, reverses again over points and stops at the other end of the bye-coach. The same conductor couples them together and the tram's ready for the return journey. Sounds a bit complicated, but you can work it blindfolded if you've done it a thousand times."

"It's simple," disputed Alexander.

"They posted me to the 39 line on launching day of the new coach. This swapping about happens a lot in winter when conductors go down with influenza. I was put on the bye-coach, Walter Nasenroth's on duty on the motor coach. He does the uncoupling and coupling. Now the tramway people spent a lot of time and effort on this ceremony. A high dignitary from the Municipality plus our deputy manager are the honoured guests. Head Office books a four piece brass band to play *Tales from the Vienna Woods* to coincide with the send-off. They park the new bye-coach right towards the rear on the single track. The programme goes like this: await the arrival of the bigwigs in their official automobile, get them seated in the new wagon, and the first tram that comes along pulls the show piece with the luminaries to the other terminus on the *Schottenring*.

There a reception committee greets them with another band."

"Two bands? And they can't equip us with chemistry books," said Rudi.

"It's our luck. Nasenroth and me trundle up just after the high and mighty have been escorted to their brand new window seats. Nasenroth does the necessary, after the manoeuvre he couples the exhibition coach to the normal bye-coach. The motor coach and my bye-coach fill brimful with passengers wanting to share the thrill of the celebration journey. The driver releases the brakes, turns his hefty brass crank, the band strikes up, the throng of onlookers cheer and wave. And? Nothing happens. Nothing happens to my bye-coach and the new one hooked on behind. I see the motor coach move off, but we stay put. I see the gap between it and us getting bigger. The crowd jeer and yell; the band plays on, comes to the end of the opening bit, and, I guess, having only brought notes for the first few bars, start all over again."

"Kept their circulation going, in the cold," said Brigitte.

"I do some quick thinking. Nasenroth, day after day, uncouples *one* coach and joins up *one*. It's in his blood: one uncoupling, one joining up. But this time there were two bye-coaches, and he forgets to connect us to the motor coach, which, at that precise moment, gathers speed. I hold my satchel in front of my belly and race after it. I hear the crowd clapping. I reach for the handrail, haul myself up and face people packed like sardines. I see Nasenroth white as a sheet. He's caught up on events, thinks he'll get the sack or be demoted to maintenance, oiling the points. We fight our way to the front to put the driver wise. *He* turns as white as a sheet. He does an emergency stop, everybody falls forward but that's only by the way. He disconnects his vast brass crank, wants to push with it through the crowd, but I tell him it's quicker to do that journey on the road. Well, he gets to the other end of his motor-coach, connects his crank, and he looks straight into four foaming, equine nostrils attached to Pinzgauer horses attached to a cart stacked high with ten metre long tree logs."

"The street's very narrow just before the terminus," explained Alexander.

"And the heaps of snow. The road's only wide enough for one vehicle. Traffic has to give way to trams. But on this occasion the tree cart has followed the tram from behind. They confront each other like a tank versus cavalry, and they shoot abuse at each other. The driver screams, 'Shift your confounded menagerie to the knacker's yard,' he clangs his bell like a crazy town crier. The coachman struggles to steady the frightened animals and hollers back, 'You blithering idiot. You got to traipse your electrified perambulator to the Schottenring before you begin your return trip. Can't you savvy horses aren't equipped with reversing gears?'"

"I'd give two nights' sleep to have seen that," chuckled Brigitte.

"So the tram driver runs back again with his brass crank, proceeds forward until the road widens to let the cart through and sets about in earnest to capture the abandoned wagons. All of this of course takes time. So I had a brain wave. I hurry back to the coach of splendour. The band, for the umpteenth time plays 'ta-taa-ta-taa-ta-ta-ta-taa.' Inside I see the two celebrities smiling and waving to the crowd. They think all this ballyhoo is orchestrated for their benefit."

"A week's sleep to have been there."

"I walk up to them and produce the *Neues Wiener Journal*. I've been carrying it with me to show off Xandi's drawing and my tram tale to regulars. I ask the two gentlemen to browse through the story and look at the picture. They think this too is part of the inauguration programme. The Council man reads first, laughs and hands the page to his fellow sufferer. Then we get into conversation, they find out that I've written the story, and Xandi's drawn the picture. They're full of this and that. In the meantime the motor-coach returns and Nasenroth joins us up, the two celebrities none the wiser. And with a final 'ta-taa-ta-taa-ta-ta-ta-taa' we move off."

Richard Dufft said: "You write down that story. In English. You give it to me and your other manuscripts. I'll do something with them in England. The English have a sense of humour not unlike ours, I'm told."

"And I've made another friend. Nasenroth said he'll be my pal for life. He said he'd save me from hell fire and worse."

"Is that the good news?"

"Guess what comes next." Rudolf's lips lengthened into a smirk of anticipation.

"You found a ten schilling note," said Alexander.

"No."

"We won the lottery," came from Pauli.

"No."

"They're going to print my Bread poem in the *Neues Wiener Journal*," observed Rudi.

"Your pal for life offered to buy you a goulash with a beer," was Brigitte's contribution.

"Listen: Today they called me into the office at the depot, and they asked me would I want to become an inspector."

The three boys shrieked with delight. Next time, at school, when they were required to state trade or profession of father, they would do so with the self-assurance of the offspring of teacher, doctor, solicitor or official *Beamter*.

"I declined."

"You declined!"

"Briggi, I couldn't do it. The job means informing on my fellow tramway men when they make mistakes. Inspectors do it all the time. That's the reason for their existence. The keen ones set traps for conductors. I couldn't do that."

Brigitte's chin muscles tensed, but she understood. The boys were less beholden to their parent's rectitude.

"Cheer up, that's not the end, I told them I wouldn't be an inspector, but I'd like to become a driver."

"A driver!" exclaimed Alexander.

"Do drivers get a higher wage?"

"Yes, Briggi. Not as much as an Inspector, but more than a conductor. They asked me how old I was. I said 'forty nine.' - 'Rather old,' they said, 'we don't train men over fifty for drivers.' So I told them I wouldn't be fifty until October, and I insisted I was quick at learning, which is true."

"Can I stand next to you when you drive?" asked Alexander with gleaming eyes.

"So they put their heads together, and after a little while they said: 'Head Office commends you. Sievering and all that. All right, Anzendrech, driver you shall be. Our next training school starts on the eleventh of March."

"We're aiming to catch the train for England on the first of April," said Herr Dufft. "Remember, our wedding in London is in July."

***

"Happy birthday, Xandi."

The boy spun round. Martha stood at the bottom of the staircase, her arms stretched out, her palms supporting a box of coloured crayons. "I've brought you a present."

"Thanks."

"Will you draw a picture of me?"

Alexander shrugged his shoulders. "If you like."

"I'll be nice to you. Ever so nice. And I'll sit very still when you do the drawing. What other presents did you get?"

"My friend Stubenegke bought me a box of coloured crayons, my father and mother gave me a drawing set with compasses, drawing board and set squares, Rudi gave me a box of coloured crayons, Pauli presented me with a pencil and pen set, Herr Dufft gave me oil paints, my Uncle Hans and Aunt Anna came round with a box of coloured crayons."

"That's what you get when you become a famous drawer," said Martha.

The 18th of March

At seven o'clock in the morning, March eleventh 1938 Rudolf Anzendrech, a little nervous, left the Milk Block to start training as a tram driver.

At ten o'clock in the morning, March eighteenth, the drone of aeroplanes hung over the city. Leaflets fluttered in the air like large, grey snowflakes. They carried the message: *National Socialist Germany Greets National Socialist Austria.* Alexander collected the leaflets as the reverse sides offered drawing space for his coloured crayons. The schools locked their doors.

Several windows displayed red flags with white circles around black swastikas. A man came up, raised his arm, said, "Heil Hitler."

Alexander said nothing.

"Don't you know the German salute, my boy? Here, run along and shove a leaflet into everybody's letterbox. Or are you a Jew?"

Alexander took the offered handbills and hurried away. He looked back, the man wasn't following. He burrowed below kitchen rubbish in a dustbin to lay the wad of papers to rest. He quickly put distance between this burial place and himself and aimed for the All Saints Park. Outside the church, men with swastika armbands opened boxes, taking out red flags with white circles surrounding black swastikas. An arm-banded man handed him four flags instructing him to hang them from his family's windows. Alexander walked into the Engerthstrasse and saw that it had been transformed into a sea of red, white circles and black swastikas.

Frau Rosenfinger, the neighbour, came over to see whether the Anzendrechs were flaunting flags. Brigitte asked whether she was. Frau Rosenfinger said 'no'. Rudi and Pauli hurried into the street and scanned the houses for other barren windows to boost morale. They saw men with swastika armbands conducting a similar survey. A little while later someone knocked hard on the Anzendrech door. Herr Kristopp, wearing a swastika armband, wanted admission.

"Frau Anzendrech," he said, "I see no flags in your windows."

Brigitte asked: "Is that the new law?"

"I'm sending Frau Kristopp down with flags." He slammed his heels together, his arm shot out as if to swat a fly in mid-air. "Heil Hitler!"

Frau Kristopp, complete with flags, bounced in, bursting with excitement: "What d'you know, Frau Anzendrech, he's an *Illegaler*. My man's an Illegal. I never knew he joined the Party in secret. Schuschnigg was sending the Illegals to prison. There's nigh a milli'n Illegals altogether, and there is a milli'n oxen waiting to cross the border at Passau, only it don't exist no more, the border don't. Them oxen are to go to the slaughter houses. We'll have meat to eat, and the rivers will flow with milk and honey. Hitler has been sent to us from" - her eyes cast at the ceiling indicated the direction - "and the Jews will pay for everything from now on."

Rudolf came home at one o'clock in the afternoon. A bitter taste stuck in his throat. A self-conscious grin hung below his nose.

"Briggi, what are we going to do?"

The news that Herr Anzendrech got the sack because he was Jewish-born, rocketed through the Milk Block. It created a sizable ripple in the overall turbulence. Herr Kristopp added the name Anzendrech to his list. Frau Kristopp chose to believe that the family suffered from an incurable disease, and whilst they could be pitied like lepers, they must also be shunned like lepers, for it wouldn't be worth a milli'n schilli'n to catch the malady. Frau Bitmann shut her toothless gums so that her wrinkled mouth pouted into a snout and she chewed away without parting her lips. Herr Junge, the invalided war veteran, explained to nobody but himself, that Frau Bitmann's jaw motions meant to convey, that all things said and done, all things chewed and swallowed, ended up pretty much the same way. Three Milk Block housewives, who regularly visited the All Saints Church on Sundays for Holy Mass, landed in a dilemma. If they could not condemn Lord Jesus for having been a born Jew, how could they condemn Herr Anzendrech for a similar happening? The rumour that the Führer was The Second Coming Of Pure Aryan Descent had not been officially endorsed by the Holy Father, and they sought to avoid the inconsistency by avoiding the Anzendrechs.

Frau Czarnikow, quite casually after the usual good morning greeting, asked Brigitte when she expected her husband to be shipped to Dachau concentration camp to rot.

Herr Bergmeister, the staunch Social Democrat who had been imprisoned during the short-lived civil war in the winter of 1934, appeared in brown SA uniform. Herr Posidl condemned loudly the continuation of Jew-dominated families polluting municipal housing. As an illegal pre-Anschluss Party member he claimed tenancy of the Anzendrech abode on behalf of one Gerta Posidl, his niece, who had been evicted from the neighbouring Cocoa Block some years earlier for non-payment of rent.

The rest of the Milk and Cocoa Block tenants went through the days raising their arms, yelling Heil Hitler at each other, looking forward to the things to be, and dismissing such trivialities as the predicament of long-standing community members like the Anzendrechs and the Duffts. Shouting abuse at them quashed any doubts.

And there was Frau Bauer, a thin, insignificant looking person whom the Anzendrechs hardly knew. She waylaid Brigitte. Brigitte steeled herself for the insult. But no venom came. Frau Bauer queried whether Alexander would like to join the Bauer's dinner table on Sunday.

Uncle Hans was a brave man. The sudden, all-or-nothing Nazi politics presented no choice, for nothing was a no-go alternative. Uncle Hans knew it, yet he desisted from flag waving, slogan shouting and street parading. Alexander heard him muttering strictures at the mushrooming columns of close-ranked Hitler Youth, when criticism had become safe only whispered to yourself within the locked walls of a lavatory. Aunt Rosa, to whom Rudolf's born Jewishness came as a surprise like the discovery of an uncle's preference for men, reversed the flow of flour, sugar and milk now that Brigitte's need was greater than hers. Aunt Anna sought to reassure her sister with oft-repeated utterances that the bark is fiercer than the bite, that things can't get any worse. She meant well, but Brigitte knew that the long-expected, fearful time had come. She knew, that from now on, it would be up to her whether the house stood or fell, and she prayed that she had built it upon a rock. Alexander flinched at the prospect of Angel Greti Katherine's eyes falling on his half-Aryan self. He studied Rudi, wondered how he will cope.

Manni Czarnikow interpreted his mother's decree to have nothing to do with the Anzendrech boys as an incentive to pull Alexander down into street puddles, or come at him on his bicycle at speed and quake with glee watching the half-Jew-boy jump to one side. This did not bother the young Anzendrech unduly, as he had not expected differently. Then there was Martha. Not the Angel but Martha who had spent her life chasing after him, who had presented him with coloured crayons four weeks earlier, for whom, when they were younger, he had saved sugar fish until they had become encrusted with pocket debris, who had watched with him the shunting of goods wagons from the Northwestrailway Bridge, who had sought his protection against Manni's onslaughts, who had kissed him on his mouth, who had schemed for mutual inspection of their respective anatomies; when he came face to face with Martha, standing beside Manni, she turned away. The honey-coloured freckles with a hint of forget-me-not blue at their centre, turned away.

The schools reopened. GK called for Alexander. He said "Heil Hitler" and grinned. Alexander said "hello" and grinned also, and walked beside his friend in silence, whilst the latter spoke of the great parade along the *Ringstrasse*, people screaming and the Führer himself standing in the open car, his arm bent in salute, not stretched out like ordinary people's, but like this - and GK demonstrated bringing his hand level to his shoulder - his eyes gleaming with awe at being able to salute in this fashion.

Alexander heard himself say: "I'm not pure Aryan."

Herbert Stubenegke stopped talking for a second. He picked up the word again and continued with his story as if he had not heard, or Alexander had not spoken, or - heart pounding - as if it did not matter. At the Mortara Market stalls GK bought two fig clusters and gave Alexander one.

Alexander faced the ordeal over and over again in the classroom. Each new lesson began with *Heil Hitler*, followed immediately by the professor identifying the Jews, whereafter it fell upon Alexander to confess his impurity. He was the only one with this half-and-half affliction. The seven Jewish students, although far worse off, were of a group; they supported one another, held together by a common bond. Uncertainty did not harry the Jews, they were out of it. But Alexander went through agonies of doubt at every new confrontation: how would the other person react? And whatever followed, whether the pains of disillusionment as when Martha turned away, or the pains of exaltation as when Stubenegke sealed his friendship with a fig cluster, Alexander crumbled in his loneliness.

This loneliness tutored enhanced perception. Professor Weicholz, aristocratically titled *Hofrath,* who had been Director of the school for the last twelve years and at the same time an ardent supporter of Schuschnigg's Austrian Fatherland, was and remained absent. No one questioned the reason, and no one, neither professors nor boys, ever referred to his present absence or his past presence. Herr Pflaume befell a similar fate.

Alexander also puzzled at the volume of messages that could be put into the Heil Hitler salute. The committed Nazis, like the new Director Professor Treibwasser, *Illegaler,* or like the freshly imported German professors, trained abundantly in head-bumps methodology, but less so in Geography, Physics or Latin, offered exact, heel-clicking Heil Hitlers, and demanded equally exact responses. But what of sharp-nosed Professor Heini's delivery, which went into the lesson without a break, and sounded like this: "HeilHitlerweshallbediscussinggthepronounstoday"?

Or what of Professor Schwartz saying it to the blackboard? Alexander wondered whether he pulled faces. And once, when standing close to Professor Kohlman who taught Physics, he distinctly heard him say *"Drei Liter,"* which resonated like "Heil Hitler," but meant three litres.

The hunch-backed Professor Jakubez, a wizard with Bunsen burners and titration tubes, treated it like gummy elastic, so that it came out like "Heeeeeeiiiiiil Hiiiiiitleeeeer." This went on for days, until the class, by prearrangement, replied with a similarly elongated rejoinder. It was one of the rare occasions when the Chemistry Professor indulged in a chuckle. The fanatics, who had dissociated themselves from participating in the blasphemy, reported Jakubez' amusement to Director Treibwasser, and shortly afterwards Professor Jakubez taught at the German High School for Boys no more.

Professor Osterbin set it to music. Alexander could not establish whether the composition signified super devotion to the National Socialist cause, or represented a masterpiece of satire. Professor Osterbin did it with such straightness of face, such minute attention to melody, rhythm and counterpoint. Whatever the motive, the hitherto unruly noise during harmony lessons diminished appreciably after its first performance by the school choir.

And why did Professor Reitlinger, Physical Training, scribble a *Very Good* in Alexander's school report? His Heil Hitlers were quite normal, but common knowledge asserted that Reitlinger restricted his *Very Goods* to pupils who could manage the Forward Roll on the horizontal bar. The nearest Alexander had ever come to achieving one was hitting blue bruises on his shins.

His halfway position placed him in the focal point of attention. Professors inwardly opposed to the regime demonstrated their feelings by showering him with favouritism. A few Nazi Professors, who wanted to show magnanimity, handled him with exaggerated propriety. The Jewish boys did not receive such treatment; they were ignored by the humane professors and treated like dirt by the political ones. When Professor Heibel, Illegal, whose illegality dated from three days before the Nazi take-over, and who nevertheless made a lot of song and dance about it, accidentally brushed his hand against the curly-headed Khan, he brought in a bowl of water, carbolic soap and scrubbing brush, and performed at his desk until the demonstration became a thorough bore.

The Jewish boy Scheessig, star of the class in the old days because of his unbeaten record at wrestling, recognised Alexander's isolation. He approached him and said, "Hey, come over to our group. We have such fun, in the back row."

Alexander, sorely tempted to acquiesce, clung to the instinct of self-preservation and resisted the impulse. The very same day, the skinny Planeta, offspring of an Illegal, kicked the hard-inflated football from half a metre's distance into Scheessig's face, willfully and maliciously, so that Scheessig's eyes watered profusely. Scheessig could have thrashed Planeta to pulp, but the Jewish boy knew that the instant he laid a finger on his Nazi class mate, Planeta's waiting cronies would howl and fall on him to teach the Hebrew swine a lesson for touching an Aryan. Scheessig looked through his blurred vision for a sign of support but met empty eyes. Professor Reitlinger thought it prudent to stage an exit.

When Scheessig stepped aside with hanging head, Alexander knew he did so not because he feared a beating, but because his old admirers had deserted him. You can stand up to draconian law as applied to all, or you can operate in jungle law as applied to nobody, and your spirit will not break. But what was this? Alexander understood that Scheessig's loneliness was greater than his.

The following day swastika-armbanded men escorted the Jewish group from the school. Teaching could proceed in an atmosphere not fouled by Jewish lungs.

Planeta asked Professor Reitlinger: "The half-Jew Anzendrech, isn't he going as well?"

Reitlinger replied: "No. The half-Aryan Anzendrech stays with us."

$2 + 2 = 5$

Posters pasted to walls, houses, factories, fences, wrapped round telegraph poles, stuck to billboards on roofs of trams, posters depicting heads with crooked noses dribbling snot, enriched the splendour of the city.

The posters promised *nazionale Erhebung*, national uplift, through visiting *Der Ewige Jude,* The Everlasting Jew Exhibition inside the defunct Northwestrailway Station, a short distance from the renamed German High School for Boys. Herbert Stubenegke said it would be fun looking at it during the next non-Catholic freedom hour.

"You go on your own," said Alexander.

"Come on, what you're scared of?"

"I'm not scared."

"You're paranoid. You're afraid to see a bit of truth."

"Looking at pictures of men who forgot their handkerchiefs to blow their noses on? What's so entertaining about that?"

"I bet you twenty groschen you won't come because you're scared."

"Give me twenty groschen then," replied Alexander defiantly.

Inside, soaring from floor to ceiling, gruesome paintings in gory colours, in which brilliant reds, labelled Aryan blood, gushed from Jew-inflicted Aryan wounds, and muddy purple oozed from dirt-infested sores of Jews.

"Look!" exclaimed Stubenegke, reading a caption: "Fat Jews Stuffing Themselves with Tender Chicken Meat, Whilst Starving Aryan Children Look on."

He walked to the next exhibit. "Jews Assaulting and Robbing A Poor Widow."

And yet again, "Jews In Fine Silk Counting Gold Coins Whilst German People Seek Shelter in an Urinal."

Mature men and women, by all accounts reasonably well educated, passed from picture to picture, making comments in outraged tones at the Jewish atrocities.

"Drawings and paintings," Alexander whispered to his friend. "They're not even photographs. I can draw a three-legged man. Does that mean a three-legged man exists in the real?"

"I know," replied Stubenegke, not bothering to lower his voice, so that people looked their way. "But the Jews do these things anyway. Don't you believe the Jews do these things?"

Alexander shook his head.

"The Führer says they do these things."

"If the Führer says two and two make five, does that mean two and two make five in the real?"

"Don't you believe nothing? You'll be sent to the camps if you never believe nothing."

CHAPTER FIVE (1939)

Hildebrandt Resurfaced

Sturmbannführer Hildebrandt reposed in a leather chair in his old office at 1B, Franz Joseph Kay.

Destiny had prevailed. Men assembled everywhere ready for the march in a straight line through burning debris towards the white-robed Teutonic damsels of his visionary hallucination. His scarred cheek glowed with grandiose nostalgia when reminiscing of the struggle in the Brigittenau district during the early years, when men like *Parteigenosse* Brunner, mistakenly taken for a renegade, sacrificed his life for the Movement, and when seemingly staunch party members like Smaliz turned traitors. He saluted the course of fate which steered unshakable men like himself to devote his entire life to the Great German Aryan Cause.

He was collaborating with Parteigenosse Kristopp in Jew-cleansing Brigittenau's municipal housing. He had the full support of the local police, including Police Chief Halbkrank, formerly known by the politically illiterate masses as the Skeleton, of the Engerthstrasse Police Station in the heart of the Brigittenau. His wider brief was to mould the city's school system into line with National Socialist doctrine

Two years earlier Hildebrandt had married a blonde, Teutonic, Düsseldorf *Parteigenossin* who had presented him with a blonde, Teutonic, future Party member. Frau Hildebrandt was busily refurbishing a five-bedroom suite overlooking the Augarten, recently the home of a family of a Jewish *Obergerichtsrat,* a high official in bygone Austria's judiciary.

The move from one city on the Rhein to another on the Danube successfully accomplished, allowed him time to pursue private matters. The years prior to his flight to Germany in 1933 rose before his eyes. Vikki. Where was she? He walked, for sentimental reasons, along the familiar Meldemannstrasse where he had first met her, and to the Prater spot where her fortune-telling booth had stood. He had promised her certification of pure Aryanship. As an officer of the German SS, he will keep his word, obtain Hitler's endorsement and elevate her to the status of his mistress. She'll bear him a son. For the

Führer.

He had searched for her before and had found her. He will search for her again and find her. He told himself history, like destiny, repeats itself, and first call on the road to her whereabouts was the tram conductor Anzendrech. He pictured the boy, Alexander Anzendrech, the Valhalla Hero he had heard of in 1929, now a strapping young National Socialist clad in the white-shirt of the Hitler Youth.

Hildebrandt learned that providence did not always follow the philosophy enshrined in Hitler's book *Mein Kampf*. When asking for an update of Alexander's family through *Parteigenosse* Kristopp, his scar showed signs of rupture when told that Rudolf Anzendrech was a born Jew, Frau Brigitte Anzendrech Aryan, and the boy, the Valhalla Hero? A Mischling, a half-Aryan, a half-Jew.

Hildebrandt prided himself to be reasonable and pragmatic considering the intended rendition of the half-Gipsy Vikki to Aryan status. He thought long and hard what to do about the Mischling. Like a stroke of Destiny, a vast idea burst into his brain - the brain of the Great Researcher for the Great Good of the Great Cause! He will extract Alexander Anzendrech from the Jewish grip. He will afford to the boy, who was born under a benign star, the full largesse of the National Socialist Regime as meted out to pure Aryan youths. If Alexander Anzendrech makes good, it will be a case of the exception that proves the rule, and an application to the Führer for granting the boy *Deutschblütigkeitserklärung*, German-blood-certification, can then be initiated. If he turns out a dud, then he, Hildebrandt, will have proof for all the world to see: as you cannot make gold from detritus, you cannot produce an upstanding German Aryan citizen-soldier from a squalid Jew source.

Broken Bricks

Brigitte organised contingency plans should the worst come to the worst, should an eviction order with immediate effect, arrive. Rudolf and Xandi were to stay at Aunt Anna's; she herself and Pauli at Aunt Rosa's; the Evangelical Protestant Church of the Lutheran Creed of Augsburg undertook to find a roof for Rudi, and gave Brigitte, after the interview, two loaves of bread and a cabbage.

The fight for survival was on. Whatever lay in store for herself and her husband, her three boys had to be got to safety. There was no time now for sentimentality and pessimism.

In addition to appealing to the church of their documented faith - their birth certificates said so: Religion: Protestant According to the Lutheran Creed of Augsburg - Brigitte argued, pleaded, cried, waited, at the Swedish Mission, the Delegation of the Society of Friends, the Representatives of the Methodist Church of the United Kingdoms, the Refugee Children's Movement, the Christian Council for Refugees, the Red Cross, the Peruvian and Uruguayan Embassies, the Immigration Departments of Canada, Australia and the United States of America.

To be classified a born Jew was no encouragement for excursions in broad daylight on SA and SS Men littered streets. She kept Rudolf indoors. And he, obsessed with guilt, could not even be entrusted with simple housework and cooking. For years she had used newspapers to protect the shiny white oilcloth, which in turn had preserved the surface of the kitchen table. On the first day she had left him in charge, the oilcloth received a stain and a cut. And what was so difficult about placing the larger soup saucepan on top of the smaller kale saucepan? The arrangement had never collapsed on her.

Come dusk Rudolf slipped into his boots, the soles of which had been reinforced with glued-on oval shapes cut from discarded Mistgstettn rubber tyres long before commercial stick-on soles became available. He said he needed exercise and waited for darkness to avoid meeting a brand-new Hitler Youth or SA Man, with whom, in their human form, he had played a friendly game of chess a few months earlier. This stroll took place night after night. The family worried because he declined company. One night Alexander followed him, and caught up with him on the deserted, dimly lit Commercial Quay.

"What are you doing out here alone, Xandi?" he scolded.

"Oh, nothing. Just wanted to see whether the Danube Meadow's under flood."

"In January?"

Alexander saw broken bricks embedded in lumps of cement, the whole nestling in a cradle of string, the ends of the string wrapped round his father's wrist.

"Are the bricks from the derelict building site?" he asked.

His father nodded. "I walk up and down in the dark where there's no people, so nobody sees me carrying bricks. If they saw me they'd think I'm crazy."

"Are they heavy?"

"Yes. I've picked big ones. I'm not crazy. You see, the tram conductors who are Jews, or like me were Jews before they changed religion, have all been dismissed. I've changed religion for one reason: Do unto others as you would want others do unto you. That's what Christ taught. But the Nazis don't buy that. They've come for the Jews, they've put them to hard work. Walter Nasenroth couldn't take it, he's already dead. They haven't come for me yet because of Mother, because Mother is Aryan. But they will. Don't cry. I want to be ready when they come. I want to be prepared for the hard work. That's why I am carrying bricks. I take them into my hands and roll them about and drop them from one palm into the other. The skin on my fingers is getting really tough."

Broken Glass

The dreaded Eviction Order lies on the kitchen table. They all read it, once, twice, three times. Alexander has heard the phrase 'the end of an era', now he knows what it means.

A crash reverberates in the room. They rush to the window. Below, fragments of the glass door into Morgenthau's toy-cum-jewellry's shop glisten on the pavement. Hitler Youths in white shirts stand around. Several manhandle Dufft, forcing him to lift up a chair, driving him bodily against Morgenthau's window pane. Dufft shields his face behind the seat. The pane withstands the onslaught twice, at the third time it caves in. Dufft, chair, and a shower of shattered glass fall on top of clay marbles, pencils, paint boxes, whirligigs, peashooters, and a bowl of sugar fish.

A Hitler Youth dips a brush into a bucket of tar, smears a face with a bent nose on Morgenthau's other window. He takes pains to paint round droplets dripping from the bent nose. Then the boys fall into close rank, and to the rhythmic beat of pomp, pomp, pomp-ti-pomp, they strut off and sing: *'Wir wollen weiter marschieren wenn alles in Scherben zerbricht,* we shall be marching on when everything breaks into debris.' The street lies in silence. Heads hang from windows, none speaks. Then a lone voice: "Disgraceful."

Further words are quickly stifled, as the window from which the utterance came, slams shut. In quick succession heads disappear and windows close.

Herr Dufft, dazed but miraculously unscathed, sits up and extracts himself from the chaos. Brigitte, who has held her hands pressed against her mouth whilst watching, hurries into the street. She leads him back into the Anzendrech dwelling. Frau Rosenfinger brings a mug of cocoa. The liquid gushes down Herr Dufft's throat in intermittent, noisy gulps.

"The glass went with the chair ahead of me. That's why none fell on me." He sounds as if he owes an apology for his blood-free exterior. He makes an effort to rise. Brigitte holds him down.

"I have to go," he says, "I'll get you into trouble."

"Nonsense, stay a while," says Brigitte.

"They think he is God. If a photographer could catch Hitler, sitting on the lavatory pan, picking his nose, that picture would save the world."

"Hush," says Brigitte, "walls have ears."

"I'm past caring. I must go. If they find me here, they'll take you away too."

Frau Rosenfinger leaves the room, whispers that the staircase is empty, walks back to her own abode.

Brigitte says to Dufft: "You've had a shock. Rest a little."

"I'm a dead man. They want a slow kill. Goodness knows what's become of Mama."

He sits quietly for a while. Alexander sees he wants to talk, talking would bring him relief.

The Hounding

"I wanted to go to a prayer meeting. God knows why, I am a non-believer." Dufft paused for some time before resuming: "Defiance? Pride? Stupidity? I walk to the Volkert Place. The square's full of people. SA Men chasing old men from the Synagogue. They beat them, knock them to the ground. They cut off their beards. They drive them back in, they make them bring out their prayer books. They force them to pour gasoline over the books, they give them matches and order them to set fire to the books. Then they command the old men to sing and dance around the burning books, to urinate on them. People laughed and clapped."

Herr Dufft drained the last drops of cocoa.

"Why? If they haven't got any humanity, they have brains. Where is the logic of it? Grunblatt tips me off, they're after me. They want a show trial of a Jewish saboteur. They've chosen me. Explosives. I'm supposed to harbour explosives. They're concocting the fable that I've planted the bomb on Brunner, you know the laundry supervisor of years ago, the bomb which killed him. That's what Grunblatt tells me."

"This is absurd," murmured Brigitte.

"If we'd planned to go a month earlier Mama and I would be safe in England."

"They won't let you leave?"

"Gusti got away in time. Perhaps there *is* a God of mercy. For her. Grunblatt is the crime reporter; he and I have worked together for twelve years. He types out an assignment note for Brno, Czechoslovakia. For me. Something about child molesting in a girls' high school, needs a woman's touch. So I can take Mama along. I still got my press card and it says nothing about my Jewish molecules. They stamp our papers. We arrive at the border. SS Men, soldiers and border police with rifles and fixed bayonets everywhere. We sit and wait. A train from the Czech side pulls up alongside us. We sit and wait. Mama's nerves spill over into mine. So I go to the toilet, wash my face to cool down. I come back, and there they are. A policeman inside the compartment, an SS Man in the corridor. I want to squeeze past him, but he puts his hand up and orders me to go back to my own compartment. I am just on telling him that this is my compartment, when the policeman sticks his head through the door and ..."

Dufft raised the empty cocoa mug to his lips.

"... and he says: 'Dufft'. The SS Man consults a list and says: 'Yes, Richard Dufft.' - 'This one's a woman, Rebekka Dufft', replies the policeman. He scribbles something in his notebook, asks Mama: 'Are you travelling alone?' And Mama, looking straight into my eyes, knowing that I'm on their list, says: 'Yes, I'm travelling alone'. So what do I do? Do I stay there to be arrested?"

Again Herr Dufft lifted the empty cocoa mug to his mouth. A shiver ran through his body as he put it back on the table.

"I sit myself down in a vacant compartment and do some quick thinking: if they arrest me, they'll arrest Mama. If somehow I could give them the slip, they might leave Mama alone, even let her through. I stuff the contents of my briefcase into my pockets, and with it gaping wide open, I run down the carriage and hail the passport men: 'I must go back to Vienna. I've left my papers behind. I'm a journalist.' I flash my press card past their noses. If they look closely, if they ask my name, the game's up. 'There's the Vienna express', says the SS Man. He leads me off the carriage, beckons a soldier and tells him to conduct me to the Vienna train. I choose a window seat looking out at Mama. Then I pray to God that her train would move off before mine, so I know she's safe. I pray, not for the earth to open to devour the Nazi gangs, not for a thunderbolt to strike them to everlasting heel clicking, but just that the passport control on the Vienna train takes a few minutes longer than the passport control on the Brno train. Not much to ask. Any run of the mill Divinity could arrange that. But no. We move off first."

Dufft lifted the empty cocoa cup yet once more off the table. Alexander noticed it, no one else did, not even Herr Dufft himself.

"Back in Vienna, what do I do? I meet the next two trains from the border. No Mama. I telephone the paper's permanent man in Prague. He's a Nazi, he's no help. I go to see Grunblatt. Somebody else is sitting behind his desk. Grunblatt's been taken away. Gestapo. The men in the newspaper office stare at me as if I'm poison. I fear they'll detain me, so I rush out. I think of Quentin Quelle, I met him in Berlin. Five years ago. They were after him then. He knew of a hiding place here in Vienna. Rossigasse. I can't remember the number. I dash up and down the Rossigasse, near the Augarten, for a sign or something. But they don't write on front doors: 'This Is A Safe House For Framed Saboteurs', do they? I go back to the flat. Perhaps Mama has returned, perhaps she'll telephone. I walk right into their hands."

"Stay here with us, Herr Dufft."

The hunted man managed a smile. "You're off your heads. If they find me here, your heads *will* be off. I go back to the flat. There they are, carrying away the files, the manuscripts, the books, the silver, the ornaments, the clock, the radio. SA Men throwing our bedding, our clothes, our cooking utensils, our furniture into Mama's bedroom. Then comes Herr Kristopp. 'Where's Frau Dufft?' he asks and grins. This tells me they've got her. He hands me an address in the Leopoldstadt and says I have one day to remove the pile from Mama's room. The new place is a hovel. I get hold of a wagon, can't get everything on it in one go. Second time round, Kristopp shows up again. He scatters the remaining chairs and table onto the street. He says he's looking for explosives. Boys run off with the cushions, others break the lamp. Kristopp plays cat and mouse. He says he won't arrest me yet but I must be available for interrogation. Any attempt to leave Vienna means dispatch to Dachau. They want this show trial, you see. They want to plant something. Then the Hitler Youths come marching past. Kristopp has his little joke: he hands me over, on loan. What happened next, you know."

Herr Dufft turned the cocoa mug round and round. "Explosives. I wish I had explosives so I could blow the entire gang, jackboots and all, into a heap of pure Aryan raw flesh."

Brigitte's voice trembled; "Herr Dufft, if they hear you say that."

He raised his eyes: "Forget the God of Mercy. I have been waiting for a religion that hasn't been invented yet. Well, I've invented one. It is run by a God of Revenge!"

He went to the window. The Anzendrechs followed him. They saw a chair placed against the wall. Herr Morgenthau, a broom in his hand, eyes closed, sitting on it. A mountain of shattered glass mixed with merchandise had been swept into the gutter.

"Perhaps he'd care for a game of chess," said Herr Dufft sardonically.

A loud knocking.

"They're here. I shouldn't have stayed."

Brigitte pushed him into the lavatory, then opened the door.

Alexander's Synesthesia

"Heil Hitler! Are you Frau Anzendrech?"

"You know me, Manni," answered Brigitte.

"Our orders are to deliver this letter personally to Frau

Anzendrech." Hitler Youth Manni Czarnikow extracted the envelope from his leather wallet attached to his leather shoulder strap. "Are you Frau Anzendrech?"

"Answer!" snapped Hitler Youth Otto Bergmeister.

"Yes. I am Frau Anzendrech."

"Here." The boy pressed the letter into Brigitte's hand, and clicked his heels. "Heil Hitler!"

Brigitte looked at the stiff white envelope, a single swastika decorating its centre.

"Haven't you learnt how to salute?" shouted Hitler Youth Manni Czarnikow.

Brigitte stared at the swastika in the centre of the white envelope.

"I said we want to hear you say the German salute." Hitler Youth Manni Czarnikow jerked her elbow into the air. "Quick, quick! Arm up! Heil Hitler!"

Brigitte closed the door. Four fists thumped on it. She opened it again.

"You are insulting the uniforms of the Third Reich." Hitler Youth Otto Bergmeister tried to put depth into his voice. "Our orders are to hear you say the German salute. You are Aryan, although an Aryan whore living with a Jew."

Brigitte looked over the boys' heads at Herr Rosenfinger who had come out, alerted by the racket. He nodded slowly and persuasively.

"Heil Hitler," said Brigitte.

The receding footsteps of the Hitler Youths echoed in the stone staircase. Herr Dufft emerged from the toilet. Brigitte read the note taken from the envelope.

"I have to attend the Engerthstrasse Reich Rehabilitation Centre tomorrow."

"They'll give you a new place," said Herr Dufft, "like they did in my case." He sighed. Alexander noticed a faint trembling of his right hand. "I'll fight them to the bitter end. One can only die once."

"Herr Dufft!"

"I'll stack every piece of furniture behind the rotting door to my new palace. *I'll* pour gasoline on it and set the pile, them and me, on fire if they break through."

"Herr Dufft!"

"What else can I do? I predicted all this, didn't get out in time, didn't take Herr Quelle seriously enough to retain the address of his safe house. Do I let them have their fun with me? They got Mama. Ooouuugh!"

The sound escaping through Dufft's clenched teeth grated on Alexander's ears like Treibwasser's wayward chalk against the blackboard. In the boy's mind a sequence of colours appeared: silver-grey = 2, light green = 7, rust red = A, grey green = 5, ochre-brown = 3.

"I've stayed here too long." Dufft breathed in heavily and offered his hand to everybody.

Alexander sneaked out quietly ahead of him. Half way down the stairs, making sure they were alone, he said: "Rossigasse twenty-seven A, Staircase five, Door three."

Protestant According to the Lutheran Creed of Augsburg

Some thirty men, women and children filled the room when Brigitte entered an hour before the appointed time. No one spoke, and Brigitte's good morning was acknowledged by nods. She stood near the only item of fixtures in the room: a wooden picture frame on the wall, displaying a newspaper. Her eyes settled on the cartoon in the middle of the page: two men, one carrying a lantern, amongst a multitude of people with bent noses. The caption: 'What are you doing with the lantern, Friedrich?' - 'I have heard a rumour that there are decent Jews about. I am searching for one, but it's like looking for a needle in a haystack.'

Brigitte turned away. Time went by. She was used to being on her feet. Even so, standing in one place differed to moving about in the kitchen. By late morning she felt a tugging ache in her hips, her knees emitted an inaudible, low frequency vibration. Women with young children sat down on the floor. A baby-faced SA Man entered, manhandled them onto their feet and threatened dire consequences if discipline lapsed again. Two little boys cried because they needed to go to the toilet; wetted themselves.

"Anzendrech."

Brigitte followed the baby-faced SA Man into an office in which

Herr Kristopp, wearing a swastika armband, sat. He requested her to shut the door behind her. The red cloth on the wall with the huge black swastika in the white circle lent stature to the thin figure behind the desk, like a horse does to a rider. The colour reflected off the polished surface of the desk, so that it shone in a deep, black-red glow and impinged on the pale orange folder marked with a large green J.

"You are privileged to meet with me in my private office, Frau Anzendrech. It's more congenial here than in the interrogation quarters. Sit down. I want to speak to you about a matter which will turn out agreeable for you and me. Your husband is a Jew, a born Jew. You are aware that an Aryan spouse married to a Jewish-born partner has grounds for divorce."

Brigitte's wont, when confronted with a particularly nasty perversity, to fall into a transfigured stare, which pierced a person and focused beyond in infinity, made it difficult for Herr Kristopp to catch her eyes.

"I asked whether you were aware of that fact?" he said in raised voice.

"I have read about it."

"Well?"

Herr Kristopp tapped his fingers on the reddish sheen of his desk. "In cases where the Jew-born partner has failed to reveal his Jewish birth before the wedding, such marriages can be annulled. The word of the Aryan spouse is taken on trust in such cases."

"I knew of my husband's religion when he was a young man. It was one of the first things he told me."

"Offspring of such unions can, upon divorce or annulment, apply directly to the Führer for an uplift in status to *Deutschblütigkeitserklärung*. If the Aryan spouse is the woman, and she declares her offspring to have been fathered by Aryan sources, such offspring can under certain circumstances be reclassified as full-blooded Aryans. Think what this would do for your boys."

Brigitte's unbroken study of distant infinity ruffled the patience of the interrogator. "Did you hear what I said? Do you understand what I am offering you? I am offering you a future in our expanding German Reich's culture, I am offering your three boys places in the Reich's youth movements, participation in the Reich's Health

Through Joy activities, the Hitler Youth, the Wehrmacht, even places in the National Socialist Party. The alternative is the label of Jew-whore, your boys half-Jews, the family dragged down along the road earmarked for Jews. It is not a pleasant road. Believe you me, it is not a pleasant road." He opened the folder, turned over pages. He wrote a word on a blank sheet and asked: "Your maiden name is Hochbauer, yes?"

"Yes."

"A good German name. You can be proud of it. We have looked into Rudolf Anzendrech's forerunners. You know by what name they went?" He lifted the paper on which he had written, and Brigitte, coming back from infinity, read *Wanzendreck*, Bedbugmess.

Herr Kristopp resumed: "Well, we are lenient. For the time being we'll make it short. We'll settle on Wanzen." He scribbled notes into the dossier. "What would you rather be known by: Frau Wanzen or Fräulein Hochbauer? And your boys? Alexander Wanzen or Alexander Hochbauer? Think about it. You are under notice to vacate your dwelling, Frau Wanzen, are you not?"

"We have less than two weeks. Herr Kristopp, if I could speak to you about that."

Herr Kristopp, the artist, the artisan, the neighbour from the top floor, laid a buff coloured paper on the desk with the red sheen. "Of course you can speak to me about it. That's what I am here for. Come, stand beside me."

Brigitte rose and walked round the desk. Herr Kristopp turned his chair so he faced her. "I would much rather you with your three upgraded Aryan boys occupied the municipal Milk Block dwelling than certain parties of dubious past political affiliation, like for instance Gerta Posidl. You are still a young, strong, attractive German woman, Fräulein Hochbauer."

Brigitte glanced at the form and perceived amongst other printed matter black letters spelling out D-I-V-O-R-C-E.

At the same time she felt the cloth of her best frock brush against her shins, the cold touch of strange skin above her knees, fingers seeking to slip underneath the elastic of her old-fashioned under-garment. Herr Kristopp's hand engaged in acrobatics. She was aghast. She struck the man's cheek. Then she backed away towards the window.

Herr Kristopp jumped to his feet.

"You lousy Jew whore!" He shouted. His cheeks, the punished one and the other, competed for redness with the sheen on the desk. He followed her to the window, cupped his hands over her breasts and squeezed until his fingers ached. Brigitte groaned. She pushed against his shoulders. Footsteps outside, the turning of the door handle. Herr Kristopp's hands dropped. The baby-face SA Man pushed the door ajar.

"The interview is not over yet," snapped Herr Kristopp.

"I heard you calling. You called me?"

"Bring me coffee."

The boy withdrew and Herr Kristopp returned to his desk. "You are under notice to vacate your dwelling. Have you found another?"

Brigitte pulled herself out of shock. She must keep her wits. The future of her boys depended on it.

She shook her head. "No."

"Go back to the waiting room."

For three hours Brigitte's brain grappled with the trial confronting her: how to save her marriage, her children and her person. Then she was called again. This time the baby face led her into a room only large enough to accommodate one small table and one chair upon which the neighbour from upstairs reposed. He pushed the buff divorce form into her hand.

"Sign at the bottom."

"I am here," said Brigitte, holding the paper away from her body like an uncovered culture of a contagious disease, "because we need to be given a place to live in."

"You are here," replied Herr Kristopp, "to initiate divorce proceedings."

"No."

"But you are married to a Jew."

"I am married to Herr Rudolf Anzendrech who is a Protestant according to the Lutheran Creed of Augsburg."

Herr Kristopp struck the table with the palm of his hand. "He was born a lousy Jew. Once a Jew, always a Jew."

Brigitte laid the buff paper carefully on the table. Herr Bergmeister, in SA uniform, entered through a second door and said: "He married you under false pretences!" The words reverberated between the bare walls.

Brigitte's fingers curved inwards as if gripping an iron bar. "I knew he was Jewish by birth, and that as a young man he changed his faith and became a Protestant According to the Lutheran Creed of Augsburg." Her instinct told her to cling on to the phrase: Protestant According to the Lutheran Creed of Augsburg.

The SA Man placed the orange J-coded file on the table. Herr Kristopp scanned again through the pages and said: "Let me put it to you this way: You, your family, your boys, live next door to dangerous Bolsheviks, whose activities are well known to us. They will not escape the wrath of the German people. You and they have been observed to enter each other's abode frequently. The Jew-Saboteur Dufft, who has been plotting to blow up vital security installations, and has been instrumental in Parteigenosse Brunner's death, has also been a regular visitor in your flat. He and his collaborators won't trouble us much longer. Our task is to weed out the hangers-on. My duty as defender of the Reich is to establish whether your association with Bolsheviks and saboteurs was an act of folly due to ignorance, or whether you and your boys are connected with the Jewish conspiracy. Your eldest son is a student of Chemistry. Knowledge of Chemistry is required in the manufacture of explosives! We have had reports of your youngest son that he has been molesting Aryan girls. This could be idle gossip, on the other hand perverse tendencies to degrade Aryan blood is common among young Jews. Your sons attend the German High School for Boys. In Paul's class a sum of money has been stolen. The thief has not been found. So far. As to the matter of divorce, your signature on the form is required."

Brigitte's chin trembled. Rudolf's survival depended on her, and on her action now. If she let go of him for the sake of her boys, he will perish. Desertion now will destroy him. She prayed with silent words: "God help me. I have not been a church-going woman. I have seen You in mountains and rivers and in trees and in creatures, not in vaults of stone and gilded artifacts. Have I been wrong? What was it I learnt in school, so long ago?"

She said: "My husband belongs to the Protestant Church According to the Lutheran Creed of Augsburg, and I am a born Roman Catholic. The Protestant Church frowns on divorce, and the Holy Roman Catholic Church forbids it. For a Catholic, divorce is a mortal sin."

"But you are not a Catholic. You are a Protestant of the Lutheran Creed of Augsburg," snapped Herr Kristopp.

"Once a Catholic, always a Catholic."

"Nonsense, woman. You can have your marriage annulled."

"And to have conceived children out of holy wedlock? It is a mortal sin to conceive children out of holy wedlock, to be punished by eternal hell-fire."

"Woman, you are making this up!" Stormed SA Man Bergmeister.

Brigitte shook her head. "This is fundamental to all Catholics."

"You don't believe in this hell-fire rubbish no more than I do. You are a Protestant According to the Lutheran Creed of Augsburg!"

"And so is my husband, and so are my children: Protestants According to the Lutheran Creed of Augsburg." Brigitte's chin trembled on, for courage is not born of fearlessness, conversely so, it springs from the womb of fear.

"You are an obstinate woman, Frau Wanzen!" Herr Kristopp's face was devoid of feeling, like a slab of stone. "Don't come to me pleading for mercy when it's too late. But I am a patient man. I shall see you again. Make sure you are making the right choice then!" He produced a scrap of paper. "Here. The address where you are to live. Arrange removal within the next seven days. There's National Socialist people waiting for the dwelling in the Milk Block."

CHAPTER SIX (1939)

For the Glory of the Third Reich

Herr Rosenfinger said: "Horse and cart will be here Sunday morning. I've arranged for Sunday, as I'll be off work and able to lend a hand. The Nazis are on parade then, so we won't have any trouble from them."

Brigitte thanked him and said: "My sister's husband will help as well. We've already shifted crockery and things which break easily. The boys found an old perambulator on the Mistgstettn, and we wheeled it over twice."

"What's it like, your new place in the Untere Augartenstrasse? It's not far from the Inner City."

Brigitte said nothing.

"If I do this," Alexander stretched out his arms, "I can touch opposite walls."

"It's an old paddock. One between two dozen," said Rudi, "Instead of horses they've squeezed two dozen families into them."

Pauli pinched his nose: "And only one shit house. For everybody in the yard. You need a jungle knife to cut through the pong."

"There's no water, from a tap," said Alexander.

"They thought we wouldn't need one," said Rudi, "because the walls are providing enough water for a swimming pool."

Rudolf, like Brigitte, said nothing.

Frau Rosenfinger sought words of encouragement: "We'll come and see you. You won't be alone without friends."

At this Brigitte managed no longer to keep dry eyes. Neither did Alexander. Like his mother, a tear ran down his cheek not because of the ordeal ahead, but because there were decent people around, still. The Rosenfingers continued to do their utmost to uplift the Anzendrech's spirits when once again loud banging reverberated through the room. Brigitte opened the door. Herr Kristopp entered.

"Heil Hitler!" He shouted. "Ha, what have we here? Quite a gathering: Jews, half-Jews, red banner people, communists. Where's Herr Dufft to complete the conspiracy? You know where he is? Is he hiding here?"

"Heil Hitler!" Rudi's heels clicked and his arm shot out in perfect timing. The action would have scored ten out of ten in any Heil Hitler salutation competition. A half-Aryan was, by law, granted the privilege to heel and heil. "Herr Dufft, in a near state of collapse, after being pushed through Morgenthau's shop window, was with us a week ago. He drank a cup of cocoa before passing out due to delayed shock, a biological condition, which like breathing, eating, defecating, sleeping, feeling pain affects Jews and Aryans alike. After regaining consciousness he left. We haven't seen him since. End of report. Heil Hitler."

"Hm," said SA Man Kristopp, "are you in the Hitler Youth?"

"No," replied Rudi.

"Why not?"

"The Hitler Youth Movement does not accept sons of mixed marriages."

"You are a student at the Polytechnic?"

"Yes."

"You study Chemistry?"

"Yes."

"You are familiar with the properties of potassium nitrate, sulphur and charcoal mixed together? You know that these are used in manufacturing explosives?"

"The study of chemistry embraces the properties of all known compounds, including those you mentioned, also the quest for new ones, including substances for medicinal use beneficial to mankind. I aim to specialise in such."

"How many more years?"

"Three years to the diploma examination."

Rudi did not tell him that he had received, this very day, a letter from the Society of Friends which informed him that the sponsor, Mr Brast of High Bentham, Lancashire, Great Britain, had accepted responsibility for the eighteen year old Rudolf Anzendrech's board and lodging in return for the latter's agreement to embark on an agricultural career on Mr Brast' lands. And as all the papers and formalities appeared to be in order, arrangement for the departure to High Bentham should be made as soon as possible, third class rail ticket to be collected from the Society's offices.

Herr Kristopp said: "The Reich needs qualified men who can shoot straight. Yes. If I were you, I'd tell you to shoot straight, and aim right, your shots will hit the right target."

"When we shot arrows on the Danube Meadow, two years ago, I missed." Rudi replied.

His thoughts were with Greti Katherine. She was spending her free time with an aunt suffering from old age, and Rudi had not seen much of her. In a way he was glad for her absence, for how could he introduce her to the squalor of the stable for browsing over stamps, or other pursuits.

"We live in different times now. Sharpshooters missing their targets are no use to us." Herr Kristopp turned to Brigitte: "I said I'll speak to you again. Sturmbannführer Hildebrandt is taking an interest in your circumstance. Sturmbannführer Hildebrandt is a high-ranking officer in the Führer's SS. You could be a lucky woman, and your sons' lucky boys. Especially young Alexander."

Alexander didn't say he was scheduled to leave for Riversmead near Grindleton, Clitheroe, Lancashire in three weeks' time. His thoughts homed also on Greti Katherine.

"Sturmbannführer Hildebrandt would much prefer dealing with a boy called Alexander Hochbauer than Alexander Wanzen, or Alexander Wanzendreck. Make up your mind, Frau Wanzen, time's running out." SA Man Kristopp veered round for departure.

Brigitte hastened to let him out.

Before he reached the door, he spoke again: "If you come across Jew Dufft, tell him we shall be calling on him to answer a few questions. Tell him also that Frau Rebekka Dufft is safe, in protective custody, and that we are asking *her* a few questions. Heil Hitler."

The Anzendrechs convinced themselves that moving into the sodden, single room basement in the Untere Augartenstrasse near the Danube Canal was a blessing in disguise as Rudi's and Alexander's absences would not be noticed in the new neighbourhood.

Ten minutes' walk from their new abode, Hildebrandt in his plush office, wrote in a dossier: If Valhalla Hero Alexander Anzendrech fails, he and his brothers will not be allowed into battle stations where true German heroes will fight for the Glory of the Third Reich. Their destinies will be in line with the fate of Jews, a fate which the Great Mind of the Führer is working on.

Rudi's Exit

Rudi hoisted the big rucksack upon his shoulders and walked into the street as if embarking on an excursion into the Vienna Woods. Rudolf, his father, followed ten minutes later with a tarnished, brown suitcase as if on a trip to the pawnbrokers. Brigitte, his mother, Alexander and Pauli, his brothers, waited a further ten minutes before setting off. They all met inside the Westbahnhof, the Westrailway Station.

They panicked when Alexander was nowhere to be seen. A plan of the station layout, showing railway lines, points and platforms had captured his attention. He had stopped to study it so he could reproduce it on his father's soft table top as a farewell gesture to his childhood game. Then he remembered that the item of furniture, the same table where Rudi and Greti had exchanged stamps, had been given to Uncle Hans for firewood, as there just had not been room for it in the stables of the Untere Augartenstrasse.

They stood on the platform, Rudi's head leaning out from the window, Brigitte's fingers touching his cheeks, saying something about washing socks. Suddenly flaming red hair mingled with Rudi's light brown curls.

Greti Katherine, the Angel, said: "Herbert told me, only an hour ago."

They looked at Alexander: had he spilled the closely guarded secret of Rudi's flight to his friend GK? He blushed.

Rudi forgave him, they all forgave him.

Then came the moment. Then they stood in silence on the platform as the wind-tossed curls on Rudi's head merged with other curls on other heads on the train accelerating towards the vanishing point.

£. s. d.

Thirty-seven half-Aryan Mischling boys, with their mixed parents, hung to the lips of the courier on the rostrum answering questions. Yes, there was a river, called the Ribble. No, it wasn't as wide as the Danube, not near Riversmead, but it broadened out to twenty kilometres at its mouth.

"Twenty kilometres!"

"English rivers are like that. And they flow in two directions: downstream and upstream. With the tide."

Strange.

The boys skimmed through the information sheets. Under the heading English Money: Twelve English pennies (d) make one English shilling (s), twenty English shillings make one English pound (£), twenty-one English shillings make one English guinea.

Strange.

Strange under the heading English Weights: Sixteen English ounces (oz) make one English pound (lb), fourteen English pounds make one English stone, one-hundred-and-twelve English pounds make one English hundredweight (cwt).

Why? Why 'd' for a penny, 'lb' for a pound? Why twelve, and twenty, and twenty-one, and sixteen, and fourteen, and one-hundred-and-twelve?

Worse was to come: English water freezes at 32 and boils at 212 degrees.

Under English distances appeared the numbers twelve, and three, and one-thousand-seven-hundred-and-sixty. When it came to English area it seemed that numbers had been exhausted as none was given for the English acre. How big an English acre, how many English square yards?

Alexander Anzendrech asked, but the man on the rostrum didn't know. The youngster wondered whether English chaos would await them on their arrival at Riversmead.

A last stroll over the Northrailway Bridge to gaze down into the Danube and to imagine how it would be if, like the English Ribble, it were to flow upstream. But there was no nonsense about the Danube. It was definitely a one-way river. And there was no nonsense about the sky-threatening guns, which had been mounted onto platforms straddling the arches of the bridge.

Wanzen

Sturmbannführer Hildebrandt shared a brandy with Director Treibwasser. The SS Man had delivered his oration to the assembled staff and pupils in the hall of the German High School for Boys, at the conclusion of which everyone stood, right arm stretched forward, and sang the German National Anthem followed by the Horst Wessel song.

"We revamped our teaching methods," said Treibwasser, "we operate in line with National Socialist curricula."

"The boys understand how fortunate they are to have a leader of Adolf Hitler's calibre?"

"Such a man comes once in a thousand years," endorsed Treibwasser. "My pupils love him. You saw the tears rolling down their cheeks shouting 'Führer you lead, we follow.' "

"'And lay down our lives for you'," added Hildebrandt.

"Such enthusiasm gives us the strength to overcome all pitfalls. Our biological superiority ..."

"The Wehrmacht will overrun Europe in a matter of days, when..."

"...England and France are stupid enough to declare war." Treibwasser's five-on-dice like face sparkled, knowing that he grasped the politics of the time.

"When the Führer gives the signal. The school is free of Jews?"

"We got rid of Jewish teachers on day one. Jewish students followed shortly afterwards. We still tolerate a handful of half-Aryans."

"Details?"

"They're quitting on their own volition. There are the three brothers, now down to two. The eldest left two weeks ago, another is due to depart in three days."

"Good. The sooner the school rids itself of all Jewish influence and connections, the better. We don't continue to pollute our registers with names like Grünspan or Veilchenduft."

Treibwasser agreed, but observed that names alone could not always be relied upon.

"This brings out again the cunning, conniving Jew," rejoined Hildebrandt. "Living under false pretences. The names of these half-Jewish characters?"

"Anzendrech but ..."

"Anzendrech?" The pulsating of his scar betrayed Hildebrandt's rise of emotional tension.

"They've been renamed. Hitler Youths call them Wanzendreck. To us they're just Wanzen, bedbugs sucking blood."

"The full name of the one that's gone?"

"He still went under the name Anzendrech. Rudi Anzendrech. Had he stayed a week longer he would have been known as Rudi Wanzen."

"And the one that's still attending the school?"

"He's known now as Paul Wanzen."

"The one preparing to leave in three days?"

"Alexander Wanzen."

Hildebrandt tapped his chin with his little finger. Destiny.

The Experiment. Will it be Alexander the Valhalla Hero, or Alexander the Wanzen? In either case the boy is going nowhere.

"You have dossiers on them? Send them to my office in the Franz Josef Kay. Today."

Westbahnhof

The Vienna-Hook van Holland express has been lengthened by three coaches on June 16th nineteen hundred and thirty nine.

Families arrive early, and soon a mass of people pack the platform. Confusion. Armed railway police with set lips guard the locked doors of the three rear coaches. Jewish officials jealously prevent spillage of their Kindertransport children into the Protestant half-Aryan contingent where a courier with a 'Riversmead' armband battles to line up his charges in alphabetical order. He checks and rechecks that names tally. Five windows of the third but last coach display 'Riversmead' notices. The space to the end of the train has been allocated to the Jewish escapees. The noise is deafening. Alexander Anzendrech sees the hands of the Westbahnhof clock creep to 9.15 pm. Departure is scheduled for 9.30 pm. Passengers, non-refugees, board the train. They look at the tumult of shouting and crying humanity, say to each other "Jews" by way of explanation as to why it has to be kept on the platform in a state of turmoil.

The doors swing open. The Riversmead boys lunge onto the train dragging rucksacks and suitcases along. The sweating courier struggles to fill the compartments in the same alphabetical order to enable speedy, final name checks. Alexander finds himself in the first compartment along with boys younger than he. The children push against the locked window; eyes cling to mothers, fathers, brothers, sisters. The smaller boys climb onto the wooden seats to gain window space. A railway policeman enters and orders them down.

As oldest Alexander feels compelled to speak up: "Out there are our mothers and fathers, brothers and sisters. We don't know when we shall see them again. Do you?"

The man turns and leaves. Perhaps he has children of his own. The Nazis have not yet succeeded in dehumanising everyone. Out there, a windowpane away, Brigitte signals frantically to Alexander to be quiet. A gentle jerk, movement. Out there, a window pane away, all hands rise as if pulled up in unison by a common chord. And in every hand flutters a white handkerchief. Vienna's Westbahnhof resembles a sea of white handkerchiefs, and looks like a field of white lilies in silent protest at the outrage.

Mothers and fathers and brothers and sisters lower their hands, which clasp the white handkerchiefs, down to their eyes. They whisper to each other; they do not move away.

Sudden commotion as two men rush onto the platform. One dressed in black SS regalia, the other in a policeman's uniform sporting a swastika armband and carrying a black briefcase.

"It's gone!" From the custodian of the law.

Hildebrandt, the SS Man, swears.

Calming down he says: "It's a long journey with many stops. Get in touch with Linz. We'll get him off the train in Linz. See to it."

Wahnsinn (Lunacy)

The boy next to Alexander says: "Don't be sad, don't cry. It'll be all right."

Alexander replies: "I'm not crying."

He isn't. His compatriot's face looks like a girl's.

Alexander says: "My name's Anzendrech. What's yours?"

"Drehbank."

The other boys introduce themselves: Dren, Blutwurst, Eulenhaut, Durstig, Arne. Arne is very small. One boy sobs and doesn't speak. Eulenhaut, the biggest after Anzendrech, has jet-black, curly hair, full, rosy lips and wears expensive shorts. Alexander judges him to be about thirteen years old. Blutwurst sits by the window, he looks pale.

Blutwurst says: "I'm dying for a fag. Anybody got a cigarette?"

Arne, skinny, subdued, fetches his miniature rucksack down from the luggage rack, fishes out a sandwich spliced with Liptauer cheese and paprika. He chews at it. Others follow his example. They eat or nibble, not because they are hungry. Alexander opens his small travel case. It contains bread, a whole stick of salami, a penknife, writing paper and three envelopes, a fountain pen, a towel, soap, a tooth brush, tooth paste, shoe polish, a spare handkerchief, a book and expensively packaged chocolate. The chocolate is special, thick and heavy. It is built up from small bars, individually sheathed in different colours, visible through a cellophane window. It has cost two marks fifty pfennigs. Alexander has first encountered a similar specimen in happier times, when the price has been two schillings fifty groschen, and he has then equated ultimate ecstasy to possessing one. But family treats have always been anchored to affordable practicability: twenty groschen chocolate bars on birthdays, fifteen groschen bars on the yearly outing to the Prater, ten groschen bars when father has made his pipe tobacco last two days longer.

Mother has pushed the confection into the travel case at the last moment, when Alexander hasn't been looking, to give him a surprise. She has written his name on the packaging like she has labelled all his possessions, every item of clothing, toiletry, and personal things. On the chocolate she has added: *mit einem Busserl von Mutter,* with a kiss from Mum. He takes out the chocolate, touches the smooth cellophane window, but does not break it open. He never breaks it open.

He reaches for the book, its title 'A German Hero'. The cover depicts crouching Wehrmacht soldiers behind a figure in Hitler Youth attire, mouth open, rushing forward, heaving up a swastika flag. The book has been a parting gift from his class. Emotionally touched when Herbert Stubenegke has handed over the brown paper parcel, now he doesn't know what to make of the present. Does it represent a genuine gesture but an ill-chosen title, or is it a piece of studied nastiness, a kick to speed him on his way? GK cannot have been party to that, GK has remained his friend. He feels low, decides the book has no role in Riversmead. He stretches to open the window, forgetting it is locked. A pink envelope falls from the book's pages. On it is written: To be sent to Rudi in England. Alexander knows who the sender is. He pushes the envelope into his pocket and feels better, even though he is harbouring the Angel's words for his brother.

The courier comes into the compartment to check names against his list. The lit-up shapes of carriage windows fly over the grasses of the railway embankment. Pandemonium further down in the Jewish section. A female voice screaming: "I'll send you back to Vienna if you don't do as you're told."

They cannot sleep. Blutwurst turns ashen. He says if he doesn't get a cigarette, he'd die. Rosy-lipped Eulenhaut comforts the boy who has been crying. Skinny Arne farts. They laugh.

A pair of blue eyes peers into the compartment and ask whether anyone is smoking. At the same time a hand presses a majestic wave of blonde hair into place. Blutwurst slouches into the corridor to become closer acquainted with this fair boy. Alexander slides into Blutwurst's window seat, intending to give it up again on the smoker's return. Rosy-lipped Eulenhaut reads rhymes from a picture book to the boy who has been crying. The smallest, Arne, sits quietly, looks at nothing. Blutwurst comes back, less pale. He settles in the place Alexander has vacated. He tells Anzendrech to keep the window seat. He pulls two deep breaths from a cigarette end before squeezing out the glow. He shoves the stub into his lapel pocket.

Drehbank with his girl face stands on the wooden seat, raises his arms and swings himself to and from to the luggage rack. Others follow his example. They cannot sleep.

Timid Arne pulls funny faces. Girl-faced Drehbank asks whether he has the bellyache because he has eaten too much Liptauer cheese. Arne wants to go to the lavatory, doesn't know where it is. As oldest Alexander feels compelled to take charge. Perhaps the tiny boy fears to be on his own in the dimly lit corridor. The nearest toilet is occupied. Walking down to the far end of the carriage they look into the compartments. Little bundles sitting around, unable to sleep. Alexander sees Blutwurst's blue-eyed, fair-haired smoker friend talking demonstratively, his arms whirling round like a windmill's sails. They pass the courier's compartment. The man comes out and asks what they are doing. Alexander explains. The courier says they are approaching Linz. The train smells as trains smell at midnight.

Linz. Respite from the jolting of the carriage. The station empty.
Except two black attired SS Men who climb aboard: "Wanzen. Where's Wanzen!"
They burst into Alexander's compartment. "Heil Hitler. Your names! Quick. Your names."
The boys recite their names.
"Where's Wanzen?"
Alexander says: "We are A, B, and D and E's. W's are further down the coach."
The courier appears, demands to know what is going on.
"Where's Wanzen?"
"Wanzen?"
"You have a boy called Wanzen."
The courier shakes his head. The SS Men push him aside, break into the next compartment. And the next, and the next. The courier follows behind. They reach the last Riversmead berth. The boys there give their names.
"Vetterlein."
"Ulrich."
"Wahnsinn."
"Wanzen?" The SS Men elect to hear no difference between the sounds of the name Wanzen and Wahnsinn.
"It's him," from one SS Man.
"Get your things, come with us," from the second SS Man.
The boy called Wahnsinn shakes.
The courier steps forward. "What's happening here?"
"Wanzen's coming with us."
The boy called Wahnsinn cries.
"No one's coming with you," the courier blocks the door. "His name's not Wanzen. It is Wahnsinn."
"Out of our way!"
"I'm responsible for the boys' safe transit."
"My responsibility is obeying orders."
The courier does not shift. The first SS Man draws his revolver, points it at the courier's chest. "Out of the way I say!"

The courier remains firm. Brave.

The second SS Man says: "There's an irregularity with the papers of this boy. If it's sorted, he'll follow later."

"What? An eleven year old, all the way to Lancashire, England? On his own?"

"He'll be sent on."

The boy called Wahnsinn becomes transfixed, like a statue. The SS Man prods the revolver harder into the courier's chest.

The courier says: "I need a written statement. I need in writing, that the Linz SS are removing Ferdinand Wahnsinn from this train, and that I, Felix Krobinski, in charge of the Riversmead refugee boys, object and protest, and that the Linz SS are threatening my life at gun point if I further attempt to stop them in their action."

A sour smell pervades the compartment. The boy called Wahnsinn cries bitterly. He places his hands over his rear.

"We haven't got time to write our life history. The train's late as it is." The SS Man shoves his gun into its holster, reaches for his notebook, scrawls on a page: 'Alexander Wanzen taken off Holland express by order of Vienna High Command,' hands it to the courier.

The courier shouts: "His name's not Wanzen, it is Wahnsinn. Ferdinand W-a-h-n-s-i-n-n."

The SS Man grabs the whimpering boy called Wahnsinn, threatens other boys in the gangway with instant arrest and removal if they don't at once return to their places. The second SS Man asks which is Wanzen's luggage. Vetterlein points to two suitcases. The SS Man takes one, leaves the other behind.

The courier suffers from breathlessness and palpitation. So do the boys.

The express moves on. The lit-up shapes of the carriage windows fly once more over the grasses of the railway embankment. They cannot sleep.

Blutwurst retrieves his cigarette end. He asks if anybody has a match. Nobody has. He leaves the compartment to seek out the blue-eyed boy with the wave in his fair hair.

Still they cannot sleep.

Passau.

They cannot sleep.

Regensburg.

The train smells like trains smell in the early hours of morning.

Alexander thinks of the boy called Wahnsinn. Will they clean his soiled trousers? He thinks of his mother and father and Pauli. What are they doing right now? He thinks of GK and Greti Katherine. How long will it be before both forget him? He thinks of Martha Bitmann, he thinks of Manni Czarnikow the loudmouthed Hitler Youth, he thinks of his school, the professors, Herr Pflaume who has disappeared, of Frau Petersengel, the bald headed Quorgel man, the boat on the Danube, on the Danube, the Danube...

"Is this the Danube?"

Alexander opens his eyes. He sees girl-faced Drehbank looking through the window at a colourless mass of rolling water. All else is colourless too: fields, sky, houses, streets.

"Is this the Danube?" asks rosy-lipped Eulenhaut.

"Where are we?"

"Don't know."

"What's the time?"

"Ten past five," says Blutwurst.

"Must be the Rhine," mutters Alexander. "Look at the castle."

Eulenhaut says: "It's no match to our castles on the Danube in the Wachau. Have you been to the Wachau?"

Alexander hasn't been to the Wachau on the Danube. He doubts whether the castles there are any better than the one before his eyes now. He has been to Greifenstein on the Danube. With his class, five years ago. With Martha. He thinks again of Martha. He thinks of her kisses, of her turning away when he faced her, a half-Jew. He thinks of Herr Dufft, Frau Spagola, Poldi, Berti, Herr and Frau Rosenfinger, Greti Katherin...

Before The Cock Crows

A sharp rattle wakes him. A man in a pale blue uniform pushes the sliding doors apart. The train is stationery. Twisted boy's bodies, heads lolled to one side, eyes closed. The man pulls the door to within a few centimetres gap and creates an earsplitting rattle drumming a steel rod against the edge of the door and the partitioning. The boys stir.

"Heil Hitler. Border control."

Still in the grip of sleep, they stare at him, not comprehending.

"Where are you going?"

Blutwurst is the first to get his wits together. "England."

"Ah! You show the British what German Youth is made of! When are you coming back?"

"We aren't coming back."

"You cannot leave the fatherland. The fatherland needs young blood."

"We are refugees."

The man's face, grim before, becomes grimmer. "Your passports. Let me see your passports."

The courier appears on the scene out of breath. He flourishes papers and documents under the uniformed man's nose. A long examination. The official, now augmented by an SS Man, enters the compartment. He commands the boys to collect their luggage and open it. He pokes his steel rod into Arne's dwarfish socks and shirts very much in the manner of the policeman who examined Gusti Spagola's little suitcase in the Engerthstrasse during the uprising five years ago, fishes out flimsy underpants, lets them slide off the rod onto the floor. He transfers a gold locket from rosy-lipped Eulenhaut's trunk into his pocket. He comes to Alexander's travel case. He lifts out the chocolate wrapped in many colours. He weighs it in his hand. He gets hold of the book, scans through the pages.

"Whose?"

"Mine," says Alexander.

"Good story." He scrutinises the boy through narrow eyes.

"My class gave me the book. My mother gave me the chocolate."

"You don't look like a Jew."

Alexander says: "I'm not a Jew."

"Refugees are Jews."

"Three weeks ago I was confirmed in the Protestant Church According to the Lutheran Creed of Augsburg. On that day the vicar asked me to show them in England what German Protestants are made of. I'm not a Jew." Alexander insists for the second time.

The man returns the book and the chocolate into Alexander's travel case and directs a narrow gaze at rosy-lipped Eulenhaut: "You look like a Jew."

Drehbank says: "He is a Protestant."

Blutwurst adds. "We are all Protestants."

And Alexander says: "Protestants according to the Lutheran Creed of Augsburg." And for the third time: "We are not Jews."

The SS Man asks: "Where are the Jews?"

The courier, terrified of further forcible removals, volunteers: "They are in the last two carriages."

Left to themselves Alexander feels shame. Yet he has spoken the truth. He has been accepted into the Protestant Church According to the Lutheran Creed of Augsburg. It is also true that he has never come in contact with Jewish traditions. His father is a born Jew. So? He is a Mischling, half-Aryan. Half Jewish? So? He has sought safety in stressing that he is not a Jew. So? In Nazi eyes being a Jew is a crime. In a few minutes he will be in Holland.

But he feels shame, as if guilty of betrayal. At his Lutheran confirmation he had listened to the story of Saint Peter who had wept bitterly after he had denied knowing Jesus three times before the cock crowed.

He is not a Jew. What the hell does it matter what he is.

In a few minutes he would be in Holland, in a different world. He opened his travel case and took out the chocolate wrapped in many colours. Once again his wet eyes read the inscription. 'With a kiss from Mum.'

PART 2

CRICKET ON THE RIBBLE

CHAPTER SEVEN (1939)

Mr Wooseley

Mr Woosely was a lucky man. He knew it, although he had lived through his share of misfortune. This had nothing to do with the number three. People may ascribe all manner of good or bad luck to the third digit, but he, unlike his widowed daughter, upheld a strictly conventional angle on the metaphysical.

Mr Woosely was a lucky man because the upper windows of his house commanded a view of Pendle Hill, of green fields and stone walls in front of it, of the shady Ribble and the picturesque Clitheroe bridge. His good fortune embraced a neat garden, a neat wife and a neat life-style, scarcely troubled by scanty news of brutal civil fighting in Spain, of ugly events in Germany and talk of a pending war.

Past adversities revealed a misspent youth in French trenches, and in later life the absence of little boys' pitter-patter in his household. Whether God assumed responsibility for this, Margaret's hormones or his own essence, did not feature for debate within the walls of his castle. Teaching geography in Clitheroe's Grammar School for Boys compensated for the deficiency of sons of his own. Now, in retirement, with a comfortable pension, he devoted more and more time to the demands on a Scoutmaster.

He was a good Scout Master. Slow but good.

The troop had settled on a field within the grounds of the abandoned Hydro Lodge Riversmead near Grindleton.

"Neeveer miind," he patted Peter Strathon's fingers which grappled with the ends of two strings, striving to curve them into loops which should bind the chords together but so far hadn't. "Wee'll tryy aanootheer tiime. Iit's Llwyyyngwryyyl neext weeek wiith Miisteer Toownsend."

Boys in blue shirts, shorts and broad-rimmed hats, who had mastered the Knots of the Woodsman's Test, responded with: "Woon't iit bee fuun sleepiing iin teeents."

Mr Woosely didn't mind the mimicry. Boys will be boys. He leant backwards (in spite of recurring aches in his shoulder blades) to ensure they profited from their endeavour. Now with Riversmead opening up again he was looking for alternative sites. At the

Grindleton Methodist Chapel farmer Gibson said: "ay, provided fillies aren't interfered with" in reply to the Scoutmaster's petition for use of the field by the Ribble just before Chatburn Bridge. The spot was ideal for camping, bathing and driving cricket stumps into the turf.

Sister Helen

Sister Helen loved God, and whenever possible, her neighbours.

First among her hero figures, which included Florence Nightingale and Jane Eyre, came The Good Samaritan. She could think of only one improvement to the Biblical character, and that was giving him female gender, not because she disliked men, but simply to reflect reality. Compassion belonged to women, to Sisters and nurses and to nuns, to mothers. A woman Samaritan would have nursed the robbed man back to health herself!

She found it hard to love all her neighbours. As a child, when the telegrams came, she could not bring herself to generate affection for the Kaiser, and now she faced difficulties vis-à-vis Adolf Hitler. Fortunately Sister Helen excelled in overcoming difficulties. She took religion as reflected in the light of reality. She was a pragmatist. God's world was as it was. It contained love and beauty. It also teemed with irritating contradictions, because God moved in mysterious ways. If He created devils as well as angels He had reasons for doing so. She strove to be a good Christian, love God at all times. But she kept the love of mysterious works within the bounds of common sense.

He had endowed her with plenty of the latter, and to help matters along, also with an abundance of self-discipline. In fact she brimmed so full of self-discipline that under pressure it spilled over, separated from the 'self', and manifested itself by demanding discipline from others.

When in her teens her fellow Methodist students had vowed at no time to succumb to the lure of alcohol. She had given no such pledge, but had never indulged in a drop, and expected similar abstinence from staff directly answerable to her.

She regularly reminded herself to help her fellow creatures. When it fell upon her to choose a hymn in the Methodist chapel, she always selected one mirroring that theme, like 'When wilt Thou save the people, oh God of Mercy, when.' At sixteen she had enrolled to be trained for a post in orphanages. Now at the age of thirty-three she had applied for overseas work, but the National Children's Homes and Orphanages urged her to accept the pressing appointment of looking after the welfare of some sixty-eight boys who had been driven from their less than fully Aryan homes in Vienna and in German cities by the Nazi regime.

Other reasons for taking on the job at Riversmead were likewise compelling. First, in early summer of 1939, the likelihood of war in Europe trembled on people's lips. Travelling at such times to far away Bangladesh, where devastation came predictably from rising rivers rather than unpredictably from falling bombs, seemed a cowardly option. Second, the home for the refugee boys lay opposite Pendle Hill, a mere stone's throw from the no less imposing heights of Ingleborough, on which she, as a young girl, had organised expeditions with the daughters of farmers all around. So if war came, and with it trouble, it would be good to be within reach of her own home. Third, dozing in the back of her mind, and kept from waking by vigilant self-discipline, nestled the thought that Riversmead would be staffed with teachers, probably mostly male.

Sister Helen was not married. To be mother to a multitude of children born to other mothers diminished the need to have babies of her own. But not necessarily the wish, though dormant, to have a man of her own. Here the mysterious contradictions with which He had stocked the universe trickled into human nature. She feared, ridiculed the very idea, secretly hoped, that somewhere, a man was waiting for her. But sisterhood did not provide for meeting new faces as an everyday event. Sisters owed allegiance to orphanages. Walking out through the gates accompanied by twenty seven children left little room to see, let alone become acquainted with, even the most patient of waiting men.

That he might be waiting for her within the walls of Riversmead, however laughable the notion when looked at square on, became nevertheless a slumbering thought. And sleeping thoughts, like dreams, do not adhere to the rules of logic. Knowing this and countering it, she methodically set in motion the routines designed to make Riversmead a flourishing home before anything else.

The building was out of this world. When she first saw it she expected a dormouse and a March hare to emerge from the entrance. The tall, central Tower, topped with a sloping roof, connected to the two-storied North and South Wings. The North Wing carried a high gabled roof; the South Wing bore a pyramidal roof, which reminded one of the pagoda style. Corners ended in onion shaped masonry, which reminded one of the Byzantine style. Extending to the front of the Tower, some sixty yards in length, ran the Gymnasium, covered by a rounded, trunk-like roof, reminiscent of the elephant style, if such existed. Behind the Tower, protected from the weather by a low gabled roof, lay the expanse of the Great Dining Hall. Windows along the far end let in the morning sun, reflected from side to side by eight floor-to-ceiling mirrors lining opposite walls, which created the impression of infinite space. Two feet high clay figures, purporting to portray Henry The Eighth and other by-gone kings of less notoriety, stood on pedestals between the mirrors.

Kitchen and larder occupied the space below the Tower. Several outbuildings housed the boiler plant, the laundry, and a workshop. The whole ensemble had originally been erected to cater for paying guests taking the waters, a hot spring gurgling in a nearby spinney providing the raw material. When the spring had stopped gurgling, the enterprise had become insolvent. After lying empty for some years, the consortium of The Children's Homes, the Methodist Church and the Society of Friends converted it into a home for refugee boys.

Sister Helen directed the creation of bedrooms, common rooms, classrooms, and staff rooms. The shortage of washrooms led to the conversion of a workshop, the dire shortage of lavatories to the hiring of Mr Gibson's farmhands for digging a twenty yard long trench across the grass tennis court, to instructing the on-call handyman to knock together a twenty yard long bench and secure it to the ground in front of the trench, to surrounding the earth work with a canvas fence, and to erecting a board with the legend 'WAY IN' near the way in. At the same time she ordered the construction of an annex to the converted washroom to house eight flush toilets.

Sister Helen engaged Mr Wooseley's daughter, Mrs Knowles, as cook. She hired kitchen help from Grindleton, making sure they were mothers, Methodist chapel goers, and middle-aged. She arranged regular milk supply from farmer Gibson, bread delivery from Clitheroe. A coke mountain appeared outside the boiler house. Beds, furniture and Methodist hymn books arrived. She attended to the procurement of kitchenware, not forgetting seven buckets, three for potato peeling, three for floor scrubbing, and one spare.

She stocked the larder, bought emergency clothing, shoe polish, soaps and tooth powders, first aid kits, disinfectants against lice and bedbugs. She booked Mr Stroller, barber, to call once a week. She approached Mr Woosely to organise a scout troop at the earliest opportunity. She made sure that the one hundred and one items, including the summoning bell for assemblies, were ready and in place. She compiled a list of orderly duties.

She felt sympathetically drawn to the three House Sisters, each with visible anxiety awaiting their allocation of gibberish speaking, foreign habits displaying, boys. Sisters Frances, Laura and Cicely would, in line with her sentiments, have nursed the injured victim in ancient Palestine to health themselves, and, human nature being what it is, would have given the parable a chapter 2 with a living-happily-ever-after ending.

But Sister Helen could not account for the presence of Sister April, who had done little apart from smiling whilst washing her hands in air. Sister April, as Head of the Home, looked like carrying on doing little, except when the task was gathering credit for what had been done. Sister Helen shrugged the matter aside, told herself that her purpose in life was to alleviate the suffering of mankind, not to revel in shouts of praise. She imagined, if Sister April had walked from Jerusalem to Jericho, she would have meekly stood by the roadside, wrung her hands and given smiling approval to her deputy cleaning the victim's wounds.

One of her duties was to hand over to Sister Helen a list of the refugee boys' names in alphabetical order. The very first one spelled Anzendrech, Alexander.

The Road to Jericho

The Riversmead Staff gathered in the Common Room to iron out last queries regarding the arrival of the first contingent of boys from Vienna the following day.

Sister Helen's lack of German posed no deterrent to her enthusiasm. She expected the boys to acquire speedily an understanding of basic English relating to orderly duties, summed up in the behest "quickly now." She sat upright and passed the time studying the teachers, judging them in the light of their likely behaviour towards the injured man on the Jericho road.

Of the two doctors, one of philosophy, one of medicine, she first singled out the School Head himself, Dr Vittauer, the thinker. He was German, unmarried. He was going to teach Religious Studies, English History and English literature. Whether he was, in her unconscious dreams, waiting, could not be ascertained at this stage.

Dr Kupfer, the physician, on the other hand, was not waiting at all. Although he had a wife, he heaped pleasantries upon the five sisters, but not upon teacher Miss Zimmermann. Sister Helen made sure she responded to Dr Kupfer's chivalry with large doses of self-discipline. He, German, was going to take charge of Surgery, as well as Sports and Games. To operate these he needed and demanded discipline, which he got. But it had nothing to do with an overflow of self-discipline.

If the two doctors were to slip into the mantle of the Samaritan, Sister Helen thought, Dr Vittauer would stroll along so engrossed in scheming up an Utopian world, that he wouldn't see the wounded man at all. Dr Kupfer would stop, blow his referee whistle to rouse him from unconsciousness, and order him to cease malingering.

Next, Mr Foutain, of uncertain origin, perhaps Hungarian, who spoke several languages and articulated perfect English, was to be responsible for Geography, Elementary Philosophy, English Grammar, and also for implanting Conversation English into the boys' brains in out-of-lessons hours. Of darkish complexion Mr Foutain exuded enigma. He seemed to have a past, the nature of which eluded detection, all of which placed him outside the category of waiting men. As life in the Home settled down, his trips to London, for reasons kept to himself, enhanced the air of mystery. The Sisters thought he visited an ailing relative, Dr Vittauer suspected something more portentous. If he had journeyed on the road to Jericho, Sister Helen had the feeling that the robbers, on seeing his approach in the distance, would have postponed the attack on their victim until he had passed by.

Then came Mr Gru*n of Art and Crafts. Though single, he did not aspire to the basic qualifications, which Sister Helen took for granted from waiting men. His perpetual sore throat needed perpetual warming by a thick scarf round his neck, worn indoors as well as outdoors, and gave rise to perpetual hoarseness of voice, which, coupled to his guttural German accent, would have made his whispered sweet nothings into her ear sound like the mating call of a frog. This would have led to a tug-of-war between her self-discipline and her sense of humour.

Whether her self-discipline or her sense of humour would have triumphed belonged to hypothetical speculation, because Mr Grun's croaked whispers were directed exclusively into the ears of Clitheroe femininity, of whom he painted many portraits, half-length and full length, half clothed and unclothed. Besides, Mr Grun feared Sister Helen. Her self-discipline demanded adoption of an upright posture at all times, which gave rise to thrusting back her head, and to balance this, pushing forward her ample bosom. Whilst Mr Grun was versed in the artistic and soothing merits of the female torso, he could not visualise Sister Helen's bare breasts as a vivifying place for mind, head or sore throat, but more like a pair of naval guns, uncapped. He might have enjoyed painting them, on canvas, for Art's sake. A Samaritan Mr Grun would have set up his easel by the roadside to capture the anguish on the dying man's face.

Mr Dottis, single, another German, spoke English like a Yorkshire man. His function in Riversmead was to be tutoring Horticulture, overseeing Recreation and carrying out everyday tasks like replacing washers in taps, repairing crumbling cement, restoring fuses. The most vociferous at the meeting, he interrupted Dr Vittauer frequently, putting forward alternative options in matters of syllabus, Sunday chapels, even diet. He carried a bee in his cap. The bee buzzed away: "You ought to be in charge here. Dr Vittauer is incompetent." Mr Dottis didn't much entertain the idea of waiting, and clearly not for Sister Helen. He would hurry by any dying man on the roadside, looking the other way.

Apart from Mrs Kupfer, who appeared for meals but rarely at other times, and would have taught needlework had there been girls amongst the expected refugees, one other female complemented the school staff. Miss Zimmermann was to teach Physics, Biology,

Physiology, Chemistry, Nature Studies, Botany, Zoology, Ancient Greek History, Ancient Roman History, and Guitar Playing. Guitar Playing because she knew how to play a guitar, and because she had one. Miss Zimmermann wore trousers or long, colourful skirts, spoke in a high-pitched, husky voice, possessed a large nose, carried her hair combed backwards, lived twenty years ahead of her time. She would have made an excellent candidate for Flower Power, but neither she, nor Sister Helen, nor anyone else, knew that. Sister Helen could not stifle the thought that had Miss Zimmermann come across the victim in Jesus' parable, she would have searched out the robbers and joined them, albeit with the object of rendering guitar tuition, so as to provide them with an alternative way of earning a living.

CHAPTER EIGHT (1939)

The Arrival

On 17th June 1939 a corridor-less, red-upholstered, dusty LMS railway carriage emptied bewildered boys beneath rain-swept Pendle Hill.

The Bedbug in the Apple

Ribble bathers split up into four groups so as not to swamp the river by an overdose of swimmers.

Alexander Anzendrech tagged on to Mr Grun who croaked warnings of unexpected deep water, slippery moss-covered stones and steep banks. Having outwitted the perilous Danube, to be warned about the tranquil Ribble, seemed to Anzendrech like cautioning a lion tamer of the vagaries of a pussycat. But lion tamers may grow fond of kittens. Dipping into the smooth river in the summer of 1939 marked the beginning of learning that things, which are different, should not be shunned because they are different.

Anzendrech lay on his back on the peat-tinged, but otherwise clear water, paddling gently with his hands. He gazed at flakes of snow-white clouds wafting across an azure-blue sky. He clambered up the succulent, emerald bank, lay in the long, deep green grass, shivered. But what bliss when the sun found clear sky and bounced warming rays onto his goose pimpled skin.

Mr Grun had brought a collapsible stool, a sheet of thin plywood, his scarf and tubes of oil paint. He sat himself half way up a sloping, dung bespattered meadow, and groped with his eyes the Lancashire paradise: in the foreground an oak tree, its low branch hovering two inches above a solitary sheep; fields, speckled with grazing horses and black cattle, falling away to the winding river; lines of stone walls, in the distance the bare, elongated, purple-green Pendle Hill.

Alexander walked up the incline to look at landscape art in the making. Mr Grun saw him coming and greeted him with a friendly nod. He had previously watched the youth draw Vienna trams in coloured crayons for the benefit of homesick refugees. Mr Grun had croaked encouragements and in return Alexander desisted joining in the chorus of frog noises whenever the sore throat sufferer passed a group of boys.

"What do you think of it?" asked the brush-wielding wizard, offering his work for inspection.

Anzendrech perceived flakes of snow-white clouds wafting across an azure-blue sky over the distant, bare, elongated, purple-green Pendle Hill, in the foreground a ten inch diameter flesh-coloured apple, a realistic bite taken out of it revealing a brown, spindly legged creature creeping out from a hole, the apple skin displaying two round swellings with pink centres.

"Where's the sheep?" queried Alexander, realising that his question sounded either stupid or sarcastic.

"The sheep?" Mr Grun thought a little. "The sheep's taken the bite from the apple after which it was no longer content to remain inert underneath the tree. If you ask me where the tree is, I can tell you, the tree is inside the apple, in the pip."

"Why the ... insect?"

"It started off as a maggot, but I changed it into a bedbug. I don't know whether bedbugs feed on apple. Probably not. It's there to show that things aren't always as we expect them to be."

"And the circles on the apple?"

"The river. The river of life springs from woman's breasts."

Alexander saw that the swellings assumed the form of a shapely girl's bosom. He blushed and succumbed to a state of inadequacy which caused his tongue to tie itself into knots and his brain to empty itself of everything in it. This irksome reaction when coming face to face with matters appertaining to the opposite gender had manifested itself shortly after arrival on this side of the English Channel, and had grown ever since.

"Now you are embarrassed." Mr Grun cleared his throat, but not his croaks. "You're still a boy. Things appear differently according to when we look at them, how we look at them, from where we look at them, who we are when we look at them. To you boys my scarf is an object of fun; to me it's a comfort. What is it really? The fibres grew once on a sheep, maybe one which liked sheltering under a tree before it got bored. Our sheep's gone to join other sheep. Driven by its herd instinct. Men are driven too. All the time, every minute of the day."

Oskar

Oskar Nabravowitz acquired blue-eyed boy status in metaphor and reality.

Of the sixty-eight youngsters (thirty-two from German cities had joined the Vienna contingent) sixty-seven answered to their surnames, he alone paraded as Oskar. This came about because he sported a grandiose wave in his blonde mane, first observed by Anzendrech on the train journey from Vienna when the super-boy enquired of the compartment's smoking habit. Brylcreamed and pressed into one rolling sweep, this undulation together with his charismatic personality captured adulation, alike with boys, staff and people wherever he went.

He excelled in games. After the 'WAY IN' sign finally disappeared and grass grew again where the trench had been, he held a tennis racket in his hand for the first time in his life and beat Sister Frances six-four after their third session.

He was good at old wives' quackery. During one of Mr Dottis' practical gardening lessons for all age groups, tiny Arne cried out: "Something's bit me."

Oskar said: "That's a bedbug."

Mr Dottis flicked the offending creature away, stroked soothingly Arne's hand. "A bedbug?"

"I know a bedbug when I see one," said Oskar.

"Here?"

"He brought it with him from Vienna. Probably wrapped in a fold of his shirt." Oskar scooped up a thimbleful of earth, kneaded it between thumb and forefinger, softened it with a liberal quantity of bubbly spit and pasted the mix over Arne's reddened skin. The little boy's face lit up in exultation.

So sixty-six boys called him Oskar. Anzendrech, to the blue-eyed boy's consternation, adhered to the surname rule. He did so because he believed hero worship should be discouraged, and because he was filled with envy. Dr Vittauer, Mr Foutain and Sister Helen likewise continued to speak of him as Nabravowitz.

Oskar summoned the six Prefects to form the Club Primarus. He appointed himself President, claiming universal approval. The club members withdrew into a corner of the Upper Lounge, a chamber which had been dedicated exclusively for use of the over fourteen olds.

There, separated from lesser boys, Oskar began: "I'm President. Everybody can speak, but when I say 'Silencium' everybody shuts up."

"Including you?"

"That's a stupid question, Anzendrech," replied President Oskar.

"If it does, Nabrawovitz, we'll be observing silencium for evermore."

"Not a bad idea, perhaps," said Prefect Kleeblatt from Berlin, the wit amongst them.

"Where's our gramophone?" Asked rosy-lipped Prefect Eulenhaut.

"Dotti's getting us one," said President Oskar.

"Dotti wants to run the show," remarked Prefect Malig, the oldest, and after Oskar, presumed the wisest.

"We'll get better grub when he takes over," said Prefect Schaumberg, the fattest.

"I got a currant loaf," said long-eared Prefect Blitz, likewise from Berlin, "got it from the larder when Mrs Knowles was leaning against the table with her eyes shut."

"We'll have a midnight feast," Schaumberg, the fattest, squeaked expectantly.

"We can meet up in my bedroom, climb in by the outside staircase," said Eulenhaut.

"Don't give none to Eulenhaut," said Schaumberg," he's a greedy Jew-boy."

"Who's calling me a Jew-boy?"

"I am. Because you look like a Jew."

"Schaumberg, shut up," scolded Anzendrech. "We left the Jew and Aryan nonsense behind. We're in England now."

"He stinks like a Jew," persisted Schaumberg. "He stinks like a *Beulenhaut,* like the skin of a boil."

"You're as fat as a rancid pig," rosy-lipped Eulenhaut hit back.

"Silencium!" said Oskar. "We're discussing a midnight feast with a currant loaf."

Blitz said: "I give bits of my current loaf to whoever I like."

Schaumberg said: "I don't give nothing of mine to anyone I don't like."

"I give kicks in the arse to anyone I don't like," said Eulenhaut.

"Silencium! If any of us get things, we share them."

"I won't share my things with a smelly Jew," said Schaumberg.

"Go and join the Hitler Youth," said Anzendrech. "You're a half-Jew like the rest of us."

"I'm not," said Schaumberg sulking, knowing that he was.

"Silencium I say! Where's the loaf?"

"Hid it in my locker."

"I'll scrounge some jam from Mrs Knowles," said Oskar. He knew the kitchen staff belonged to his ardent admirers.

"My bedroom. Outside staircase, OK?"

"We'll meet in the new lavatory block," Oskar contradicted. "Half past eleven. Bring some fags."

"It's draughty there. There's no doors and no windows yet. And it's dark."

"No one will see us then."

"Dottis goes on the prowl at nights. I've seen him," warned Anzendrech.

"Dottis is on our side," said Oskar. "Dottis has got Vittauer by the balls."

"Vittauer's not the only one he gets by the balls," said Schaumberg.

Mr Dottis' Affliction

Mr Dottis began with the Prefects.

He told them they lacked freedom, their recreation facilities fell short of a gramophone, their light weight dinners did not fulfil the demands of growing men, peeling potatoes and scrubbing floors were beneath their Prefects' dignity, they should not be exposed to bedroom vermin like bedbugs. They listened and grumbled. Younger boys listened to the Prefects and grumbled also. Sister Helen listened but couldn't get to the gist of the business, because the boys grumbled in German. Morale dropped.

Then the wheelbarrow incident happened. Mr Dottis asked Mr

Gibson whose farmyard and stables bordered on Riversmead's land, for a bit of organic fertiliser to boost the Home's onion and lettuce growth. He dispatched his favourite pupils: big Oskar for his verve, little Arne for his fervor. The little boy, originating from Vienna's dusty industrial atmosphere, had developed, since breathing Lancashire air, an affinity for earth, mud and greenery.

Farmer Gibson pointed to a shovel and a mound of equine droppings mixed with cattle dung. He spoke. The two boys responded like statues. The English they had so far acquired excluded the farmer's Lancashire version. Mr Gibson recognised the futility of prolonged monologue and withdrew. Just then Josie Gibson, the daughter, entered the yard. Mesmerised by the blonde wave, blue eyes and gold Prefect badge, she began a conversation, which, like her father's beforehand, created little literary impact. But a great deal of feverish longing. After lengthy finger gesticulation, Josie managed to convey to the blue-eyed boy that she would show him the luxurious interior of the barn, if he so wished. Oskar so wished, and the two departed, leaving tiny Arne with shovel and dung heap.

The skinny minor struggled with the steaming wheelbarrow towards Riversmead territory, and since Mr Dottis had uttered the request to "bring here" the manure when standing inside the entrance hall, Arne pushed his cargo, with difficulty, through the swing doors, whereupon, loosing balance, he tipped the lot upon the recently orderly-scrubbed, red floor tiles.

Mr Dottis was not pleased to see this.

The School Office was situated at the top of the staircase. When tangy gases penetrated its door Dr Vittauer left his desk and sniffed his way to the source of the blight. Within seconds several Sisters, teachers, Mrs Knowles and half the compliment of giggling boys gathered round the reeky heap and red-faced Mr Dottis, who tried in vain to extract an explanation from the tearful Arne.

Mr Dottis' ego suffered. Seeing himself the laughing stock, his ambition to rule the roost received a severe blow.

"What's happened to Oskar?" He screamed at Arne in German.

The boy at last told his story, which of course the English Sisters found difficult to follow. Then Oskar appeared.

"What's the meaning of this?" demanded Mr Dottis.

Oskar replied that coming upon the manure, the odour

overpowered him. He felt sick and he made his way into nearby trees, where he rested to recover which unfortunately took a little time. His account conflicted with Arne's, and no one conversant in the German language had any doubt as to the truthful one. Whereupon Oskar's status amongst the boys rose several notches higher.

But deeply wounded Mr Dottis saw Oskar in a different light. He tore off the Prefect badge, and ordered him to clear up the mess forthwith. Sister Helen requested translations, which Dr Vittauer provided without mentioning Josie Gibson. She then called for dispersal to orderly duties of all idle, juvenile onlookers, said "quickly now" and retired with the three House Sisters to have a titter before inspecting the tidy-up operation. Oskar, left alone, was joined by four devotees of tender age who did the removal work, scrubbing and disinfecting.

The Club Primarus members met and Oskar, the President, announced: "Dott needs to be taught a lesson. We can't let him take over."

"He's got us the gramophone," objected fat Schaumberg.

"The clapped out thing from the Ark? And only one record: Boots, boots boots boots marching up and down again. And not even a woman singing it."

"Arne's pissed his bed since the business in the showers," observed long-eared Blitz.

"Dottis is not fit to run Riversmead," Malig, the oldest, agreed with Oskar.

"He's a pansy," said Schaumberg.

"Let him try it on me!"

"Arne's afraid to tell anybody."

They elected Malig, the oldest, to inform Dr Kupfer. The physician approached the Head of School, and together they summoned Mr Dottis who explained that the incident in the showers had been a matter of no importance. There had been a little horseplay, boys splashing about and throwing soap at one another, Arne got hit in a vulnerable spot. He had doubled up, and he, Mr Dottis had gone to inspect. No injury had occurred, none had therefore been reported. That was all.

There the matter rested. But some of it reached Sister Helen's ears. She began to watch the horticulturist's conduct. She noticed his interference with her well organised orderly duties: relieving boys of brooms and shoving cricket bats into their hands, and in so doing brushing against their groins. She discovered he coaxed them to convey to Mrs Knowles they were hungry. Then Sister Frances came with the story that having overheard a conversation between Anzendrech and Schaumberg, she had gathered that the boys expected Mr Dottis to oust Dr Vittauer.

Sister Helen consulted Sister April. Sister April reacted by washing her hands in air. So Sister Helen went to Dr Vittauer. He said Mr Dottis would have been sufficiently frightened by the interrogating interview to desist from any further molestation. Vexed by this lack of vigilance, she said that she had put body and soul into making Riversmead a happy home, and would not stand idly by seeing it destroyed by a schemer who went for little boys. She revised the role allotted to him on the Jericho road from looking the other way to stripping the shirt off the bleeding victim.

Sister Helen continued watching. He, in turn, continued stirring up unrest. The sloppy orderly work and grumbling continued.

She wrote a letter to the Reverend W W Shimpton.

The Opening Day

The official Opening Day fell on a warm summer Sunday.

The Riversmead Committee, including the Reverend W W Shimpton of the Christian Council for Refugees, came in shiny automobiles. Invitations to attend the ceremonies and to look over the building had been sent to local dignitaries high and low. On the day not a speck, not a smear, disgraced the sparkling tiles of the Entrance Hall. Sister Helen did not entrust the work to orderly duty. She rose at six in the morning, went down on hands and knees, and scrubbed herself. Then she locked the doors until the arrival of the first guests.

Several boys wore yellow ribbons over their shoulders signifying some knowledge of English, and were assigned to act as guides. Arne, though not yet ten, had outstripped everybody else in amassing vocabulary, and was able to conduct a flowing dialogue in the new language:

Arne: "May I show you the house?"

Guest: "Yes please."

Arne: "This is the Entrance Hall, and now we go into the Common Room."

Guest: "What do you do in the Common Room?"

Arne: "In the Common Room we have lessons for instance Singing, Playing, Drawing and Elementary Philosophy. But today it is the tearoom for the guests."

Guest: "Have you a piano for singing?"

Arne: "Yes we have. But today it is in the Gymnasium where we need it for the acrobats."

Guest: "You have acrobats too?"

Arne: "Yes. The boys will jump over the horse and do many other things. Then we shall sing: My Bonny Lies Over the Ocean, and a Prefect will say the English poem: Our England Is A Garden."

Guest: "Is this the Dining Room?"

Arne: "Yes. But stop. I have quite forgotten to show you the Reading Room. Therefore here is the Reading room. When it is raining the boys read many German and English stories which are lying here. So and now I will show you the Dining Room. Here the boys eat breakfast, dinner and supper. We sit in Houses. Each House has a Sister: Sister Francis for Luther House, Sister Laura for Schweitzer House, Sister Cicely for Wesley House."

Guest: "Yes, this is very nice. But where are your bedrooms?"

Arne: "I am just going to show you the bedrooms. There are the bedrooms in the South Wing. But first here is the office of Sister April and next to it is the Surgery. When a boy is ill he goes there and sees Doctor Kupfer. And now we go to the Tower."

Guest: "What is the Tower?"

Arne: "In the Tower are the bedrooms of the small boys. So and now we go upstairs."

Guest: "Oh, this is a very nice view. This is Pendle Hill."

Arne: "Yes. Now we go down to the shower rooms and the bathrooms. Every boy has one shower and one bath every week."

Guest: "Oh, that's very fine."

Arne: "Here is the Upper Lounge. It is the room for the Prefects. And now I will show you the Gymnasium. There are the lockers. Each boy has a locker. He can put his things in it."

Guest: "It is very lovely here, and I thank you very much for your kindness in showing me your Home. I shall ask Dr Vittauer whether you may come to have tea with us. Would you like that?"

Arne: "Yes. I should like it very much. Thank you."

Arne's guests were not the only ones to offer tea invitations. Five couples aimed for Oskar. The choice was left to him, and he selected a family who had brought with them their daughter Vera. Even Eulenhaut, whose greasy, curly hair, oily skin, puffed cheeks and rosy lips contrasted to Oskar's charisma like peat to gold, secured an invite. Malig hovered around Mrs Knowles, as the cook had dropped the remark that her niece Mary had won first prize in a beauty competition. He achieved his wider aim, and Mary became his girlfriend. Other guests had sons. Kleeblatt's life-long friendship with Peter dated from a rainy afternoon with the P Strathon's family. Anzendrech's patron had neither sons nor daughters, but an Alsatian. The dog showed his affection by licking bare shins or dangling fingers. The animal's owner, the vicar of the parish of Bolton-by-Bowland, demonstrated his appreciation by practising German, which he did all the way during tea taking, leaving Alexander little time to savour the cream buns laid out before him.

The Opening Day was a success. Yellow-ribboned boys acted as guides, performed gymnastics, sang '*My Bonny Lies Over The Ocean*.' Kleeblatt recited '*Our England Is A Garden*'. The Reverend W W Shimpton stayed for supper: ham and lettuce and ginger bread. He delivered a speech which Dr Vittauer translated. He then asked the refugee boys to sing his favourite hymn: 'Lord I Was Blind I Could Not See'. The dramatic rise and fall in the minor key ensured that the melody Implanted itself in Anzendrech's memory, although he himself was incapable of rendering it in tune.

Following this the Reverend led a prayer and whilst offering it his mind wandered to the letter in his breast pocket, and to the conference to be held later in the evening. Perhaps the best course would be to transfer Mr Dottis to a post in an English Home. An English Head wouldn't tolerate any hanky-panky from a German subordinate. Send him to a summer camp until a place could be found.

He said "amen", and Dr Vittauer translated and said "amen". Dr Vittauer waited to see whether there was more before giving the signal to Anzendrech to deliver a few words on behalf of the boys. During the moment of uncertainty Mr Dottis rose to his feet and began a speech.

Mr Dottis, translating his own sentences, said that in expressing thanks he was sure he spoke for all staff, and that he wanted to pay tribute to the National Children's Homes and Orphanages for the wonderful work they were doing in providing this wonderful home for the refugee boys in these difficult times. He then put emphasis on the challenge the staff experienced in striking the right balance between the two cultures, English and German, and that the teachers not only taught, but also learnt from the boys.

"I am sure," he concluded, "on this unique occasion, in the presence of our very distinguished guest, it would be appropriate to invite the boys to speak up, so that a better understanding may be forged between the needs of the boys, and ourselves who are privileged to provide these needs."

He looked at Dr Vittauer who was put off his guard by this unscheduled item on the day's programme. The Head nodded and asked to show by hand if any boy wished to make a verbal contribution.

After a brief silence Arne raised his arm.

"What is it?" asked Dr Vittauer.

"Please, we want to have more to eat."

The Reverend looked hard at the child. Did he resemble Oliver Twist? He left the staff table, walked between chairs to the little boy, took his hand and led him into the Common Room.

"You are hungry?"

Arne made no reply. The Minister noticed that the boy carried a yellow shoulder ribbon, so he would have understood the question.

"Tell me, I am your friend."

A tear rolled down Arne's cheek. "I want to see my mummy."

The Reverend fell back in his chair as if he had received a physical blow. It had been a good day, and he, like Sister Helen, would make sure there would be many more. Yet here was misery. He wondered who was worse hit: an orphaned child deprived for ever of parents' love, or Arne who had parents but could not reach them to receive their love. He thought of his own childhood and of his cosy home. He felt inadequate to deal with Arne's sorrow.

"Are you really hungry?"

Arne shook his head.

"Why did you say you want to have more to eat?"

The boy remained silent.

"Speak up. I'm your friend."

"Mr Dottis told me to say we want to get more to eat, and he told me to say there are bedbugs in our rooms."

Two weeks later Mr Dottis was escorted down the back staircase by Sister Helen to a waiting taxi.

Dr Kupfer took over Horticulture and Recreation.

CHAPTER NINE (1939)

The Surgery

Sister Helen strode from one room to another, said "quickly now" to anyone sweeping the floor, washing up, spreading margarine on bread, peeling potatoes, or doing nothing.

Once, when Oscar on orderly duty abandoned the kitchen refuse bucket half way to Mr Gibson's pigsties because he caught a glimpse of Vera in a pink dress meandering on the road, he hurried after her, and on his return forgot delivering the animals' dinner, Sister Helen came across him in the Upper Lounge an hour later and asked him: "Have you seen Nabravowitz?" To which he replied truthfully: "No Sister."

Her mind was on other things.

Hardly had the Dottis crisis been resolved, when she noticed another looming, a consequence of Dr Kupfer concentrating his entire store of charm on Sister April.

The boys noticed this also.

The story circulated from giggling bedroom to giggling bedroom that Heilsterben and Mexler attended Surgery, one with a toothache, the other with a bruised knee, and whilst Dr Kupfer slipped away into the adjoining room for an interlude with wringing hands, they saw a packet of French Letters among an array of stethoscopes, cotton wool pads, eye and ear bowls, iodine jars and other gear. They carefully took one out, severed the tip of the sleeve with a scalpel and replaced it in its envelope.

Dr Kupfer's Penal Code

Dr Kupfer appointed himself as custodian of Riversmead's punishments. He operated the established rules: extra floor scrubbing for excessive giggling in bedrooms, extra potato peeling for sneaking into the sheltered lavatories instead of using the facility under the sky reached through the 'WAY IN'.

Until completion of the new toilet block the dry, lockable, indoor WC's were for staff use only. A few extroverts didn't mind the communal airing on the dug-up tennis court, but most boys would risk a stint of potato peeling by stealing quietly away during meal times. When Dr Kupfer got wind of the ploy, he watched out for departing boys, and followed.

Anzendrech trained himself so that his bowel movements occurred at dead of night.

Miss Zimmerman, to ease the boys' discomfiture, taught during Ancient History how the Romans built great communal houses fitted out with drainage channels underneath boards with holes, on which neighbours met, sat, shat and told jokes.

The boys' joke, which caused further giggling in bedrooms, related how little Arne, on advice of fellow visitors into the canvas enclosure, had pushed himself backwards to reach centrality over the excavation to avoid fouling the edge of the trench, had been assisted in the process by fat Schaumberg so that little Arne's sitting posture had lost stability.

Arne's frail frame became the target of unending teasing. He developed the habit of walking away from scenes of upset in straight lines with hand motions in the manner of Sister April's, muttering to himself exclamations of discontent. Like many of taller stature, he fell victim to the error of blaming well-meaning people rather than the bullies for his misfortune. So when Miss Zimmerman, taking Zoology, stressed the superiority of communal activity over solo acts in all life forms including Homo sapiens, Arne relived the disagreeable close encounter in the communal trench. He picked up a pair of scissors with which the class had cut out reptile shapes, and opening and shutting the blades in the manner of an alligator's jaws, he advanced upon Miss Zimmerman and said: "You are a stupid crocodile."

The severity of the offence caused Dr Kupfer to think up a new punishment. He placed Arne into the windowless potato cupboard, closed the door and locked it.

When Sister Helen heard of this, she confronted Dr Kupfer in the middle of the Dining Hall in full view of various boys, and sending self-discipline over Pendle Hill, admonished him that under no circumstances whatsoever were children, who had lived through the dark terror of the Nazi regime, who suffered traumas of family separations, whose fathers languished in Nazi concentration camps, were these children, she lambasted him, to be locked up in complete darkness, in punishment or in fun, ever. Then she calmed down, and added by way of explanation, that if a child needed to be reprimanded, floor scrubbing or potato peeling had never done harm to mind, body or soul.

Dr Kupfer reached for his keys and let Arne out, after which he aimed for his Surgery to recuperate from Sister Helen's outburst, but before reaching it he came across wringing hands which he followed into the adjacent room.

Mrs Knowles' Ghost

Mrs Knowles faced a shortfall of carrots. She sent word to the neighbouring farm. Mr Gibson arrived, carrying a giant paper sack filled to the brim with the vegetable. As he lifted the receptacle off his shoulder, the bottom split open, and the red roots, which the farmer had helpfully trimmed off their green leaves, rolled all over the kitchen floor.

Mr Gibson, although a staunch Methodist, nevertheless enjoyed the invigorating effect of a sup on special occasions. He left to let the cook gather up the ingredients for the evening's soup, but returned a few minutes later with a hidden flask of gin and two glasses, taking great care that the misdemeanor about to take place would not reach any Home dwellers' eyes.

After two days absence Mrs Knowles explained: "Ghost of Pendle Hill Witch frightened living daylight out of me. I heard noise, clanking noise like Blackburn tram thumping over points in Penny Street, and through wall floated apparition."

Apparently the spectre's attributes had been a displeasing sight: haggard hair, bare bosom like two huge, dried up, flattened carrots, ripped rags and rusty chain, all hanging down. Then to crown it all, it had quaked in a tremulous quaver:

"Crimson on the kitchen floor, crimson in the air,
Crimson on this very earth, crimson everywhere."

It had weakened the Riversmead cook's tenacity to the extent of having to spend a day and two nights indoors at her father's house. It set tongues wagging in folk around her, who offered explanations as to the meaning of the vision: namely the advent of fire and brimstone in Europe's affairs.

"People are right in their prophecy," observed Mr Foutain, exercising his brief to converse with his pupils in English which they didn't do when left to themselves. A frequent visitor to the Prefects' Corner he thought it proper to stimulate awareness of what went on in the wider world. "Fire and brimstone's been around for some time. You may have heard of Guernica. Crimson corpses of women and children everywhere."

Anzendrech recalled the scene on Vienna's Danube Meadow some two years earlier, when a woman accompanying a fugitive, the *Quorgel* Man, had handed crimson leaflets to him and his friend Herbert Stubenegke.

"That was the Civil War in Spain," he said.

"Correct. I reckon Mrs Knowles's Ghost of the Pendle Hill Witch gave a forewarning, like Shakespeare's Witches in Macbeth. You heard of Shakespeare? No? You will. I'm sure Dr Vittauer will rectify that neglect. To return to ghosts ..."

"I've seen the ghost of my aunt Ursula sucking the end of a crimson chicken bone," said rosy-lipped Prefect Eulenhaut.

"You sure it was a chicken bone?" came from reinstated Prefect Oskar.

The query sent fat Schaumberg tittering as he guessed what the Club Primarus President was hinting at.

"I believe in ghosts," said Prefect Malig, the eldest, in a loud voice, at pains to keep the discussion from drifting into frivolity.

"That's your right," replied the teacher of Elementary Philosophy and Conversation English, "in a free country like England."

"What do you believe in, Mr Foutain?" queried Prefect Blitz with the long ears.

"Well, you may call it Science."

Science

"Not everything can be explained by Science," contradicted Malig. "Some things are beyond Science."

"What for instance?" queried fat Schaumberg, wishing to side with the teacher.

"God, for instance," replied Malig

"There's no contradiction here." Mr Foutain stretched his legs and clasped his hands behind the back of his head. "God created the universe with its laws and everything in it: the sun, the earth, ghosts, bedbugs, us, our ability to formulate the laws of the universe, catalogue and manipulate them into science, which enables us to predict certain events, build skyscrapers and make fountain pens."

He reached for his fountain pen inside his breast pocket, rolled it between his thumb and forefinger. He continued, "I say ghosts are part of science, because science is simply the study of what, how and why things happen in nature, in the universe. All things, including ghosts."

"Careful you don't drop your pen." warned fat Schaumberg.

"What happens if I do?"

"Makes an inky mess on the floor," said Prefect Kleeblatt, the one gifted with wit.

"Makes an inky mess on the floor. A forecast based on past observation." Mr Foutain tried his best not to appear supercilious. "Why does it fall to the floor?"

"Things fall to the floor," said Malig. "Happens time after time. It's gravity."

"Gravity. Objects or in scientific lingo masses, attract each other, and the Earth, being a huge mass, attracts every other much smaller mass to itself. We've studied that phenomenon, we've discovered its laws, and the whole caboodle's entered into the realm of Science. So when you say my fountain pen falls to the floor if I let go of it, you make a scientific prediction. As Malig has revealed, things fall to the ground, happens time after time. Ghosts don't happen time after time. They happen rarely, so we are unable to study them closely, so we can't establish laws governing them."

"Don't ghosts appear at the stroke of midnight and vanish at the first cock's crow in the morning," said Anzendrech.

"Well noticed. Even folklore finds it convenient to assign rules to supernatural events. Mrs Knowles' ghost may be the exception that proves the rule. The witch with her massive attributes appeared in broad daylight."

"The witch's massive attributes," fat Schaumberg whispered," banging against her belly button must have sounded like..."

"Big Ben?" Mr Foutain's sharp ears gathered up the opulent

Prefect's remark. He understood the ruckus wrought in boys at pubescence, and he aimed to guide it into educational channels. "That's the bell in London's Houses of Parliament."

"I'd like to go to London to see a bit of life," said Oskar, "instead of being stuck up here where nothing happens except a ghost walking through a brick wall."

Mr Foutain resumed his analysis: "Mrs Knowles' apparition produced a noisy clatter from its trappings hanging down. This means they are made of mass and are therefore subject to gravity. A brick wall is no barrier to the spectre's horizontal movement. So the Earth's surface won't stop it being pulled down vertically by gravity. So Mrs Knowles' ghost ends up at the centre of our globe, huddled together with trillions of other ghosts."

"But people do see ghosts," insisted Malig. "How do you explain that?"

"I don't." Mr Foutain breathed in heavily: "Making a loony guess: perhaps some ghosts, by yet undiscovered means, are catapulted now and then into the atmosphere, like lava from a volcano. As I said before, the event doesn't happen on a regular basis. And irregular occurrences scare people."

"If ghosts coming *through* walls happened as often as bedbugs creeping *on* walls, Mrs Knowles wouldn't be scared of them, would she," said Oskar grinning.

"Speak for yourself, Nabravowitz," returned Mr Foutain, "English people are very house-proud. An Englishman's home is his castle, and he won't tolerate any uninvited intruders, be they two-legged, four-legged or six-legged."

"I was thinking of the tenements in Vienna," said Oskar.

"My living quarters in that city always reeked of naphthalene which kept a moth, ghost or bedbug at bay."

"You lived in Vienna, Mr Foutain?" asked Anzendrech.

"For a while, in the Brigittenau. My fairy godmother got me out before the Nazis arrived. I changed my name and appearance during my travels."

"You changed your appearance, Mr Foutain?" Kleeblatt asked, intrigued.

Anzendrech interjected: "I lived in the Brigittenau, near the Danube. I learnt to swim in the Danube. I often wish I had a fairy godmother who could arrange a swim in the sea for me."

"What was your name before you changed it, Mr Foutain?" Kleeblatt continued the interrogation.

"Enough for now." The teacher explained he had yet to mingle with younger pupils for conversation English, and left.

Fat Schaumberg said: "I've been to the sea. Near Trieste in Italy. The women there, when they strip off..."

"English women," drawled Oskar, purporting to have had experience in the matter, "are as hard as eggs boiled for two hours. It's hard work breaking them. Back in Vienna, I had something going on with a skirt every two months."

"So did I," said Blitz.

"So did I," said fat Schaumberg.

"Me too," said rosy-lipped, curly-headed Eulenhaut, unconvincingly.

"What about you, Anzendrech"?

"Me?" He felt unrest steal into his brain. "Yes, something going on with a skirt. You mean dancing, Nabravowitz?"

"For shit's sake, grow up," growled Oskar. He had not forgiven Anzendrech for using his surname.

"I think Mr Foutain's wearing a wig," said Kleeblatt.

"I think he's a spy," said Malig.

Llwyngwryl

Mr Wooseley learnt a lot about Riversmead from his daughter, Mrs Knowles, during her day's recovery.

She told her favourite story: "I've mislaid key for broom cupboard, and asked tiny Arne to go to Sister Cicely for loan of cupboard key. She has spare set. Back comes Arne, carrying tiny cup of tea. He mistook 'cupboard key' for 'cup of tea'. Talk about laugh: here's poor Sister boiling away tiny kettle on tiny stove in tiny room to send me tiny cup of tea in kitchen amongst galaxy of kettles."

Her father smiled dutifully. His bigger interest lay in the Home itself, barely two miles away: a refugee Home for sixty-eight boys, who, as Sister Helen had already pointed out, were in need of the Boy Scouts Movement.

The Riversmead Committee convened a meeting, which Mr Wooseley and industrial tycoon Mr Townsend from Birmingham attended. The wealthy businessman concerned himself with the welfare of boys. He financed two annual summer camps in Llwyngwryl on the Welsh coast at the foot of Cader Idris, one for Boy Scouts, one for orphaned boys. The Scout jamboree had already taken place, so he proposed a contingent of Riversmead boys for the orphan camp.

"I can accommodate six," he said.

"Two seniors, two from the middle group, two youngsters," recommended Dr Vittauer.

"I'm prepared to make the selection of who goes," said Dr Kupfer.

Sister Helen intervened. "Let's leave it to their fairy godmothers. Put names in three hats, seniors, middle ones and young ones, and take out two from each."

Mr Foutain seconded.

The names drawn from the senior batch were Anzendrech and Oskar; Drehbank and Arne were two from the younger groups.

Mr Wooseley then suggested starting a Boy Scout Branch at Riversmead, which the committee agreed to have in place as soon as financial and practical means allowed.

The sight of the Irish Sea shimmering silver in the glow of the sun sent the hearts of the six lucky ones into a frenzy of excitement and expectation.

Tents were already up when they arrived in Mr Townsend's spacious car. The English orphans kicked at footballs or rolled in the grass, some threw tree branches onto a great pile, others busied themselves with plates and cutlery in a big marquee, all activity proceeding in very much do as-you-like fashion. Two biggish boys directed very loosely what, if anything, others should do.

Martin and Bob appeared, shook every Riversmead hand and presented themselves as guides for the duration of the camp. With eight weeks' accumulated English and a repertoire of hand signals, a tour of the camp commenced. They came upon Mr Townsend talking to a young man on a motorbike.

"Meet our X-boy who's grown into manhood," The camp chief

introduced them.

"How do you do?" said Anzendrech, wandering whether the motorcyclist suffered from a mathematical syndrome X like his friend GK had done once in Vienna.

The Riversmead group split up. Oskar took charge of two younger boys. Walking to their quarters, he monopolised Bob's attention by demonstrating with both hands how the X-boy's motorbike needed to be handled, which necessitated his protégés carrying his belongings.

"You come with me," Martin said to Anzendrech, "bring your two infants along. Tell me their names."

"This is Drehbank, this is Arne."

The tents were of conical shape, supported by a centre pole, each sleeping eight. Martin lay down on a ground sheet, feet against the post, and asked Anzendrech's contingent to follow suit by way of practice. Their bodies radiated outward like petals of a giant daisy.

"I'll be in the grub marquee to see what damage our new cook is doing. He's Mr Dottis, he came from your place, didn't he, Riversmead," said Martin taking his leave.

Anzendrech swam in the sea.

His English grew by leaps in Martin and Bob's company. However when squatting around the evening campfire, he could neither grasp the connection between one, two or more men, Ventimo, his dog and a meadow, nor understand the Rary, which required a long way to be tipped.

Sitting on the stone parapet of the Llwyngwryl Bridge, awaiting the call for dinner by the sound of a gigantic wooden spoon striking a dustbin lid, the Riversmead boys and English orphans watched Llwyngwryl youth lick ice cream and call out to one another in total gibberish. To their surprise Martin and Bob suffered from the same deficiency of comprehension.

"There's a village no more than thirty miles away," explained Martin, "which needs fifty-six letters to write its name. Nobody except a few inhabitants ever learnt how to spell it."

They became aware that three girls leant against the wall diagonally opposite. The maidens conversed loudly in the unintelligible parlance, shooting glances into the boys' direction.

Straight-cut fringes topped the round faces of two look-alikes, perhaps twins, the third let her reddish hair flow loosely down her neck over a bright green dress. Anzendrech's saw a vision of Greti Katherine, followed by a state of incompetence, used to it by now, which caused his personality to shrivel into something like a wet sponge.

But Oskar pushed his comb through his yellow wave, and next instant stood on the other side of the road, spelling out English and German words, and being taught Welsh ones in return. The rest witnessed his ardour in admiration mixed with jealousy, and trotted off at the first sound of wood hitting galvanised metal.

The food marquee covered three rows of trestle tables and benches onto which the orphaned youths streamed in a disorganised manner, settled down amidst an orgy of shouts, got up again to collect plates of the soup variety, and proceeded with them to a steaming pot attended by a very tall orphan dishing out with an enormous ladle enormous portions of meat stew, beans, and carrots. Everyone stood in line, and as the ladle emptied its fill, the giant said "nuff?" and the receiver of food said "yes."

Observing this ritual several times it dawned on Anzendrech that the monosyllabic dialogue referred to an enquiry as to sufficiency. He ate his meat broth smarting at the thought of failure when it came to competing against Nabrawovitz in the quest of the feminine. But his spirits rose at the sight of the pudding: stewed plums with custard. He persuaded Drehbank, when asked "nuff?" to both answer "no."

The tall orphan ladled prunes, juice and custard with infinite care up to the brims of their soup plates, drowning supporting thumbs. They hadn't meant him to respond to their voracious pleas in such generous manner. So here they were, Anzendrech and Drehbank, flushed with embarrassment, taking three-inch long steps to avoid spillage, all eyes on them. Martin, Bob and a few others spurred them on to race each other to their places. When nearly there, Bob tickled Anzendrech's ribs, the plate wobbled, and pudding dripped onto the trestle table. As he sat down everybody clapped. He thought it best to play along with the act, he took a bow, wiped his spoon on his shirt as Charlie Chaplin did in films, smacked his lips, and the applause grew louder and wouldn't stop.

So he took another bow, patted his stomach, and still the

cheering went on. Then he saw Oskar walking in the marquee. He realised the clapping neither hailed him nor Drehbank, but Oskar. Word had gone round of his conquests on the bridge, and now he came in late, and he knew they were paying tribute to his valour, and he grinned in acknowledgement and pressed the wave of his hair into shape.

"What idiot spilled custard all over my place?" he asked looking at the overflowing plates. "Who's going to wipe it off? When I come back I want to see a clean table. Stupid to fill plates up that high. Trust Anzendrech to think of that."

He walked away. Arne fetched out his handkerchief and mopped up the yellow blobs onto which a fly with pulsating wings had settled. Applause soared up again. Oskar, taking three-inch long steps, carried, in both hands and drowned thumbs, his plate filled to the brim with Irish meat broth. Bob tickled him. Brown broth spilt upon the spot which had just been cleaned of plum flavoured custard.

Anzendrech remarked: "What's more stupid: thinking up a stupid idea, or aping a stupid idea?"

"Hercules with the ladle thinks us from Riversmead are starving," said Oskar.

They ate in silence, after a while Oskar leant over to Anzendrech: "Alwyn wants to see you. She's the one with no tits, with the red hair in the green dress."

Anzendrech's heart missed a beat, his tongue stuck to his gums.

"I said no chance," Oskar continued. "I said to Alwyn, that's Anzendrech, he's immature. I don't think she understood. She wants to see you."

The rattle of spoons against trestle tables ended Anzendrech's nightmare of a stammering rendezvous with Alwyn. The ex-boy stood on his feet.

"Lads," he said, "tomorrow we're climbing the mound. Rise at six, breakfast finished by seven, away by eight. It's a hard slog to the top. The aim's to get there, don't matter how long it takes, who's first, who's last. It's not a race. Whoever reaches the top wins, and we'll all make it. Cader Idris is one of the highest mountains in Wales, 2929 feet. Mr Dottis, our new kitchen man, is coming with us."

Anzendrech caught Oskar's eyes and saw in them the desire to take advantage of the ex-boy's anti-competitive words. He saw in them the ambition to present himself to Alwyn and her friends as the perpetual number-one-boy. So there was to be a race after all, one having two runners. That Mr Dottis had reappeared on the scene seemed of little consequence to either.

To the Top of Cader Idris

Rugged rocks and clusters of boulders with craggy cracks on a one-in-one incline confronted the sweating, puffing rivals on the last couple of hundred feet climb. They clambered up, Anzendrech some thirty feet ahead.

"Oskar!" The cry came from the spread out party below.

"Oskar! Oskar!" reverberated about their ears.

The blue-eyed boy stopped, looked down. Anzendrech also.

"Oskar! Arne's in trouble. He got stung. By an insect. Can you come and do your magic cure?" Mr Dottis waved his handkerchief above his head.

"Another bedbug?" Oskar hollered.

He glanced at Anzendrech who shrugged his shoulder, but remained otherwise immobile.

"Come quick. Arne's calling for you. He's in pain."

Oskar started to descend.

Anzendrech wondered: did his contender do so over concern of Arne's plight, or over the opportunity of an excuse for failing to be first on top? Anzendrech resumed his climb. He set foot on the summit, but as the ex-boy had said, it wasn't a race. Still, he felt good daydreaming that the winner's name would somehow reach Alwyn's ears.

As the ex-boy had predicted, all made it to the top. There the Riversmead boys joined the orphaned boys triumphantly shouting at the glittering Irish Sea to the west, and all of Wales to the east:

"Llwyngwryl, Llwyngwryl, rock, rock, rock!

"Llwyngwryl, Llwyngwryl, rock, rock, rock!"

Anzendrech thought, if this were his Vienna class on top of Schneeberg, they would stand to attention in close ranks, arms stretched out forward, and yell:

"Sieg Heil! Sieg Heil! Sieg Heil! Sieg Heil!"

CHAPTER TEN (1939-40)

Tennis

The new washroom-toilet block opened without fanfare. The 'WAY IN' trench disappeared to be topped by strips of Mr Gibson's grasslands.

The farmer motored his seven-foot field mower over the turf. Mr Grun and Mr Foutain dug holes and cemented the old tennis posts into them. The House Sisters closed gaps in the net with black twine. But Sister Helen would not be moved to endorse the erection of a surrounding fence. This led to a shrinking reserve of tennis balls, especially during Dr Kupfer's massed classes, due to the court bordering on one side with Mr Gibson's fallow field of high weeds.

After five or six airings the school tennis racquets resembled framed holes of disintegrating spider webs, and were laid to rest in the games cupboard. After which lessons ceased. Play on the court became restricted to those who, equipped with wholesome gear, could also afford regular renewal of balls. None of the boys could. So no one played, except Oskar. The blue-pupilled boy's instinctive eye for a ball assured that he was sucked into the salary-earning Riversmead tennis fraternity, of which Dr Kupfer was the principal proponent.

This annoyed Anzendrech. Here was another pursuit in which he would not outshine Oskar. However he determined to have a go. He disentangled two racquets from the abandoned pile, and with Kleeblatt spent one afternoon restringing them with overspill of the Sister's black twine. A search in the border weeds revealed three blackened, weather-worn, bald balls, which, upon hand pressure, regrettably squashed into pancake shapes. Barefooted they commenced play.

When Mr Foutain saw this, he took pity. He brought his own racquet and with Sister Frances' approval, hers. He also held between thumb and middle finger one still off-white, still hairy, still firm, tennis ball and offered the two boys the lot on loan. He emphasised that on no account were they even for a split second to take their eyes off this ball, a piece of advice primarily given to avoid losing it, but which would go some way in raising the standard of the players' game.

The door to the adjoining Dining Hall had barely closed behind Mr Foutain, when it opened again to let Oskar through.

"You got to come off," he said and walked to the centre of the net.

"We've only just started," said Anzendrech.

"I need the practice," Oskar retorted as Dr Kupfer, white-shirted and white-trousered, filled the doorway. He held two tennis racquets under his arm, and he carried four dazzling tennis balls in a yet unopened, green-netted pouch.

"We need the practice too," said Anzendrech, striking Mr Foutain's ball.

Dr Kupfer scooped it up, as by ill-gotten chance or miss-hit, it rolled towards him. He pushed it into his pocket.

"The ball belongs to Mr Foutain," shouted Anzendrech.

"I shall see that it is returned to Mr Foutain unharmed," Dr Kupfer replied.

Anzendrech seethed with anger. He picked up the three spent balls, and lashed out at one, hoping it would reach Kleeblatt. It flopped into the net. And so did the second, and so did the third.

"That's no way to behave on a tennis court," warned Dr Kupfer.

"Stealing a ball is?" asked Anzendrech.

"What?" Shouted Dr Kupfer.

"Mr Foutain lent it to us so we could play, as otherwise we never get a chance."

Dr Kupfer's eyes focused on Anzendrech's feet. "You've been told you must not step onto the court without wearing proper tennis shoes."

"Bare soles don't do any damage."

"Quazzel nich!" The doctor, emotionally charged, abandoned the school's decree that staff address the boys in English only. "Shut up! Go now, quietly. Argument won't foster our friendship."

"I'm not sure I'm that keen on it," Anzendrech replied under his breath.

"Anzendrech," said the doctor, "you will report to Sister Helen for three buckets potato peeling."

The Blackburn Concert

A poster outside the Queen's Hall, Blackburn, announced a concert by the Riversmead Boys Choir singing traditional German and English songs. Organised by the Methodist Church, it aimed to uplift Riversmead's image in the community.

Thorough rehearsals were called for. Dr Kupfer assumed the role of Musical Director, and proceeded to arrange 'Oh My Darling, Clementine' into four part harmonies. Anzendrech had neither inherited his mother's sonorous voice nor acquired his father's gift for reproducing melodies. He liked listening to songs, was able to hear them in his mind, but could not keep in tune singing them. Dr Kupfer, after placing his ear against the stricken mouth, stepped back, curved his forefinger repeatedly in a beckoning manner, which meant that Anzendrech needed to be separated from the choir. The doctor then decreed that the visit to Blackburn applied to singing boys only.

Anzendrech did not understand the harsh treatment. Could not the Doctor have asked him to mouth the words without producing sound? Or was the Choir Master still nettled over Mr Foutain's intervention in the tennis ball incident and the subsequent lifting of the potato-peeling sentence?

Blutwurst and Arne also stayed away from the coach ride to Lancashire's renowned city and jelly trifle tea. Their forced abstention related to punishment for more serious misdemeanours than singing off key. Blutwurst had been caught three times smoking woodbines in the new toilet block; and Arne, reprieved from his stint in the potato cupboard, suffered Dr Kupfer's alternative disciplinary measure.

Pendle Hill

Anzendrech concluded that exploring untamed nature would be a morale-boosting substitute for the missed incursion into Blackburn city culture. The broad flank of Pendle Hill had been smirking at him for the past ten to twelve weeks, and he wanted to subdue it by direct assault, like he had Cader Idris. Would that Alwyn knew of his exploits! Blutwurst said he'd come along. Arne's meek disposition deterred him from joining.

Once over the Ribble and railway line, the two explorers kept to a straight line. They climbed over walls and fences. Cultivated fields gave way to wet, clumpy, thickly-tussocked bog of a generally upward trend, continued over humps and ridges before ending at the vertical-looking slope of Pendle Hill proper. Blutwurst dropped onto the dry, stony incline, declared that he could not take another step until he had strengthened his lungs. He lit four stumps one after the other.

On top the land squelched water as the bog had done below. They saw grass and sky, nothing else. Populated England had vanished, obscured by the never-ending crown of Pendle Hill. A sense of timelessness filled their young souls, a feeling that here nothing had changed, would change, come Hitlers, wars, pestilence, gloom, joy or Witches. Anzendrech felt that something of him could take root here, as once, a long time ago, something of him had taken root on the Danube Meadow.

Having climbed one side of Pendle Hill, it went without saying they would not turn back until they had looked down the other side and had seen what there was to see. The other side took a long time in coming, but when it came, it arrived with a bang, a bang not for ears but for eyes. Below: chimneys, smoke-belching chimneys. Tall chimneys, short chimneys, middle sized chimneys, as far as vision would take them: chimneys. The horizon stacked with smoking chimneys.

Low Gill Junction

"Fire and brimstone. We're in it now, all of us," announced Mrs Knowles on September 3rd 1939.

Dr Vittauer spoke to assembled Riversmead, first in German, then in English. He finished with the words: "It will be difficult for our English friends and protectors who have given us a home, it will be difficult for us. We must and we will face the challenges ahead, we must and we will remain loyal to our host nation, we must and we will think of and pray for our loved ones left behind in what are now enemy countries." He then asked everybody to stand and he said a prayer, in which all joined in.

The rituals of Riversmead life continued without noticeable change.

When Sister Helen learnt that Anzendrech's brother, Rudi, resided at farmer Brast, with whose daughter she had climbed the slopes of Ingleborough, near High Bentham a mere sixteen miles away as the crow flies, she set about arranging a visit for the Riversmead boy. Letters traversed the sixteen miles. Rudi and his Quaker Friends suggested Alexander come by train to Low Bentham.

Sister Helen opined that Clapham or Ingleton lay nearer to Mr Brast's farmstead. "Ask for a ticket to Clapham rather than Ingleton," she instructed Anzendrech giving the matter final thought as he set off at eight o'clock in the morning. "You've got to change at Hellifield. You'll be there in about an hour and a half."

Alexander did as advised. The ticket office at Chatburn consulted a huge book and located Chatham on the southern side of the River Thames to the east of the metropolis of London. Alexander knew this wasn't what Sister Helen had in mind. He had mixed up the Chats and Claps. He said he was told to change at Hellifield.

The ticket man shook his head, muttered something about swapping trains in Manchester and said: "I'll give you a ticket to Hellifield, ask them there."

To avoid the risk of being hauled to the Distant South, Anzendrech opted for Sister Helen's other choice of destination, Ingleton, when standing in front of Hellifield's ticket office.

"Second train through Platform One."

Anzendrech never discovered what went amiss. Perhaps they told him wrong, perhaps he miscounted, perhaps goods trains didn't count as trains. So he had the good fortune of journeying north on the spectacular Settle line. He travelled over long viaducts, into dark tunnels, along broad valleys, in and out of towns, Kirkby Stephen, Appleby. The grassland sodden with wet, the bleakness, held him spellbound. He had seen nothing like it before.

Eventually the train bounced over a great number of points through a confluence of railway lines on which a multitude of steaming engines puffed away. Slowing down he realised he had come to a large town. He alighted and showed his ticket to the nearest human being in uniform. The man led him up stairways, across bridges, to a far-away platform and impressed on him to catch the next train and change at Low Gill Junction. So Anzendrech had the good fortune of journeying south on the spectacular Lancaster line as far as Low Gill Junction.

There was nothing at Low Gill Junction. The one person, the ticket collector, said the next train to Ingleton would leave at 7.17 p m. The Station Clock indicated half past three in the afternoon. He showed Anzendrech where to wait, and rode off into nothingness on a bicycle. Alexander had three pennies of the large 'd' variety. He popped them into a wall-mounted chocolate dispenser and extracted a late lunch of three red-sleeved, dark chocolate bars. He walked up and down the platforms, then up and down the solitary road flanked either side by nothing.

At seven o'clock it was pitch dark: war-time black-out enhanced by the blackness of nothing. Anzendrech noticed a faint flickering light. It turned out to belong to the ticket collector on his bicycle. The man recognised the juvenile blob against the station wall, came up and told him to be careful to count six stations, and get off at Ingleton, the seventh.

The youngster remained deeply indebted for the railway man's advice. The night was black. He saw nothing from the train, when moving, when stationary. He was the only occupant in the corridor less compartment; he wondered whether another heart besides his and the engine driver's beat on that train. He counted six stops, hoped they all took place in stations, and got off at the seventh.

He found himself on what felt like a street. He placed his hand some distance from his eyes to test whether he could see it. He could not. He heard footsteps, he ran towards them, bumped into something soft and said: "Please, can you help me."

The footsteps had feminine voices, which by chance, or by Heaven's intervention, or perhaps they belonged to kinsfolk of Sister Helen, had heard of Farmer Brast. The ladies knew the layout of the town blind-folded. They walked him to some roller shutters, banged on them. Someone opened and they were ushered inside. Light flooded the scene. The greengrocer, proprietor of the roller shutters, possessed a telephone. Farmer Brast also possessed a telephone.

Alexander narrated how he had travelled to Ingleton via 'Carleeslay', hence the late hour. Rudi corrected his brother's pronunciation of the town on Scotland's border, told him that half of Bentham's population and the whole of Lancashire Police had been looking for him since the hour of his non-arrival on the Hellifield-Bentham train twelve hours earlier.

"Why didn't you get a ticket to Low Bentham?" he queried.

Alexander elucidated: "Sister Helen said Ingleton or Clapham were nearer."

Mr Brast sat up: "Sister Helen? Would that be Sister Helen Webston?"

"Yes."

"Ah!" Mrs Brast's eloquent contribution suggested Alexander's answer explained everything.

"So what did you do all day long?" asked Mr Brast.

"I waited for a train at Lowgill Junction."

"Ah," said Mrs Brast.

The three days with Rudi were wet. Mrs Brast lent the brothers her umbrella. They splashed through puddles to Quaker Friends' Meetings. The war was on everybody's lips, a problem for the Friends who were pacifists, and a problem for Rudi and Alexander who were enemy aliens.

Rudi said: "I'll be sent to an internment camp on the Isle of Man. Actually it may be a blessing in disguise. I know a bit of Chemistry, I can identify the gases escaping from decomposing vegetables through olfactory analysis. But this doesn't cut any ice with Mr Brast. He makes me shovel the muck about just the same. So escape from here to anywhere is welcome. And when the British Government realises that people who have been hounded by the Nazis are not England's enemies but her friends, they'll let us out again. They'll be glad of our efforts in helping to fight our common foe."

"I've heard from mum and dad," said Alexander, "through the Red Cross. They're still alive. The Nazis call them Wanzen. Did you get the letter from Greti Katherine? I sent it on to you."

"Yes, thanks Xandi."

"What did she say?"

"Nothing about you."

Be Prepared

"Whaat aare thee uuses oof thee Scout staaff?"

"To lead a Scout troop through a flooded river."

"Yeees." Said Mr Wooseley, and waited for more.

Kleeblatt whispered into Anzendrech's ear: "To trip up Mr Grun during woodwork lessons."

"To ward off a wild dog," said Oskar, remembering what he had studied so diligently all morning.

"Yeees." Mr Wooseley nodded agreement.

Oskar had run out of ideas, so Eulenhaut butted in: "To ward off a wild cat."

Mr Wooseley removed his Scout hat, scratched his head, and said: "Yeees."

"To ward off ..." Oskar looked pleadingly at the troop.

"A wild mouse," Kleeblatt came to his assistance.

"What about when you come across an injured man lying by the roadside?" Mr Wooseley queried.

"Like on the road from Jericho to Jerusalem?" asked Anzendrech.

"Juust soo."

"To ward off a wild vulture," said Oskar.

Malig came up with: "To make a stretcher using four Scout staves."

"Veeryy gooood."

This completed the theoretical part of the test, the practical bit followed. The boys in blue shirts, shorts and Australian-type headgear had to get a fire going using wood only, no paper of any sort allowed, and restricted to one match. This, in moisture friendly Lancashire, at the end of March, was indeed a tall order. The boys gathered sticks and branches, and built an imposing heap. The honour of striking the single match fell upon the senior troop leader Malig. The flame flared up between his thumb and forefinger, he pushed the fire into the pile. It went out.

"Neeveermiind," said Mr. Wooseley.

He pulled a dozen of the thinnest sticks from the stack, snapped them into shorter lengths, and arranged them into a loosely interwoven pyramid-like structure. He laid a freshly lit match under the slenderest twig. He made a tent-like shape with his large hands, placed them, whilst in a kneeling position, over the struggling glow for protection (or in prayer, as Kleeblatt whispered to Anzendrech).

Blowing with baby breath from a circular shaped mouth into the triangular opening created by his palms, he nursed the flickering sparks until crackling wood signified fire. So the boys passed the practical test as well. Mr Wooseley congratulated the troop and distributed badges.

"Youu muust soow theem oontoo youur shiirts youurseelves," he said.

Oskar knew there'd be many young admirers competing to do the job for him.

To celebrate the satisfactory outcome, Mr Wooseley invited the troop leaders: Malig, Kleeblatt, Anzendrech and Oskar (Mr Wooseley having acceded to the popular practice of calling Nabravowitz by his Christian name) to tea. This raised high expectations, especially for Malig, as both Mr Wooseley and Malig's girlfriend resided near Waddington. Oskar immediately set up a plan in which he with Vera and Malig with Mary would spend an hour or so for a get-together in the village after tea. Kleeblatt and Anzendrech were not incorporated into the scheme. Neither took kindly to the idea of hanging around whilst the other two amused themselves, since the four were expected to keep together in a team. So Malig suggested to Oskar that they could ask Vera and Mary to bring along two further girls. Anzendrech's brain immediately experienced a void.

"A girl for Anzendrech," jeered Oskar, "you're joking? He don't know that girls got naught between their legs. Anyway he's totally besotted with Alwyn. He wouldn't want to be unfaithful to Alwyn."

"You never told me," Kleeblatt turned to Anzendrech, "who's Alwyn?"

"She eyeballed him in Llwyngwryl last summer," volunteered Oskar.

"I never spoke a word to Alwyn!" Anzendrech objected, inwardly fuming.

"That's just it," said Oskar. "Vera won't be very happy when she finds out I've lumbered a dumb ninny on her friend Maisy."

"Maisy's for Anzendrech? Who's the lucky one I've got?" asked Kleeblatt.

"Gladys."

"Maisy and Gladys, are they wild?"

"That's for you to find out," replied Malig.

"Because if they are," said Kleeblatt "we reserve the right to make use of our Scout staff."

The blank look on Oskar's face prompted Kleeblatt to elucidate: "To ward off wild females of the human species!"

Malig and Oskar approached Mrs Knowles to deliver a note to her niece, Mary.

The appointed day arrived and the troop leaders set forth on their trek to Waddington in anticipation of Mrs Wooseley's acclaimed, delicately cut, brown bread cucumber sandwiches, to be followed by thrills in the darker alleyways of the village. Anzendrech had accepted to be prepared, according to the Scout motto, for any eventuality including outwitting a knotted-up tongue and empty brain, not only to impress Maisy, but also to be on level terms with Nabrawovitz. He was rehearsing things to say, like: 'England's a nice country with nice people.'

The Air Raid

A mighty roar gushed down from above.

The aeroplane's fuselage barely missed the Tower, the wings covered the width of the North and South Buildings. The Scout troop leaders looked up, picked out the pilot and a crew member targeting a machine gun at them. The markings near the tail end were that of the German Luftwaffe. The aircraft disappeared behind Gibson's farm, reappeared over the Cement Works near Clitheroe, made a U-turn, flew back along the Ribble valley to thunder again over Riversmead. It retraced its previous flight to the Cement Works, dropped two bombs and vanished over Pendle Hill.

Riversmead was not prepared for this. The Scout troop leaders, alas, were not prepared for this. Mrs Knowles rocketed into the bricked-up workshop, which had been designated as air raid shelter. Boys, sisters, kitchen helpers, troop leaders, Mr Grun, the Kupfers,

Mr Foutain, everybody, rushed behind the cook into a mighty panic laden squeeze.

Two minutes after the bombs had exploded Mr Foutain said: "He could have wiped out the lot of us."

Five minutes after the bombs had exploded Dr Vittauer's telephone rang. Clitheroe Police strongly advised the Headmaster that in order to forestall possible angry scenes, it would be wise for enemy aliens to remain within the precincts of the Home for the foreseeable future.

After ten minutes an All Clear siren sounded.

After fifteen minutes Mr Vittauer opened the door to the workshop and said: "You can come out now. But don't go anywhere. Beyond our fences is out of bounds for everybody."

Then he telephoned the Wooseleys. Anzendrech's tongue received a reprieve.

Three hours later four disgruntled teenage lasses twiddled their thumbs in frustrated expectancy on Waddington bridge, listening to the sentiment expressed by passing villagers:

"We'll teach the Kraut a lesson yet."

CHAPTER ELEVEN (1940-41)

Exit Sister April

Sister April left quietly. Dr Kupfer saw her off standing behind a window in the Common Room, Mrs Kupfer did likewise behind another in the Reading Room.

The boys, in their classrooms, didn't see her go, but knew of the moment when they heard the slamming door of the taxi.

"She's cooking a redhead in her oven," said Oskar.

"You got see-through eyes, Nabravowitz?" asked Anzendrech.

"No, I don't have see-through eyes, but I know *Kupfer,* Copper, is red."

"Dr Kupfer?"

"Yes, Dr Kupfer," mimicked Oskar.

Heilsterben and Mexler grinned and hunched their shoulders up, shortening their necks in a gesture of dissipating guilt.

The Riversmead Committee did not look for a replacement. Sister Helen had effectively managed the Home by herself from the start, and by all accounts would continue to do so. But another problem loomed.

Mr Foutain went off on one of his lightening visits to London, and on his return he endorsed what the local police bobby had already hinted at, that the entire German staff would be shipped to the Isle of Man for internment.

Darkening Days

As the German teachers were removed one after the other, English replacements had to be found, however difficult the process, especially when every able-bodied male candidate underwent training to throw the Wehrmacht back over the Siegfried line.

"I pray that in these darkening days this fresh upheaval may prove a blessing in disguise for the boys," said Sister Laura.

"So do I," from Sister Frances.

"And I," from Sister Cicely.

"I also." The thought that amongst new English teachers might be a man of waiting breed, resisted immediate dismissal, but after a second's fantasising Sister Helen's self-discipline regained control. "Let's all pray that the Lord bestows common sense upon the leaders of nations so they stop this senseless war, that He grants fortitude to whosoever is caught up in it, that He protects our departing German friends who are innocent like the rest of us."

"Like Dr Kupfer?" whispered Sister Cicely. She had cherished a passion for the doctor herself, but had been too astute to let her secret out.

"Like Dr Kupfer, like Sister April." Sister Helen continued: "That He grants us the wisdom not to judge others as we are all sinners, and that we shall become friends with our new English colleagues."

"Amen."

Anzendrech took from his locker the old, pre-war correspondence. His father had said to him if something needed to be written which would give the Nazi censors reason to torment the family, he would compose the words in such a way, that the first letter in each line read downwards spelled out the forbidden sentence. The paper in his hand, dated August 1939, told of the hot summer, the unbroken sunshine and that everything was in place for brother Pauli to leave for England on the fifth of September. The vertical message read:

w a r i s c o m i n g h o p e p a u l i w i l l g e t a w a y i n t i m e

Four months since his last twenty-five words home. He could write another twenty-five. The Red Cross would see that father and mother got them. What can he say in twenty-five words including address? 'I am well. I get plenty to eat. I have friends. I study a lot. I love you.'

The Dragon

The new Headmaster, Mr Hozell, arrived with a Dragon.

The Dragon had born him two little girls. Mrs Hozell's concern, keeping her offspring and herself from coming into contact with the resident, vermin-infested refugee boys, occupied her from morning to evening. She commandeered the rooms along the North Wing corridor, which had given shelter to the entire German staff before their internment. She decreed the area out of bounds for boys and vociferously discouraged visits from House Sisters. She and her daughters never appeared for meals in the dining hall. Kitchen staff wheeled separately prepared food on dainty, specially bought trolleys to her apartment. Her strategy to keep aloof suited both the boys and the Sisters, as neither were skilled in cultivating manageable relations with gall spitting dragons.

On one occasion Anzendrech met Mrs Hozell coming down the main staircase whilst he was going up. She redrew the boundary of her private domain then and there, included the stairs, and gave him four debit points for the transgression of trespass, which cost him 2d. This was one week's pocket money, equivalent to the price of a potato crisp bag containing a small screwed up blue paper packet with salt, which, when poured into the bag, produced perhaps a bland crisp which had missed the salt avalanche followed by one which had not and was like a taste of heaven.

Mr. Hozell made it his brief to transform German customs into traditions guarded by the Union Jack. He was too busy to undertake regular teaching himself, but filled in whenever he felt in the mood to acquaint the boys with the legends of Sir Walter Raleigh and tobacco, Francis Drake and bowls, Guy Fawkes and parliament, 1066 and All That, the MCC and Cricket.

His three chief noticeable accomplishments focussed on the possession of a large, forward pointing chin so that his lower front teeth encompassed his upper, and with which he could produce an explosive "no Sah!" in reply to a boy's plea for the use of the football instead of cricket stumps; the possession of a dragon; and carrying arms permanently stuck to his sides and protruding out horizontally at the elbows, ending in drooping hands, the sight of which always arousing in Anzendrech the urge to hang his shirts over them.

According to Sister Helen's intuition any robbers on any road would take to their heels at the distant sight of the Dragon, thus abandoning any plans of immediate attack. And Mr Hozell, nurturing a fastidious disposition, would not venture into bandit territory without having his wife in tow.

Another replacement was Mr Storm MA, in matters of health not unlike Mr Grun. He was single, undernourished, suffered not only from a lung ailment which had disqualified him from military service, but also from insufficient years, (twenty) which ruled him out as a waiting aspirant in Sister Helen's eyes. He was to teach English and all subjects connected with English like English Songs, English Weather, English History, English Diet, English Swear Words, the last unofficially. Sister Helen speculated that had he ventured onto the Biblical Road, the robbers would have kept off the victim in the parable, and attacked him instead for easier meat.

Mr Sidge, afflicted with conscientious objection, was to be engrossed with teaching Sciences, Natural and Theoretical, and with keeping his slim, nineteen-year-old wife Holly at bay from the older boys. This preoccupation precluded him from much other activity, and certainly, Sister Helen guessed, from getting embroiled with a robbed man lying in a roadway.

The Gebirges

The school, after running for twelve weeks on a stretched staff, saw the arrival of the Gebirge family, fifty per cent British, fifty per cent Austrian. Mr Gebirge's subjects were Mathematics, Geometry and Technical Drawing. His wife would assist in mending boys' clothes, and having trained as a nurse, attend to the Home's medical needs. The fourteen year old Bruno Gebirge, when introduced by Mr Hozell, would be just another boy like any other.

In 1926 Herr Gebirge had pulled an attractive young lady from an unfriendly lake at Zell-am-See during high winds whilst on holidays. He had travelled to the Tyrol from Linz, she from Manchester. The rescued girl liked the little Austrian tourist town. He took a fancy to both.

He tended to blame himself for his shortcomings, including his craving to carry on doing whatever he was doing. Having a good time in Zell-am-See for a week was reason to carry on having a good time there. He secured a teaching job in the local Gustav Mahler School, and married the Mancunian, who found work in the local hospital.

Herr Gebirge's larger than average corpulence stemmed from his habit to carry on eating when he was eating. Paradoxically, stomach gripes followed frequent hurried breakfasts due to his propensity to continue sleeping when he was sleeping.

His erotic drive obeyed the general pattern of keeping to the status quo. For weeks the proximity of soft, female skin did nothing to rouse him. Then, once roused, his never-ending lunges wanted to make up for lost nights. After the birth of Bruno he felt responsible when his wife moved into a separate bedroom, because his snoring, once started, did not cease until his waking. It disturbed the baby and caused him to cry. The resulting cacophony kept the mother from refreshing slumber.

Then came 1938.

The changes in ritual, which the new regime introduced, did not divert him from keeping to a set course. He failed to understand that saying "Heil Hitler" at the commencement of a lesson would ease penetration of the Binomial Theorem into the voids of his pupils' heads. Saying it was also a new thing, and it happened that he forgot to say it. And just as in 1914 he had argued against militarism partly from conviction and partly from the desire to maintain the run of a stable lifestyle, he pushed forward similar views in the staff room of the renamed Hermann Göring School.

His colleagues did not take kindly to his unpatriotic talk. They connived together and, in collusion with newly appointed Nazi security officials, contrived to unearth a plot against the Reich fostered by the twelve year old Bruno Gebirge who was found in possession of geometric drawings depicting spherical and oblong objects, and who, to underline his criminal intent of sabotage, declined to join the Hitler Youth. Very soon the father, teacher in Technical Illustration, husband to a British born national, faced charges of espionage with the prospect of incarceration in a concentration camp.

To escape this eventuality Frau Gebirge turned for help to an acquaintance she had known prior to the life-saving incident in the lake, and who, during the days of political turmoil, had risen to high rank in the National Socialist Movement. She had retained her good looks. The Gebirge family found themselves on the Hook-van-Holland to Harwich ferry in May 1939 with passports, exit and entry visas, but little else beyond Herr Gebirge's struggle to come to terms with his wife's compulsory infidelity.

Internment

One year later Mr Gebirge met Mr Foutain in the Internment Camp on the Isle of Man. Their common teaching background led to mutual rapport. Mr Foutain spoke with feeling of Riversmead, set in beautiful, rural Lancashire, as a refuge for boys and staff. He said he hoped to return to it, as soon as the War Office had completed the task of sifting spies from real refugees.

He kept to himself that British Intelligence had requested him to assist in the Camp's sifting process.

"I understand the fears of the British." Mr Gebirge accentuated his statement with a nod. "The Nazis have their fifth columns and spies everywhere. They have them in France, they had them in Spain. And it wouldn't surprise me if a lot of the young men here fought against Fascism in Spain."

"Like me for instance," remarked Mr Foutain. Again he did not disclose that throughout the civil war he had kept contact with England.

Mr Gebirge went on: "We should let the British know, that if the Germans overrun this country, God have mercy on us. The first thing they'll do is shoot us."

"That's why Dr Kupfer, he's an ex-Riversmead man, says he's heading for the United States as soon as they let him out. That's why Miss Zimmermann, another ex-Riversmead teacher, is warming to an inmate here with Zionist leanings. The pair plan to journey via Argentina to Palestine at the earliest opportunity. And Dr Vittauer, the Head, has applied for a position with a university in Vancouver."

"Daydreams," said Mr Gebirge, "once here, you stay here."

"And poor Mr Grun, the last of them, lies in hospital with acute pneumonia. I'm under no illusions. Hitler must be stopped from overrunning us. If the Nazis mount an invasion, I'll opt for the resistance. In the meantime there's the job in Lancashire. And it strikes me you're perfectly cut out for work with the lads in Riversmead."

"I have a wife and a boy."

"Your wife's English by birth. She's a nurse. You'll fit in like an axle to a wheel. I reckon the Home's having difficulties recruiting English replacements because the war is denuding schools of teachers by putting them under steel helmets. Our teaching in Riversmead aids the war effort, it releases men for the forces. Apply for a Riversmead job."

When, weeks later, Sister Helen opened the door to show the couple their room, there was an embarrassing silence.
"I have a dilemma," said Mr Gebirge at last.
Sister Helen looked quizzically at the rotund newcomer.
"I crave your indulgence," said Mr Gebirge in accented English.
"What is it?"
"I'm to blame," he said apologetically, "I plead for two rooms."
"Two rooms?" queried Sister Helen.
"Mrs Gebirge and I sleep apart."
"You are married?" This slipped out unintentionally.
"We are married. It's really my fault that we need separate rooms."

Sister Helen faced two problems: one of understanding, one of organisation. She thought that not only God, but also over-weight Austrians and their attractive English wives, moved in mysterious ways. She solved the situation with her customary pragmatic skill. She clawed back for Mrs Gebirge the last room in the North Wing corridor, currently serving as Music Chamber for the Dragon's little girls. It contained a mini piano at which the two infants pounded their palms and outstretched fingers, so that the tabletops in the adjoining dining hall resonated like sounding boards and set the cutlery jingling during music hours.

The Dragon objected to Sister Helen's remedy on grounds that it would contravene the out-of-bounds rule for boys in the event that any of them, and most likely Bruno, should have need to call upon Mrs Gebirge. She requested her husband to arbitrate upon the matter (in her favour). But Mr Hozell, anticipating a cessation of the racket if the music room was given over to Mrs Gebirge, said: "The boys, if wishing to visit Mrs Gebirge, can use the outside staircase."

The Taming of the Dragon

Sister Frances deposited upon a table in the dining hall thirteen shirts and nine pairs of shorts, which had suffered torn sleeves or button loss. She arranged them in a neat pile when Sister Helen pounced through the door.

"Quickly now," she said, "come with me."

"One moment. I'm carrying these to Mrs Gebirge."

"Arne's throwing a fit. They're bullying him. In the Gymnasium." She turned to several boys who were passing through the hall. "Quickly now, Bruno, take these to your mother's room. Anzendrech will help you."

"It's coming down in buckets," said Sister Frances. "Don't let the shirts and shorts get soaked."

"The shirts and shorts," griped Anzendrech when out of earshot, grappling with a multitude of sleeves falling over his ears. "What about us? I'm not getting soaked going all the way round to the outside staircase."

Mrs Gebirge placed the clothes upon her bed, postponing the hunt for the sewing basket until the two visitors had been fed with biscuits and lemonade.

On their way back along the corridor the boys came upon the Misses Hozell involved with dolls. Seeing the approaching youths the little girls saw the rare opportunity of enlarging their game to 'Father-Mother-Child-Uncles. Bruno had always longed for a sister, and Anzendrech had no wish to hamper the children's play. They got down unto their knees, reverted to baby talk and gave away pretend presents.

The Dragon came out of her lair. She managed to cap the fumes emanating from vitriolic substances inside her body. She flounced away in search for Mr Hozell, Mr Gebirge, Sister Helen and any additional Sister at hand and dragged them into the corridor to view the spectacle.

"There!" She screeched. "I knew it. Boys. Child molesters. Creeping in here to abuse my daughters, introducing vermin into my quarters. That Anzendrech! It's the second time I caught him trespassing."

"We've been carrying clothes to my mother," retorted Bruno.

"The corridor is out of bounds for you, all of you, with or without a mother."

Hearing this Sister Helen's ample bosom began to heave.

"You've been told to use the outside stairs," the Dragon hissed on.

Sister Frances butted in: "I asked them to keep the shirts and shorts dry."

"What's that got to do with it?"

"The clothes would have got drenched if they'd used the outside stairs."

"The sun's shining!" which by that time it was. "They deliberately set out to pervert my girls." Turning to her husband: "What are you doing about it? I demand Mrs Gebirge be moved elsewhere."

Sister Helen spoke in forced calm: "Mr Foutain comes back next week from internment. Guest chambers are down to two. I'm requisitioning another room off this North Wing corridor and I shall move into it myself."

"Over my dead body."

Silence followed, not broken even by Mr Hozell.

"Either Mrs Gebirge moves out or I shall."

Silence. Eternal silence.

The Dragon's fangs transmuted into lips. Their slight trembling signified pending defeat when she said: "Did anyone hear me?"

"Mrs Hozell," Sister Helen breathed in heavily so that her bust threatened to burst through her uniform, "if you allow me." She shot glances at the two men, to make sure they listened, "Mr Hozell runs the school, I run the Home. Room allocation is the Home's responsibility. I aim to make everybody comfortable, staff and boys." She paused, recalling that she had subdued Dr Kupfer over Arne's cupboard confinement, she carried on with fresh vigour. "The Home's here for the boys. Boys who've had a rough deal, are having a rough deal. Arne. You know Arne, frail little body, hardly anything of him. Homesick, dreadfully homesick. Been crying out for his mother. Doesn't know where his mother is. Maybe in a concentration camp. Have your girls been homesick? Cried out for their mother? In a concentration camp? Mrs Hozell?"

Mrs Hozell stood still. Mr Gebirge touched Sister Helen's hand, deliberately.

Mr Hozell, as was his habit in a crisis, veered towards diplomacy.

His chin thrust forward, his lower arms held out horizontally, his hands flopping downwards, he said: "Storm in a tea cup. Speaking of tea, why not talk this matter over a nice cup of tea."

He opened the door to their living room and led the grown-up party through. A mini piano pushed against the rear wall became visible.

"This is all my fault," Mr Gebirge murmured walking to the chair indicated by Mr Hozell, "we crave your indulgence, we occupy separate bedrooms because ..." He didn't quite know how to continue. Should he say: ... 'because I snore' or: '...because Mrs Gebirge chose to fornicate with her Nazi boyfriend; sex in exchange for escape from Germany?'

Mr Hozell intervened: "Put the kettle on, Popsie"

Popsie, formerly The Dragon, withdrew into the adjoining kitchenette. Sister Frances followed to lend a hand. She believed in Christian reconciliation.

Whilst waiting for the tea, Sister Helen visualised Mr Gebirge wandering along the ancient road frequented by bandits. She saw him address the robber-in-chief: "I crave your indulgence. This is really my fault for being here." She saw the crooks, shaken by such honest confession, step aside, lead him to their tent and offer him the hospitality of waiting concubines. And Mrs Gebirge? She would simply go with the ringleader and rear him many Brunos.

With the teacups in their hands, Sister Frances recounted her favourite anecdote when tiny, timid Arne, after three weeks of bread and gooseberry jam for breakfast, had asked her: "Sister, when can I become an egg?" (The German for get is bekomme).

"I kept a straight face," Sister Frances words intermingled with laughter. "I told him that not only the boys, but likewise the teachers and Sisters refrained from becoming eggs for the simple reason that in wartime everybody had to put up with hardships."

Did Mrs Hozell get the point? She kept a straight face too, and listened to Sister Helen tell the story of Anzendrech's fiasco when visiting his brother Rudi in Ingleton.

Mrs Hozell realised she had lost the battle over the rooms. She thought of her daughters in the corridor playing with two foreign boys. It didn't really worry her. What worried her was wondering how she could become the Dragon again without loss of face.

Outside in the corridor, Anzendrech said to the girls: "Your dad won't let you touch the piano in your living room."

"We're going to have a teacher and practice scales, mummy said," replied Millie, the older one.

"My mummy says you got bedbugs in your beds," said her sister.

The Regal

The ban to show themselves on Clitheroe streets lasted eight months. Thereafter the town's more enlightened citizens thought it unlikely that Riversmead had radioed the Germans to bomb the Chatburn Post Office, and the boys were allowed out again.

The cinema during that epoch appealed to all: to cabinet ministers, church ministers, laymen, soldiers, refugees. The majestic Odeons of the metropolises displayed, during intervals, up-rising and down-dropping, triple-keyboard organs on which nimble-limbed operators enthralled audiences with scintillating sounds, whilst curtains reflected purple half-moon shapes on yellow background, changing to green on red. Small urban picture palaces, unable to supplement their wobbly projector systems with such audiovisual magnificence, installed by way of compensation, back rows of double seats.

The manager of the Clitheroe Regal frequently conversed with Sister Helen in the Methodist chapels on Sundays. Married, and therefore non-waiting, he earned her approval when he granted a concessionary entrance charge to Riversmead personnel, 2d to the boys.

And in the Clitheroe Regal Anzendrech suffered palpitation as savages poked long spears through horizontal bars of a bamboo cage at white-helmeted prisoners (here Kleeblatt whispered to him he had found another use of the Scout Staff) to be saved from the soup pot by the yodeling Tarzan. And in the Clitheroe Regal he fell in love with Judy Garland as she followed the yellow brick road.

Oskar, always, made a beeline for the back row. First Josie of Gibson's Farm, then Vera Harbotle of Clitheroe Grammar School, became aware of violent movements inside Oskar's grey flannel trousers. This caused them some alarm, as Oskar did not conceal the phenomenon. Rather the opposite, he pointed his finger at the region to draw the girls' attention to it.

The Shaming of Oskar

And when Mrs Sidge assured Mr Sidge that there would be no harm in going to see *King Solomon's Mines* with a school outing, and when Oskar assured her that there would be no harm in sharing a back row seat, and when his flannel acrobatics commenced and Mrs Holly Sidge, by accident or intent, who was to know, placed her hand momentarily on the hump, Oskar was thrown into such confusion that it brought about the collapse of his self-control, insomuch that on the walk back to Riversmead he pummeled Holly into shrubbery, there to declare his everlasting love for her.

She, flattered by the sixteen year old, good-looking boy, listened to his vehemence with her head inclined to one side, amusement on her lips. She stroked his straw-coloured wave and asserted that if things were different, he five years older, and she not bound to Mr Sidge, etcetera. In vain. Oskar felt the need to prove by physical means the magnitude of his emotion. Mrs Sidge withdrew deeper into the foliage, he followed and when his advances became dangerously energetic, she slapped his cheek.

By a twist of fate Eulenhaut had penetrated into the same bushes, not to peep, but to pee. He witnessed the chastisement, and collided with Oskar as the latter emerged from the leaves, bright red from ear to ear. The colour remained etched on his cheeks for the rest of the day. Eulenhaut enlightened every boy who wanted to know the reason for Oskar's facial metamorphosis.

At tea time the green watercress stood out in relief as he pushed it into his mouth. Boys turned their heads to fix their eyes on their shamed idol, he fixed his on Holly. She sat next to Mr Sidge, cool, calm and beautiful, chatted to her husband, and took no heed of Oskar's searching red face.

The following morning gave birth to the rumour that not Oskar but Mrs Sidge had been the force d'amour, that she had pulled him into the greenery where she began kissing him wildly on exposed bare skin. Oskar saw that they were spied upon. He signalled to Mrs Sidge to slap his face, so that it would appear she was the victim and so escape retribution which Mr Sidge was otherwise sure to unleash upon her when Eulenhaut spilt the beans. The act of gallantry in assuming the role of villain was in the boys' eyes a streak of pure Oskar. As it happened the incident, fact and fiction, remained primarily the property of the boys, and of staff only Mr Storm and Mr Foutain got wind of it and chose to keep it to themselves,

In the boys' eyes the real villain of the episode was neither Mrs Sidge nor Oskar, but Eulenhaut for snooping. Five of the most ardent Oskar worshippers cornered the dark, curly haired, rosy lipped prefect in the dining hall and slung abuse at him. Eulenhaut, his dignity of a senior under threat, returned the verbal onslaught by pushing the heads of two youngsters together, whereupon Arne jumped upon his back. Two more Oskar admirers joined in the escalating fray. The words 'potato cupboard' hung in the air, and the seven juniors overcame the struggling prefect, and dragged him towards the door.

Eulenhaut read their intention: a repeat of Arne's infamous imprisonment. With a mighty push he wrenched himself free, jumped down the stairway three steps at a time, raced through the Entrance Hall to the rear of the North Wing, shouting obscenities to his pursuers, leaping up two steps at a time on the outside staircase leading to his bedroom on the second floor. Some way up he collided with Mrs Gebirge taking a short cut from her bedroom on the first floor. To avoid tumbling down head first Mrs Gebirge's arms clung to the boy's neck, Eulenhaut's hands gripped her waist.

"Take me to your room," pleaded the prefect.

CHAPTER TWELVE (1941)

Hildebrandt's Fulfilment in Vienna

Back in Vienna Sturmbannführer Hildebrandt was luxuriating on the crest of fulfilment.

The marching men of his vision obliterated everything wherever the Führer sent them; they had flattened the already flat lands of Belgium and Holland. Right now they left nothing standing, God-made or man-made, in their advance through the Ukraine and all Russia. He planned to join them in due course to celebrate the final Glorious Victory.

Since his return to the city on the Danube he had noticed that many of his SS colleagues boasted of mistresses, and paraded extra sons for furthering the march of the thousand year Reich. His aim was to proliferate likewise. For this he needed Vikki, the object of his love in pre-Hitler days. His Parteigenossin wife need not know of it, or if becoming aware of it, would be made to collaborate with the National Socialist Doctrine. Did not the National Anthem thunder into every brain: *Deutschland, Deutschland über Alles,* Germany, Germany above All Else.

Three niggling personal setbacks needed rectification.

Vikki, so far, had eluded his search; Alexander Anzendrech, his onetime Valhalla Hero, had slipped through his fingers; the Jew saboteur Dufft had vanished from the face of the earth.

The long established Anzendrech-Dufft liaison was well documented. Two years had gone by, so why wait any longer? In the midst of issuing orders for the arrest of the remaining Anzendrechs, correction: Wanzen's, on charges of sabotage which Parteigenosse Kristopp had laid before him, he held back. Jew or no Jew, the ex-tram conductor held the key, he still believed, to Vikki's whereabouts. All right, he argued, information could be swiftly extracted from detainees earmarked for concentration camps. But it has come to his cognizance that men facing such futures were apt to finish their own lives before useful facts could be gathered.

His strategy, if other Vikki hunts failed, was to feign ignorance of Rudolf Anzendrech's (Wanzen's) Jewishness, waylay him as if by chance, and speak with him as he had proposed to do eight years ago when destiny had stepped in and decreed an alternative path to a reunion with his chosen love object.

Once again, destiny held sway.

Greti Katherine Hilde

A scourging dossier from the Joseph Göbbels School, previously known as The Wesergasse Gymnasium, was laid before Hildebrandt. It revealed that in 1937 propaganda material in the form of crimson leaflets, agitating for the Jewish-Bolshevik case of the Spanish civil war, had been introduced into the school by persons hitherto unknown. Scouring the office of the sacked and recently expired, through suicide, Director Hinterzweig, SA men unearthed, tucked away behind a massive chest of decadent history books, one of these crimson papers with the names Manfred Willberg and Fritz Wasserman written on it.

Both individuals had been then, and were still, students of the school. Both asserted no knowledge of how or why their names appeared on the handbill, and both denied any involvement in the dispersing of the leaflets. However they pointed fingers at their cousin, Herbert Stubenegke, who had let out, before the Anschluss, that he had carried out the stunt.

Upon interrogation Herbert Stubenegke, oblivious of any serious misdeeds, revealed the source of the propaganda material, and its connection with an address in the Rossigasse. This led the Gestapo to uncover Purple Pimpernel with a link based in the Angol Park, Budapest, overseen there by a fortune teller called Vikki Huber, and also to the apprehension of everybody directly or remotely associated with this perfidious, enemy abetting organisation in Vienna, including Herbert's parents and his sister, Greti Katherine Hilde.

To avoid a lengthy and bureaucratic involvement with the Hungarian authorities, the Gestapo in collusion with the SS decided on a simple way to mete out justice. Specially selected SS would enter the traitor Vikki Huber's abode at night, and whilst asleep, or not, kill her.

When all this reached Hildebrandt's ears, his scar succumbed to twitching. He commanded that no action must be taken relating to the effacement of the lady in question until he, and he Hildebrandt alone in person, gave the order to proceed.

Destiny must be allowed to take its course.

He looked at Fräulein Stubenegke through compressed eyelids to better focus on her stunning features and the flaming red-gold strands caressing her shoulders. If Adolf Hitler was the prophet of the Aryan doctrine, the vision sitting here was the pure embodiment of it. If she just wore a white robe instead of the orange dress!

"Name?" He commenced.

"Greti Katherine Stubenegke."

"Is that your full name?"

"Greti Katherine Hilde Stubenegke."

Hildebrandt's scar yielded to pulsating activity.

He gets up, pulls her hair, screams silently to himself: 'this is fire, *brand*. My name is Hildebrandt. Her name's Hilde. Hilde stands for battle, Brand for sword. If Destiny isn't at work here, I eat my underpants.'

He asks: "Are you Aryan?"

"One hundred ten and a half per cent."

After a pause, ignoring the sarcasm, not having understood it, he asks, "Have you traced your ancestors?"

Greti Katherine senses the SS Man's reactions to her compelling aura. Men cannot do otherwise. Nevertheless she is terrified, not knowing what comes next: 'Will he defile me? Will he torture me? Will he send me to a camp? Will he kill me?' But she retains her macabre sense of humour and replies: "I'm a direct descendant of Brunhilde."

She fantasises that the blot on his cheek, now heavily discoloured, would leap from his face.

He struggles to compose himself as he silently screams on: 'She's making fun of me. She's ridiculing ancient Germanic culture. Shall I exchange her for Vikki? Yes. Destiny demands that I do it. And do it I shall.'

CHAPTER THIRTEEN (1942)

Quentin Quelle

Mr Hozell's chair legs scraped against the floor as he stood up. The clutter of dinner crockery removal subsided; the screeching heralded the delivery of news.

He said: "To-morrow Blutwurst's aunt is paying us a visit and will be staying with us for a few days. She is the renowned vocalist Franziska Hannick who will sing for us, here at Riversmead, in your native tongue and in Yiddish and also in English. Miss Hannick is a very gracious lady; she and her companions will expect you to be at your best behaviour. Is that understood?"

The following day, when the Home was again preoccupied with the intake of food, Anzendrech's heart missed a beat. He cried out: *"Dort sitzt Frau Gusti Spagola*, there sits Frau Gusti Spagolola."

He rushed towards the staff table where one of the visiting ladies stared at him with open mouth. Mr Hozell ordered him back to his place: "Wait for a get-together with our guests after we've eaten."

That Anzendrech and Franziska Hannick's companion knew one another generated wide-spread curiosity. Sisters, teachers, boys, Franziska Hannick herself, her pianist and Gusti Schattzburger alias Spagola, gathered in the Common Room.

"*Na so was,* well, I never!" exclaimed Gusti before answering Anzendrech's rapid questioning. "Berti's at boarding school in Bristol. "We were in Holland. We escaped to England just before the Germans marched in. We expected we'd meet up with Richard."

"We drew a blank everywhere. No Mr Richard Dufft," added Franziska Hannick.

"The last time I saw Mr Dufft, I told him to go to the Rossigasse," Anzendrech said eagerly. He shut his eyes and saw in his mind the colours of the numbers and letters. "Twenty-seven A, Staircase five, Door three. I think it was a safe house for people on the run from the Nazis."

Without giving prior warning Mr Foutain thumped the nearest desk, making a pen lying thereon near the edge, jump off: "The Two P's."

"Herr Pflaume...and...Frau Petersengel?" Anzendrech's agitation brought on the stammer.

"They sent Jews and refugees to float down the Danube into Hungary. I took that route myself. "

Anzendrech looked hard at Mr Foutain and yelled out: "You're the *Quorgel* Man!"

"What?"

"You took the Orgel boat. Your name's really Quentin Qu-something. But you had no hair then, six years ago. And there was the woman with the crimson leaflets."

All eyes fell on Mr Foutain. He hesitated. His hand reached up, hesitated again, then clutched his mane. He lifted it. Anzendrech, the assembled boys, the Sisters, the Sidges, Mr Storm, Mr Hozell, Franziska Hannick beheld a head as smooth as the polished tiles of the Entrance Hall.

"Quentin Quelle, at your service. I never made a secret that I changed my name and my looks. I had no choice. Fountain is English for Quelle. I dropped the 'n'. Now I remember seeing you, Anzendrech, by the railway bridge. You and your friend brought notes to Frau Petersengel. Strange I didn't recognise you before."

"I never thought you'd be the *Quorgel* Man."

"Small world," remarked Mr Storm.

"Wouldn't it be wonderful if we could make it smaller still," said Franziska Hannick, "finding Richard Dufft. He and Gusti were to be married."

"It would indeed," said Mr Hozell.

Mr Foutain, alias Herr Quelle, tapped the desk from which he had sent the pen flying: "The Two P's or the Purple Pimpernel as they liked to be known. Their escape route ends in London. I know people there. "

Dufft's Story

"Does she know I'm coming?"

Mr Foutain shook his head. "I telephoned Franziska Hannick yesterday, she said it would be a fantastic surprise for Miss Schattzburger if you just turned up."

The previous day Mr Foutain had contacted colleagues in the

Home Office. This had led to tracking down refugee Dufft. The Riversmead teacher called on him at his work. The two men recognised each other from their meeting on the Berlin train in 1933. On hearing the good tidings, the Assistant Foreign News Editor insisted on dropping everything and zipping to Lancashire straight away.

He raised the Euston Station cup of tea to his mouth and scolded his tongue.

"I pledged myself to Gusti thirty years ago," he said dabbing his handkerchief against his lips to relieve the sting the super-heated liquid had left. "Then the First World War, then other things happen. After I met you on that train, I dwell in the realms of fantasy once again, thinking Gusti and I would get hitched. But no, other things happen. We finally arrange it, the wedding. And what comes next? Austria suffers extinction, followed by another war. I believe Gusti's somewhere in Holland. You come out of the blue telling me she's in Lancashire! And this confounded English concoction scorches my larynx so I can't shout hip hip hurray!"

"Hurray, congratulations."

Dufft blew on the tea. "If it hadn't been for the Anzendrech boy, I wouldn't be sitting here now. He knew where I had to go."

"He stumbled across the Two P's, the Purple Pimpernel."

Mr Foutain, having learnt from his regular trips to London, that railway station tea could not be swallowed if less than ten minutes separated its purchase from a train's departure, stirred the fluid vigorously in the fragile hope that heat would thereby dissipate. "When I gave you that address, I had a premonition you'd need it."

"And I forgot it. Anyway, with the boy's help I found the place. I told my tale to Frau Petersengel, the lady of the house. She consulted others, they let me stay. After a few days these good people organised a transport for someone else. The Gestapo arrested the man earmarked for the run, and Mrs P fixed it that I take his place. We wait until dusk, I get rid of all identification. I step into this boat, I and an escort. We drift down the Danube as far as Hainburg."

"Right in the corner where Austria, Czechoslovakia and Hungary meet," Mr Foutain reminisced.

"There we hit the bank in pitch darkness amongst reeds, but we can see the German patrol boats. Their search light beams flick over the river. My blood runs cold when my escort hands me a rubber sack with sleeves and leggings all in one, and an opening for mouth and eyes, also some airbags sown in to keep it afloat. Did they give you one like it?"

"I crossed the border in a boat," replied Mr Foutain, "in the civilised days of escape."

"I put the contraption on, he knots it together over my head, says it's watertight, but after two minutes in the wet, the river seeps in. 'You have a fifty-fifty chance,' he tells me. 'Lie on your back, so only your nostrils are above water,' he says. 'If the Germans catch you, they kill you. Either they shoot you straight away, or they hold you and torture you to make you talk. If you talk it's the end of the Two P's. Afterwards they shoot you just the same.' He goes on. 'So you have no choice. That's why I'm putting this pill in your mouth. Bite on it if the Germans fish you out. Don't let your teeth chatter with cold either, or you end up a stiff before your time. Sorry, but that's how it is,' he says."

"Cheered you up no end?"

"My guide's a well of inspiration. He enraptures me with: 'After Bratislava there'll be Hungarian patrols, but not so many, and they won't kill you if they catch you. So you can spit it out.' He hands me a rubbery torch. 'It's waterproof,' he says, 'hold on to it. Squeeze it hard, it lights up. After you've cleared the patrols light it up three times at short intervals. That's the signal for our men. If you miss the rendezvous you're on your own. You'll probably die of hypothermia.' That's what he tells me."

Mr Foutain now resorted to spoon-feeding the scorching tea into his mouth.

Dufft continued: "I never want to go through an experience like that again. I felt so wretched at the mercy of the water and the patrols, had they shot me I would have metaphorically jumped for joy. Anyway I made it, they pulled me out on the other side. I stayed in Budapest tucked away in a circus shed in the Angol Park where I was nearly eaten by bedbugs. To my surprise a woman I've known in Vienna in the early thirties turned out to be the second link in the escape chain. She was a fortune teller, had lived in the same house as the Anzendrechs. I can't tell you much what happened to me after that, because the British Authorities requested I don't talk about it. The escape route still exists."

"Does it? The information I picked up yesterday is different. But I can't say much more either, for the same reason."

"What I can tell you is that I arrived in London eighteen months ago. After a wrangle with the British - they made sure I wasn't a spy - they let me see the newspaper that'd interviewed me before the war. I got the job with the News Chronicle. The work must be important: they're giving me a secretary next week."

"Drink up," said Mr Foutain, "train leaves in fifteen minutes."

"English Railway Station tea! You've learnt how to handle it."

The Finest Day

Mr Hozell hoped to add the day to his collection of the finest.

The reason for this was not because he had proposed that the wedding take place at Riversmead, not because he had softened the Dragon's heart so that she lifted the out-of-bound restriction for boys on the main stairway during the festivities, not because the sun shone, but because of the cricket match.

He had been appalled from the start that German-speaking boys understood not the terms silly mid-on, silly mid-off, or LBW. He had taken many opportunities to rectify this shortcoming by both theoretical and practical toil. And now, in co-operation with farmer Gibson and Scoutmaster Wooseley, the prospect of a Riversmead Eleven pitched against a Clitheroe Scouts Eleven on a field bordering the Ribble during the combined celebrations of Augustine Schatzburger's wedding to Richard Dufft and the Home's Annual Sports Day, fired his zeal just as Anzendrech's passion had propelled him to be first on top of Cader Idris. But whereas Anzendrech had relied on his own energy for success, Mr Hozell depended on the talent, the discipline, the will to win, on his chosen team which, luckily, included Oskar.

"Make this a matter of life or death," Mr Hozell urged the gathered Prefects. "We'll aim to do well in all activities, but we must beat them with the red ball."

"Have no fear, we'll win with a cheer," said Malig, the rhyme falling on his tongue by accident.

"I always finish, not out," boasted Oskar.

"I can scale five foot one inch in the high jump," said Anzendrech.

"Yes, good." Mr Hozell flinched at Anzendrech's lack of understanding. "But we're talking about cricket." A victory at the wicket must convince his employers, nay the world, that he had succeeded in turning Central Europe boys into little Englishmen.

"Keep Anzendrech away," sneered Oskar. "He's still in his infancy. He thinks the game with the red ball is big boys' marbles."

"Nabravowitz," retorted Anzendrech, "with Mrs Sidge watching, be careful your overflow of adrenalin doesn't send the red ball flying over Pendle Hill."

"Now then!" warned Mr Hozell, but his spirits performed a somersault, as intentionally or not Anzendrech had hit on a fundamental fact. The team would be raring to go if it could impress the opposite sex. He stressed: "I'll be pleased to welcome your young ladies. They shall have tea with us."

Oskar quipped: "Anzendrech's Welsh bit of fluff's as flat as a window pane. He's been true to her for two years. He pines for her all night long," and in a loud whisper to Schaumberg: "He gets wet dreams and thinks he pissed his bed."

"Shut up, Nabravowitz. Not everyone's got a drain for a brain like yours. I can manage without girls."

Mr Hozell's thinking hit top gear. If there wasn't a female to show off to, a sibling would be a good substitute. "I believe you visited your brother in Ingleton?"

"Rudi's in Birmingham now," said Anzendrech.

"Why not ask him over for a return visit on Sports Day?"

The Secretary

Franziska Hannick emphasised the need for two bridesmaids. The problem of selecting a pair from four eager Sisters was solved by choosing none of them. Instead Mrs Knowles's niece Mary quaked with delight when asked to do the honours, and Mr Dufft's newly appointed secretary, also a refugee from the Nazi regime, accepted to make up the second.

When this secretary showed up at Riversmead, sixty-seven boys immediately fell in love with her. The sixty-eighth, Alexander Anzendrech, was already in love with her, had been for the last six years. For the girl was none other than the Angel, Greti Katherine Hilde Stubenegke, spelt with gk, complete with flaming red hair, now cut short, above an orange dress, and very much bulging chest.

Her entry into the Dining Hall caused a sensation. Oskar was the first to approach her. But Greti Katherine spied Rudi, and he her, and for them the whole of Riversmead, including Oskar, bride, groom, and everything else, dissolved into the Lancashire air, flew out of the window to the moon for all they cared as their arms intertwined.

Come evening Alexander lay wide awake. They had told him they were engaged. There was no hope. Glad in a way that Rudi had stolen her heart and not, for instance Oskar, the hurt, nevertheless, kept him from sleep.

He crept out of bed.

A clump of trees and rough scrub bordered the entrance to Gibson's farm. There he sat down on a mossy patch, shrouded by darkness so no one would see his tears. After he had suffered, he prepared to return to the warm sheets. He heard footsteps, voices, their voices. They tumbled into the grass no more than ten feet away separated by shrubs. He stalled his movement. Shall he make his presence known? How could he explain being here in his pyjamas, his wet cheeks? He knew if they discovered him, eavesdropping, they would not respond in the forgiving manner of a similar incident, four years ago in the Augarten!

He waited. Then it was too late; he had to remain very still until they moved on.

"Your little brother's got a crush on me," Alexander heard the Angel's voice, "but they all have. I'm sorry to have to admit to that."

"You love me and I love you, and the rest of the world, including my little brother, can do what they like, weep if it helps them."

"My love, I couldn't forget you after you'd left. Every day I ..."

A new tear amassed in Xandi's eye. He placed his fists over his ears so he wouldn't hear their cooing. When he removed them, words from her mouth came again through the shrubbery.

Greti's Story

"The SS Man with the scar on his cheek said I could save Herbert and my parents if I did as he told me."

"Did you?" Rudi's anxious tone resonated in Alexander's ears.

"Don't worry. Nothing like that. He told me to stay a few nights alone in an empty hut. He shoved me in his car between two other SS Men. We sat in the rear. A third crony, he was the man with the arrow on the Danube Meadow, when I first saw you, do you remember?"

"Of course I do, my darling love. Herr Kristopp, a nasty piece of work he turned out to be."

"He took the passenger seat. We drove out of Vienna, eastwards, past the Neusidler Lake, crossed the border into Hungary. There wasn't room enough for three in the back, and the men on either side pressed against my body. They behaved themselves at first, but after we've travelled a couple of hours or so, one put his hand on my lap and began to fiddle with my clothes. This encouraged the other who crossed his arms and touched me up along my chest."

"Bastards. If I'd been there," said Rudi.

"We were hurtling along this empty country road. I see this tall tree by the roadside ahead on the left and nothing else except a few haystacks in the fields. The two SS pull me about and I retaliate with my elbows. There's a scuffle. The men in front yell out, they turn their heads, try to restore order with their arms. I saw this hole in the road. The car bounces into it, spins out of control into the one obstacle for miles around."

"You hit the tree?"

"Next thing I remember I crawl back to the car. Blood's pouring from the man with the scar. He's got a chunk of glass stuck in his throat. The other three bodies, twisted, are hanging out of the vehicle. I feel weak, need to sit down, I slink to a haystack, drop behind it into the loose hay on the ground. I have this terrible pain in my chest, my blouse is wet, clings to my skin. Then I pass out."

Alexander, reposing in a kneeling position, felt a crick worsening in his shin, but he dared not move lest he drew their attention.

"I must have lain unconscious for several hours," Greti Katherine continued, "because evening was drawing in when I saw this woman, holding a bicycle, looking down at me. 'All four men dead' she says. She spoke German. I crawl to the edge of the haystack and see the burnt out shell of the car wrapped round the broken tree, no sign of any living creatures. The woman turns out to be the local farmer's wife, and they happen to dislike the Nazis."

"A stroke of destiny," said Rudi.

"She gets help, a cart comes along, and they take me to a farmhouse. They clean me up, put me to bed, nurse me. A doctor examines my wounds. From my neck down to my hips, and down my legs, all in a mess. They get me to a hospital, they ask no questions, although I've told the farm people why I've been in the car. They stitch me up. And remove my right breast."

"My darling!"

"I had to tell you, especially now that we rushed into accepting union until death do us part. If you feel you want to cancel the business, I'll understand. Otherwise you have to put up with just one, which incidentally has grown at double the normal rate."

"My sweet love, how can you ask. It doesn't matter two hoots."

"Well, it matters one boob. Look, I show you."

Alexander, in cold sweat, motionless like a lump of stone but far from emotionless, could do nothing but wait.

"My left breast, not too bad, you agree? But feel here, all shrivelled up. I wear this special brassiere, left cup's normal, the right is padding, see?"

Alexander endured listening to rustling sounds intermingled with silences, followed by her voice: "No darling, don't, not just yet."

His heart pounded.

"We'd better be thinking of going back. It's getting cold, but I feel warm inside with my love for you."

"Me too," returned Rudi, "it's beautiful to say to you: 'I love you.'"

More rustling, after which the Angel's voice hit Alexander's ears once more: "The farm people and I got on well. He collected stamps. I stayed for several weeks. Then they moved me around. Two other ladies, gypsies from Budapest, swelled the party. The older one, a fortune teller, a half gypsy really, lived in the shack which I was supposed to have graced with my presence for several nights."

"What a coincidence."

"She told me this and said, she was to be snatched away by the scarred SS Man who had passed on to another world in the car crash.

She'd been active in helping fugitives along their way, she got wind of some nasty stuff being hatched, so she and her assistant decided to do a run themselves. The younger woman later left us to join up with her family in Rumania. I had seen her before in Vienna, years ago, on the stage of the Emporium in the Prater."

Alexander only just managed to suppress calling out: "The Girl in the Shimmering Green Costume!"

He heard them rising to their feet.

"Then we tramped through Yugoslavia into Albania, mostly at night. The half-gypsy lady knew where to head for. We reached the Adriatic. They put us into wooden crates, loaded us onto a boat bound for Lisbon. In open waters they let us out. From Portugal into another ship for England. Vikki, that's the fortune teller's name, and I, we've become friends. She told me my fortune, she said great things shall await me in my new country. She'll be thrilled to bits when she hears ..."

Greti Katherine's words faded away as she and Rudi walked back to the Riversmead building.

Cricket on the Ribble

The same evening Blutwurst, in search of an isolated spot to enjoy a few puffs from half a Craven 'A' found on the Grindleton Road, heard whispers in a familiar inflection: "I've loved you since the moment I first set eyes on you. Don't fret yourself about Vera Harbotle," and fell over outstretched legs in the high grass. He scrambled off on all fours, shouted: "Damn, I fell over some logs," and ran off. He never understood why he gave voice to that utterance. Perhaps, in spite of his unsavoury tobacco habits, he cherished a charitable soul, or because he thought it unwise to be witness to Oskar's affairs, as was borne out by Eulenhaut's flight into Mrs Gebirge's arms. The encounter was never mentioned, neither by himself, nor Oskar, nor Josie Gibson.

Next morning Dufft's wedding took place at the Clitheroe Registry Office, and was followed by a short service back at the Home, led by a priest for Gusti's benefit. Then Mr Hozell made a speech in English, in broken German and in platitudes. He stressed that in spite of the woeful times, life must go on, and play must go on. He hinted that life meant marriage, and play meant cricket.

Franziska Hannick gave a rendering of Schubert's *Ave Maria*.

The guests admired the bride's dress, a creation in light green muslin with drooping bows. Sister Helen repelled one adverse comment, delivered to her by the Dragon, that the gown exhibited a noticeable shortage of length, by reminding Mrs Hozell that there was a war on, resulting in a conspicuous shortage of clothing coupons. The pale blue bridesmaid's garments had sidestepped this problem as they had hung dormant in Mrs Knowles wardrobe since 1939 when her cousin had married, and to which the cook had made a few adaptations.

Anzendrech placed a two-inch square box amongst a tea kettle, a wireless set, an alarm clock, an ironing board and other gadgetry. The box contained a brooch purchased at a Clitheroe Jewellers and had diminished his savings by three shillings eleven pence and three farthings. The adornment was crafted from a gilded ring supporting an emerald green foliage leaf on which a turquoise coloured ladybird reposed. When shown to his friends, Oskar had scoffed: "Trust Anzendrech to buy a bedbug which sucks blue blood."

Then the boys, the Staff, guests, the newlyweds, the to-be-weds, made their way to the field by the Ribble for combined Reception and Annual Sports Day. Only Mr Sidge remained behind to keep an eye on the Home.

Blitz ran the fastest one hundred yards.

Mallg's legs were first to step over the finishing line of the cross-country run.

Anzendrech reached his highest high jump: five foot one and a half inches.

Oskar excelled in everything.

Younger boys, too, topped their norms when sighting the Prefects' girlfriends.

The tug-of-war between the Clitheroe Scouts and Riversmead, seven boys in each team, happened next. The Clitheroe contingent selected their giants, the Riversmead side consisted of Malig, Schaumberg, Kleeblatt, Blitz, Oskar, Eulenhaut and Anzendrech. Weight-wise the ratio was thirteen to ten in favour of Clitheroe. The Scouts won the toss, and aware of their superiority in mass, chose as befitted English fair play, the north facing end which exhibited a slight rise.

The little red flag in the middle of the rope hovered over the centre line, shifted to the right, to the left, right, left, right, left. The girl friends yelled, Rudi and Greti shouted, Mr and Mrs Dufft roared, the teachers, the Sisters, the Dragon and her little girls, Mrs Knowles and Franziska Hannick hollered, all the spectators, the Scouts' parents, their friends, farmer Gibson, his daughter Josie called out "Pull! Pull! Pull!" Mr Wooseley delivered one long "Puuuuull."

And they pulled. The little red flag hesitated from right to left and back again. Then came the fatal slip. The shoes of the Scout anchorman slid on the grass. His body, nearly horizontal, flopped to the ground. With one mighty jerk the Riversmeadians fell back, the Clitheroe Scouts tumbled forward.

After the cheering Mr Hozell said, to reciprocate the spirit of fair play, that the advantage of the incline contributed to Riversmead's victory.

So a repeat was staged, sides swapping ends.

The Riversmead boys were still 'taking the strain', and not ready, when the Scouts, in the belief that one defeat entitled them to dispense with fair play, English or otherwise, tugged away sharply, their opponents falling to the ground.

So an overall draw was declared.

Riversmead objected, but Mr Hozell, using diplomacy, whispered that everybody in their hearts knew who had won, urged calm for the sake of harmony and said: "Let's take revenge by showing them off the cricket field."

Winners of the sports activities were presented with red-white-and-blue ribbons. Mr Hozell, Mr Wooseley, Mr Storm and Mr Foutain (Mr Gebirge acting as giver of advice) defined the boundary using farmer Gibson's yellow rope previously deployed for improvised fencing to contain his mares. They measured out for the stumps, drove them into the ground, marked out the creases. A red ball appeared, and cricket bats, and padding for shins.

The manager of the Regal Cinema and a Methodist minister volunteered as umpires. Once again the Clitheroe Scouts won the toss and opted to bat. According to Mr Hozell's record sheet, Malig's bowling included four bouncers, seven byes, one maiden, one chinaman and three no balls. Oskar delivered ten shooters, six beamers, one first ball duck, followed by another wicket catching it himself as it bounced off a forlorn looking Boy Scout.

When the score reached thirty three, and five batsmen had yet to complete the innings, Mr Gibson collected his tractor, and with Sister Helen and Mr Gebirge, brought the Home's tea urn filled to the brim, crockery, sliced meats, new potatoes, pickles and salads. Also brown bread cucumber sandwiches cut and shaped into triangles by Mrs Wooseley, fairy cakes, and strawberries, even cream.

By two fifteen the Clitheroe Scouts were all out having scored forty-five runs. Mr Hozell declared picnic break. People flocked into groups, collected their share of sustenance, chatted, teased, joked, laughed. Alexander sat on the grass next to Rudi and Greti, Mr and Mrs Dufft, Franziska Hannick and her pianist, Mr Foutain and Mr Storm.

"How different this is from the Danube Meadow," said Mrs Gusti Dufft, stroking Richard Dufft's palm in her hand.

Her new husband was aware that their drowned child Poldi occupied a place in his wife's remark. But he replied: "We didn't play cricket on the Danube Meadow."

"No Riesenrad over here," said the pianist who felt homesick, "no Kalafati, no Toboggan, no Emporium, no clowns and their old, old jokes."

For the second time in two days Alexander was reminded of the Girl in the Shimmering Green Costume. The memory eased his heartache whenever he looked at his Angel close to Rudi.

"There's an art in telling jokes. Many good jokes are spoilt by poor telling," said Mr Storm.

This prompted the pianist to comment that many good things were being spoilt these days, and what was once, was no longer.

To stop the conversation drifting into sombre territory Franziska Hannick broke into song: *'Wien, Wien, nur Du allein,* Vienna, City of my Dreams', and in order to maintain equilibrium Holst's *'I Vow to Thee my Country.'*

Mr Foutain questioned the bride and bridegroom about their honeymoon arrangement, and Richard Dufft squeezed Gusti Dufft's hand when replying they were setting off in the morning.

"Where are you heading?"

"We booked a room in Blackpool."

"You'll see all the fun of the fair, British style, in Blackpool," said Mr Storm, "I vouch you won't get better beer served anywhere else in the whole country."

Alexander pricked his ears hearing the young English teacher enthuse about alcohol, for the Home's leaning towards Methodist ways debarred liquor as an item of consumption, and of conversation.

"You may have heard this one before. A stranger goes into this pub," Mr Storm went on, oblivious of Alexander's concern, "orders a beer and observes the locals. A man gets up, shouts out a number like FIFTEEN, everybody roars with laughter. After a while another man gets up, shouts out another number like TWENTY-SEVEN, everybody roars with laughter. After a while yet another man gets up, shouts SIX, everybody roars with laughter. The stranger thinks this very peculiar, asks the barman what's going on. The barman explains: 'they've been telling these old jokes, time and time over again. They got fed up with listening to the long-winded gags so they numbered them. Now when one thinks of a funny story, he just shouts out the number, and they identify the joke and laugh.' The stranger thought this a very good idea. 'Can I have a go?' he asks. 'Yes, go on,' says the barman. The stranger takes a deep breath, shouts out with all his might: 'TWELVE'. Silence. 'Well' thought the stranger, 'perhaps it didn't stand for a good joke'. So he tried again 'THIRTY-THREE '. Not a murmur. So he tried again. 'NINETEEN.' Again dead silence, not a titter. He turns to the barman: 'What's wrong? Why did nobody laugh?' The barman bears a serious mien, folds his arms over his chest. 'Well' he explains. 'It depends on how you tell them.'"

Other groups heard the laughter, and Mr Storm repeated the joke. Even the Methodist minister chuckled. Sister Helen wanted to hear it, and Mr Gebirge obliged. She laughed already when it came to the numbering bit, and Mr Gebirge told her she needed to wait for the punch line. Which she did, laughed even more, forgot about self-discipline and steadied herself on Mr Gebirge's shoulder.

"Sister Helen's got herself an alpenstock," observed Mr Foutain and explained that Gebirge, in English, means High Mountains.

More jokes were told, one even by Mr Wooseley which took a looong tiiiime.

Mr Hozell stood up, wished the happy couple good fortune, and also announced Rudi and Greti Katherine's engagement. Everybody cheered, took a sip of tea, and as Mr and Mrs Dufft kissed each other, Rudi's lips touched Greti's. Everybody followed suit and sought out the nearest, which in most cases resulted in husbands kissing their wives and boys their girlfriends, but also in Mr Gebirge, standing closest to Sister Helen, seeking out that buxom lady, and, likewise by reason of proximity, Eulenhaut finding Mrs Gebirge.

Oskar crouched in equidistance between Vera Harbotle, Josie Gibbons and Mrs Sidge. Josie surged forward towards the handsome youth in denial that she had been superseded by Vera. Oskar saw the thunder amassing in Vera's face, turned away from Josie's advance and grabbed Mrs Sidge, who, under the circumstances of the moment, returned the caress.

Mr Foutain went to search out Sister Frances.

Mr Storm kissed the pianist, and Franziska Hannick pecked Alexander's cheek, neither actions bearing any significance.

Franziska Hannick sang Parry's '*Jerusalem.*'

Everybody clapped and fell back into jovial chatter, and nobody within a mile from the merriment remembered that Rommel was driving back the allies in Libya and that the German Wehrmacht were preparing the offensive against Stalingrad.

Mr Hozell worried that the hilarity could have an adverse effect on his batting team. He pondered over his strategy, when to put Oskar in. The star must play at the right time, not too soon, not too late. When Riversmead had scored twenty six, he called for Anzendrech. Eager to impress the Angel and his brother, Alexander marched to the crease, took up his stance and practised his swing.

"Out," said the umpire, the Methodist minister.

Alexander could not understand. No ball had past him, why was he called out?

"Out," repeated the minister. "You've knocked the bails off with your bat."

Alexander looked at the grooved lengths of wood lying on the ground, then appealingly at Mr Hozell. His practising swing had gone too far to the rear. Surely this didn't count. Mr Hozell spoke to the minister, who remained adamant.

Anzendrech going 'out' met Oskar coming 'in'.

"You're a *unbrauchbare Wanzn*, a useless bedbug," hissed Oskar as they passed.

Mr Hozell began to sweat. Riversmead scored three more runs but lost two batsmen. Then came Oskar's masterstroke.

"Six," shouted Mr Hozell, the ball still floating in the air. It never hit the ground; it splashed into the waters of the Ribble.

Mr Wooseley produced a spare ball. Mr Hozell sweated more profusely. Although the score had gone up to thirty five, only Malig and Blitz remained.

"One."

Which made thirty six. And brought Oskar back into batting.

History does repeat itself, frequently at short intervals. A hurricane hits an American city once in a lifetime, and then these mighty whirlwinds flood the same town twice within a month. And so it was with Oskar. He lashed out at a ball, it soared into the sky, flew, flew, and disappeared into the river once again.

The score stood at forty one, but no ball to produce further additions. The nearest one lay in Mr Hozell's drawer at Riversmead, one and a half miles up the road, and no sight of Mr Gibson's tractor, which had moved off half an hour ago with the empty tea urn, stained crockery and his Oskar humiliated daughter Josie.

To sprint to the Home and back, if Blitz did it, would take forty minutes. If he, Mr Hozell, did it, an hour. Blitz had yet to bat.

"Anzendrech, you came second in the cross country. Run to the Home, find Mr Sidge, and together go into my room. The cricket ball's in the middle drawer of my desk next to the window. Here's the key to my room. Be as quick as you can."

Alexander galloped off, slowed into a canter then into a mere trot up the steep hill to Grindleton. Puffing and soaked in perspiration, he reached the Home, looked for Mr Sidge. He wasn't in his room, he wasn't in any of the toilets, he wasn't in the Common Room nor the Reading Room, nor the Gymnasium. Alexander called his name, loud, once twice and again. No Mr Sidge.

Well, he had to go into Mr Hozell's room on his own. He located the drawer, opened it, saw the ball. But it wasn't a cricket ball, it was a tennis ball.

He could not return with a tennis ball, he knew that.

Running back empty handed, and the cricket ball subsequently located elsewhere, very likely by Oskar, would reflect on his ineptitude. He opened other drawers, including one filled with woman's clothes, underwear, petticoats and heavy knickers: Mrs Hozell's. If the Dragon saw him rootling in her stuff, what would she do to him? He wished he were elsewhere.

He became aware of a presence.

"Are you a poof?"

He turned round and stood face to face with Josie Gibson.

"Are you a poof? You get a kick out of feeling old women's bloomers?"

He stammered: "I ... was looking for Mr Sidge."

"You won't find him in there."

"And...a cricket ball."

"Cricket balls in knickers? You're talking about wrong balls."

Alexander's tongue stuck lame in his mouth. Why does he get into these humiliating situations? With girls. She'll tell Oskar, and he'll add the incident to his arsenal of jibes.

"Have... you...seen Mr Sidge?" He didn't know what else to say.

"He's talking to my daddy down at the farm. Prove to me you're not a poof."

She unbuttoned her blouse, slung it over her shoulders, and presented his eyes with a filled, pink bra embellished by white spots.

A burst of anger more than lusty yearning filled his person, similar to the paroxysm as a little boy when he gave the much stronger, much heavier Manni Czarnikow a bloody nose. All right, he'll swallow his inhibitions, he'll show her. He'll show her and she won't say anything to Oskar.

He clasped her in his arms, pressed his body against her body, his mouth against her mouth, his teeth against her teeth. Bend her backwards like he had seen men do to women on cinema screens.

"You're no poof," she said, breathing heavily, when he released her.

They heard footsteps and men's voices. Josie slipped back into her blouse, Alexander closed the drawer. They left Mr Hozell's room and Alexander locked it. They came across Mr Sidge talking to Mr Storm in the Dining Room.

"There you are," said Mr Storm, "forget about the cricket ball. It's beginning to rain. They decided to call it a draw."

CHAPTER FOURTEEN (1942-43)

Chapels

Two well-trodden paths led out from Riversmead: one downhill, over the Ribble bridge to Sawley, the other along the slopes overlooking the Ribble valley to Grindleton. Both ended in chapels. Both reverberated to boys' footsteps four times every Sunday. One half of Riversmead attended Sawley Chapel in the morning and Grindleton Chapel in the afternoon, the other half did this in reverse. Thus was any rivalry between the two communities nipped in the bud. Credit for paying religious allegiance alike to both villages went to Sister Helen.

The boys were not starved of the Word. However, especially in the early days, the Word was given to them in words which none could understand. Even those who had come with a handful of school English failed to make sense of the sounds emitted by Lancashire lay preachers. To compensate for the unavoidable gospel loss due to language difference, Sister Helen organised readings from German scripture. These were allocated to senior boys during an extra service held in the Dining Hall after the Sunday midday meal.

Not every senior boy possessed the skill of recitation. Schaumberg substituted for the heavy bible text easier flowing lines featuring a continuous stream of made-up nonsense words like isitimblitindl. The English teachers and Sisters sat through the performance without flexing a muscle, resigned to the unavoidable gospel loss due to language difference.

The chapels taught the boys many things including patience and control of giggling attacks. On the whole they coped all right. They watched a speck of spittle in the corner of Mr Gibson's lips progress slowly towards the middle, elongating and compressing like a piece of elastic, to be annihilated by a flick of the tongue between saying verily and verily, and a new speck born in the same corner growing fatter, ready for the journey and eventually expiring in the manner of its predecessor. They were intrigued by Mrs Sloane of Grindleton's sweet shop and her lilac hat, which looked like a sailing ship and behaved like one rocking in rhythm with the owner's total involvement, singing: "Oh hear us when we pray to Thee for those in peril on the sea."

Sometimes the boys failed.

Blutwurst had earned the reputation of out-gassing anybody. Challengers came and went, beaten ignominiously by Blutwurst's impregnable wind machine. On the occasion of Mrs Knowles' week's holidays, the traditional Monday soup was served on Saturday. The concoctions' ingredients of the leftover vegetable mix, boiled down, produced embarrassing effects on ordinary intestines, on Blutwurst's they were catastrophic.

The incident in Sawley Chapel the following morning reminded Anzendrech of his first encounter with Herbert Stubenegke on school opening day in a bygone world. The congregation's faces remained expressionless, Scout Master Wooseley in the pulpit raised neither an eyelid nor a nostril, but thirty-four boys, red faced, tears streaming down their cheeks, coughing and choking with efforts not to giggle, had to be led out by Mr Sidge. For three weeks afterwards Anzendrech did not look at anybody in Sawley Chapel. He was ashamed, for such things were not done in a place where people worship.

Miss Morris

Miss Morris, a young and pretty Methodist researcher in child psychology arrived at Riversmead. She laid out geometric shapes for everybody to rearrange, declared Arne's IQ of 141 the highest in the Home, and postulated that Nabravowitz's undoing was lack of concentration on the exercises engaged upon. It was clear from the outset that Oskar would make no headway with her. Anzendrech indulged in daydreams, that with the blue-eyed Apollo out of the race, he himself might stand a chance.

Around this time Riversmead went through a phase of made-up nonsense words commencing with the syllables 'isi'. The nonsense words fell upon Miss Morris' ears, and the young researcher deduced they were manifestations of deliberate silliness to counteract the trauma of having been torn from family and home.

Long-eared Prefect Blitz asked fat Schaumberg: "You coming?"
"Where?"

"Raiding the larder."

"When?"

"Tonight."

"Isi-pipi," meaning yes.

Blitz laid bare the plan: "There's a trap door in Eulenhaut's dormitory under his bed. The space below is full of pipes, but there's room to crawl along. Blutwurst crawled along."

"He got into the larder?"

"He found another trap door some way off over the larder."

"Isi-poko," meaning well, I never.

"Oskar's coming and Anzendrech and Kleeblatt. We'll send Blutwurst down because he's smaller than us."

"Isi-yapsi.

Equipped with rope and torch borrowed from Scout gear, the party reached the desired trap door. Blutwurst rolled over onto his belly. First his legs, then his stomach, then his chest, then his head disappeared into the dark, square hole, his hands holding onto the edges of the opening. Blitz directed the light beam at the dangling rope. Blutwurst's fist closed round it, and there followed a mighty crash. Schaumberg, who was supposed to have anchored the rope, let go when Blutwurst's full weight came to bear on it. The fallen boy disentangled himself from bean sacks and rope, got onto his feet, squinted into the torch and said: "Idiots!"

"Can you see?"

Blitz directed the light beam onto the shelves along the wall.

"How am I going to get back?"

"Look. Dates. Blutwurst, can you see the dates? D'you want the torch?"

"Isi-yapsi."

Blitz stretched his arm down through the trapdoor, shining the torch into Blutwurst's upturned eyes. Blutwurst reached for it. Blitz thought his accomplice had got it and let go. There was another thump as the torch bounced on the stone floor. All was in darkness.

"I can't see a thing," said Blutwurst.

"Find the light switch," came the reply from above.

Blutwurst groped about, blundered into boxes and sacks, knocked over jars. Then he remembered: "The light switch is outside. In the kitchen."

"Find the torch. See whether you can make it work."

Blutwurst went down on hands and knees, swept the floor area with his palms and felt a thing crawl over his fingers.

"A bedbug," he cried.

"There's no bedbugs in a larder. A spider perhaps," said Schaumberg.

"Or a cockroach," said Kleeblatt.

"Or a scorpion," said Oskar and giggled.

Eventually Blutwurst located the metal artifact. It did not respond to pressure on the switch button.

"Somebody go to the kitchen to switch the light on."

The words had hardly left Blutwurst's lips when the larder was brilliantly illuminated. The boys blinked, they saw Blutwurst on the floor amongst sacks, rolled-over jam jars, dates, raisins, tins of fruit. Silence followed by the crunching noise of a turning key.

"*Isi-Zwetschkenbaum,* isi-prune tree," said Anzendrech.

He and his accomplices withdrew their faces and quickly replaced the trapdoor. Blutwurst remained still as if cast in stone, awaiting in dread the moment when Sister Helen's eyes would meet his.

But it wasn't Sister Helen who slowly pushed the door open. It was Mr Storm and Miss Morris. They were as surprised to see Blutwurst as he was to see them.

"What are you doing here?" Mr Storm wanted to know. He released Miss Morris' hand. She was wearing a colourful dress. She looked very pretty.

"How did you get in?" she asked.

"Have *you* got a key?" queried Mr Storm.

"Have you got shut in?"

"Yes."

Mr Storm nudged his companion, at the same time pointing to the three Inch gap at the badly aligned trap door and said: "I suppose wearing pyjamas and bringing a rope and torch were actions designed to mislead Sister Helen, if coming upon you, into believing you found ingress by other means than getting shut in, for instance by lowering yourself down from the trapdoor?"

Blutwurst looked up at the ceiling and said: "Yes."

"It's Miss Morris' birthday today," said Mr Storm, "come, let's celebrate. We'll treat ourselves to a handful of nuts, and a slice of bread and marmalade each. But not a word to Sister Helen."

"Isi-pipi," said Miss Morris, the birthday girl.

Into the Lion's Mouth

Alexander wondered whether the encounter with Josie Gibson would develop into something resembling permanence.

He viewed the possibility with trepidation. He frowned upon taking up Oskar's cast-off, although holding her close had kindled a sensation craving repetition. Lying awake between his sheets he counted the girls he had cherished, and came to the conclusion that each of his romances had suffered from flawed futility.

"One: Poldi (in the Vienna days): She really did love me, but it was an innocent, different kind of love. And the Danube snatched her away.

Two: Martha Bitmann (in the Vienna days): She liked me enough, but in the hour of need her Aryan eyes turned away.

Three: (Still in the Vienna days) The Girl in the Shimmering Green Costume. The least said the better.

Four: Greti Katherine. Shut up or there'll be tears.

Five: Alwyn of Llwyngwryl: I never spoke to her, never touched her.

Six: Josie Gibson: No. In spite of the itch, I can't see myself shovelling muck in pigsties for the rest of my life.

Seven: Miss Morris: Too late, Mr Storm nabbed her."

These reflections caused him concern. Before acting out his decision to swallow his pride and accompany Oskar into Saturday's Mecca Dance Hall, frequented by Maisy, another of life's complications made its presence felt. Mr. Hozell summoned the prefects and older boys into the Common Room.

"You, who are sixteen and seventeen," he held forth, "must expect to fend for yourselves. There are plenty of interesting careers for you to look at. Get an idea of what you want to do. Talk it over with the teachers and Sisters, or me. Now and then I'll bring job vacancies along, and I'll expect you to take these up if they're suited to you."

Anzendrech talked it over with Mr Foutain.

"You're good at drawing, why not opt for a job in a drawing office."

"What about university?" asked the boy.

Mr Foutain shook his head.

"Bruno's going."

"You haven't got a working father here to push you along and come up with the cash."

So drawing office became his choice.

One senior boy after another raised his hand when Mr. Hozell read from his lists. Malig with cloth merchants in Blackburn, Schaumberg for a Clitheroe garage, Kleeblatt to accountants in London, Blitz for the Cement Works. Anzendrech waited to hear his cue words, but drawing office did not pass the Head Teacher's lips.

Then Mr Townsend of Llwyngwryl Camps visited Riversmead. He brought with him two vacancies in the Birmingham sheet metal works Smyth & Worship. He said the jobs were on the shop floor, which offered the prospect of training to become inspectors. Mr Hozell added, whilst looking hard at Anzendrech, that from inspecting to draughtsmanship required the smallest of small steps.

Anzendrech put his hand up. Oskar did likewise.

And for the two boys the Riversmead epoch came to an end. There was no doubting Sister Helen's sincerity when she shook their hands, saying: "Go into the world, love God and thy neighbour like the Good Samaritan, and the world will love you."

Anzendrech knew that the world will love Oscar Nabrawovitz, Good Samaritan or no, and he envied him.

Sister Frances packed Anzendrech's suitcase, embraced him, gave him a kiss and two half crowns.

Scoutmaster Wooseley said as a farewell motto: "Bee Preepaared."

Mr Wooseley had done his best to plant a sense of upstanding readiness in the boys, but it needed a magic wand rather than a Scout staff to bridge the world of isolated, cotton-woolled, all-provided-for, chapel-going Riversmead in idyllic rural Lancashire to that of coarse Smyth & Worship engaged on war work in rough, industrial Birmingham.

Mr Townsend handed the two young men over to Mr Worship, Director, who passed them on to Mr Johnson, Foreman, who handed them over to Arthur.

Arthur said: "You take this effing tail-pipe, and because it ain't effing round, you eff yourself pushing it over this effing chuck. Then you take this effing hammer and you hammer the effer along the effing weld. This makes the bleeder round, but not effing round enough. So you take this effing mallet and hit at the effing tail-pipe all over until it's effing round all over. Then you put it down next to the other finished effers, so the effing inspectors can effing inspect them. You do effing forty."

That was the expurgated version.

After two hours Anzendrech searched out Arthur to tell him he had done forty. Arthur came up, stared at the neat rows of well-rounded, hammered and malleted tail-pipes, turned to the newly appointed tail-pipe basher to ask whether he was bleeding effing mad. He called over several workmates to divulge to them what had been done. Mr Johnson, the gaffer, loomed up to check on the commotion.

"You do forty effers in an effing day, not in an effing half bleeding hour!" Arthur burst out at last, with more expurgation.

Consensus all round confirmed this requirement. Even Mr Johnson nodded agreement. Red-faced, Anzendrech glanced over at Oskar's pile to see how he had fared. Just six circular-shaped, ten-inch diameter, two-foot long tail-pipes stood by his chuck.

Mr Worship called the foremen to a conference, and as soon as they had shut the door marked 'Office' behind them, the two ex-Riversmead boys were surrounded.

"Are you spies?"

"No."

"Have we ever seen Hitler?"

"No."

"Do you want Germany to win the war?"

"No."

"Do you eat sauerkraut?"

"No. Not now."

"Do you like swimmin'?"

"Yes," answered Anzendrech, and eager to exploit shared enthusiasm for a common pastime, he added: "I've been swimming in the Ribble and in the sea in Lwyngwryl."

Oskar stepped away to demonstrate his dissociation from the retort. The query had been put to elucidate whether they liked "wimin".

"Do you speak bleeding German?"

"Bleeding yes," replied Oskar.

He acclimatised quickly to the conventions of the new environment, including the adoption of the Smyth & Worship vernacular in using just one or two adjectives to add luster to descriptive dialogue.

Several girls wearing faded blue overalls mingled in with the workforce. Eva, very blonde and very red-lipped, had no fixed station in the works. Her job entailed switching on and off motors, filling and emptying coke trays used for heating weird-shaped metal components no one knew what they were for, sweeping away steel shavings and scrap, carrying two-pint tea mugs to the welders, and chatting up everybody she came across in her travel. She selected Alexander as a target for continuous stares, and as this didn't lead anywhere, she switched to bombarding him with hot coke missiles.

Alexander had no wish to add her to his list of failed loves, partly because of a crude drawing captioned by her name on the wall of the Men's. He walked over to her and told her, if she didn't stop, he would clobber her with his tail-pipe mallet.

This non-conformist rebuttal of the temptress Eva sent a bustle down the workshop. Round-shouldered Spitfire-nose spinners told watery-eyed tail-pipe welders, who told finger-thickened fly-press swingers. All considered it a great laughing matter, but one like-minded non-conformist came up to Alexander to say that Eva had done the rounds, and that he needed to be careful.

Then from where, a moment ago, Mr Merriweather had been behind a fly-press, a screech like the dried-out break of a railway truck penetrated Alexander's ears. The man lay on the floor, whimpering, holding up his left hand, the region where palm met wrist thinner than normal and very blue.

Work mates gathered round, Mr Johnson, foreman hurried to the scene, Mr Worship, director, came through the door marked 'Office.' Eva brought a first aid kit and a mug of water.

"It's not that serious," commented Mr Worship, "it's not that serious. Come, Mr Merriweather, I'll drive you to the hospital in my car. Sorry, I can't. I've got an important customer ..."

"I'll take him," said Mr. Harrison of the welding section. "He can sit in the side-car."

Eva offered to go as well, riding pillion on Mr Harrison's motorbike and taking along the first aid box in case Mr. Merriweather fainted on the way.

The dissenting non-conformist turned to Alexander: "They'll be lucky if they get paid for the time they're away, you know."

Dot was a stunner. She brazed brass brackets to the aforementioned weird-shaped metal components, and this necessitated wearing darkened glasses. She pushed them up onto her smooth, velvet brow to look at whoever passed by. Alexander's frequency visiting the Men's, a journey that skirted her coke tray, increased daily. And when she smiled at him - never once allowing him to think that her white teeth could have been flashed at somebody else - he let himself fall in love with her. The snag was that he could think of no conceivable circumstance which would bring him to tell her so.

Then one day she stood next to him in the sticky bun queue. She had something in her eye, and she handed him her handkerchief so he could remove it. To his surprise he heard himself asking her out. They went to the cinema. He walked her home and experienced the urge to do a Josie Gibson repeat. But he only managed a brushing of closed lips whilst his heart pounded as if intent on rounding off a Smyth & Worship tail-pipe.

Next day another wave swept through the workshop when news broke that Alexander Anzendrech had spent all evening with Dot and had done nothing. She became Number Eight on his list.

The quantity of tail-pipes rounded per day stayed at forty even after the pep talk by RAF Officer Fripps who came to applaud Smyth & Worship's contribution to the defeat of Hitler, pointing out that no Spitfire could take off without an aluminium nose spinning fixed to the front of the aircraft, nor without a tail-pipe fitted snugly to the rear of the exhaust system.

The art of prolonging the stay of a tail-pipe on its chuck was to hit at it demurely. Alexander accomplished this by simultaneously bashing, daydreaming, and watching the inspectors emerge from the enigmatic 'Office' door, carrying two metal rings. They pushed one over the pipe, and tried the other but couldn't. This meant a pipe was OK.

He watched Mr Worship pass through the same door on his regular tours. One day, as he came by, Alexander stepped into his path.

"Please, I would like to become an inspector."

Mr Worship's look told Alexander that requests of such a nature were rare. Nevertheless the Director explained that his two, young, healthy, war service-exempted inspectors were looking after all the inspecting needs of Smyth & Worship but that he could, if he wanted to, become a welder.

CHAPTER FIFTEEN (1943-44)

Landladies

Alexander's first bed in Erdington, Birmingham, stood, with four others, in one room of seven others, held together by the crumbling, bedbug friendly plaster of 'The Lime Trees'.

Mr Townsend left him and Oskar there after introducing them to two middle-aged, chain-smoking spinsters, Maggie and Betty, sisters and owners of the establishment. The ruddy glow on their faces reflected either their philanthropic desire to give shelter, breakfast, and dinner at 6 pm sharp to those in need of such essentials, or the prospect of retiring to the Bahamas as soon as cessation of hostilities dried up the lucrative flow of Labour-Exchange-directed teenaged war workers. By way of welcoming the two ex-Riversmeadians, Maggie said if God had intended her to look after Gerries, she should really have been born in Berlin, to which Mr Townsend replied, by way of joke, which fell flat, that if God had intended people to smoke, He would have provided them with chimneys.

Frolic at 'The Lime Trees' leapt to dizzy heights every Sunday by the young guests sneaking into rooms sleeping opposite sexes and upturning the bedding therein, and all, male and female, rushing to chairs and sitting demurely reading books at the first sight of either Maggie or Betty. Alexander's and Oskar's stay lasted until a bombing raid on Coventry, when Maggie told them that they were nothing but bloody Krauts, and would they please vacate the premises.

With the intervention of Mr Townsend's good offices they were permitted to remain under 'The Lime Trees' roof until alternative accommodation could be found. The two Riversmead boys parted company. Alexander's suitcase travelled to Sheldon, to the house of Mr and Mrs. Saxon. After many evenings during which they laughed at "Can I do you now, sir?" Mr Saxon came in late reeking of liquor, switched off the wireless, walked up to his wife and hit her on the head.

Alexander sat motionless, said nothing, but when Mr Saxon lashed out again, he protested: "Don't do that when I'm around."

The head of the household stopped for a moment, looked at the youth with hazy eyes and replied: "Bugger off then."

He grabbed his wife's hair and pulled it about.

"I can't stand idly by and watch this," said Alexander.

"I can't stand idly by and watch this?" Mr Saxon mimicked the accent. "Who are you anyway?"

"I lodge here."

"Not if I can help it, you don't."

The following morning Alexander spoke of his plight to Arthur who came up with a solution. His neighbours, the childless couple Mr. and Mrs. Farquharson living in a two-up, two-down terrace house only five minutes walk from Smith & Worship, were willing to let their spare room. Mrs. Farquharson loved dogs but had none. So she got one from a pound. The canine was prone to lie motionless under the table for hours at a time, then without the hint of a yap, leap from its hiding place onto whosoever sat on the settee, regardless of whether that person drank a cup of tea, or lit a pipe, or picked his or her nose. Mrs. Farquharson took it to the vet who diagnosed a brain tumour. So she brought back another dog. The new animal looked like the twin of the former specimen, more to the point it behaved like its twin. The third dog had a normal brain, but wasn't house-trained, and refused to become so.

After three weeks' harmonious co-habitation the landlady of Alexander's next lodgings burst into his room to confiscate the gadget on which she said he transmitted messages to Germany. He was stroking his chin with a newly-acquired electric shaver. The explanation didn't convince the woman entirely. She came unannounced to check whether the light had been left on, or whether the window was shut, when on subsequent mornings he again needed to attend to growth on his face. In the end, to re-establish tranquillity and since the apparatus didn't do its job properly anyway, he gave it to Joanne who distributed Smith and Worship's wage packets every Thursday. At the same time she collected white elephants for a bazaar to raise funds for, of all things, the National Children's Homes.

A change to luck with landladies happened through Joanne. Her surname was Belfont, but had not been Belfont for very long. Eager to ease the pain of losing a son, she suggested to her new mother-in-law that Alexander Anzendrech fill the gap. His new lodgings, in a fabulous house in leafy Solihull, differed from his previous abodes as a sweet-smelling rose from garlic plants.

Time drew near for the annual week's holiday.

Anzendrech wrote to Kleeblatt in London, explaining that after several months' exposure to Smith & Worship, he longed to hear Lancashire sounds, to sniff Lancashire air, to walk on Lancashire grass, to look out of windows and see a long Lancashire hill, that he was planning to cycle to Riversmead, and would his friend care to join him. Kleeblatt wrote back acclaiming the idea as brilliant. He proposed commencing the trip from Birmingham, that he would tie a Scout Staff to the cross bar for use in emergencies, the one snag: he didn't have a bicycle.

Mrs Belfont's son had one resting on deflated tyres in the garden shed. She said Alexander could borrow it. The bicycle was a very good bicycle, except that it had lost its bell and brakes. Having enrolled as a weekend student for the Higher National Certificate in Mechanical Engineering, fitting replacements presented no difficulty for Alexander. However the front wheel brake cable was too short to reach the control lever below the handgrip. Alexander solved the problem by mounting it half way up the handle bar. There it pointed forward like the sword of a swordfish. It was extremely efficient. A slight pull on it and the RPM of the front wheel slumped instantly to zero.

Three Angels

Kleeblatt arrived and did a test ride. The shiny, new bell rang out loud, the brakes gripped, everything was tip top.

They aimed to complete the tour to Riversmead and back in a grand circle through East Anglia and North Wales. They chose the easy-to-start-with anti-clockwise route, as Kleeblatt's groin had become unused to the contours of a saddle, and his shins to continuous circular exertion. They set off into the level eastern regions.

They reached the area around Kettering. The landscape was flat as predicted, but it contained one depression, and their itinerary led them through it. They freewheeled down the slope. A road sign warned of an S-bend at the bottom. Kleeblatt came up from behind, overtaking Anzendrech who thought his friend would not get round the curve at his speed.

"Brake!" he called over.

Kleeblatt pulled the lever pointing forward like a sword. The front wheel ceased turning, his body left his saddle in the manner of an aircraft launched from an aircraft carrier. His bike somersaulted into Anzendrech's. They both flew through the air towards the ground, Kleeblatt first, Anzendrech on top of him. Anzendrech suffered not one scratch, his friend's leg was cut wide open. He hobbled to the grass verge, sat down and cried for water. Anzendrech ran for help and water. Finding neither in the dip below, he retraced his steps, and as he passed Kleeblatt he sought to cheer sagging spirits by remarking that maybe a Scout troop equipped with sufficient Staffs to make a stretcher, might by chance emerge over the brow from whence they had come. Kleeblatt's customary sense of humour failed to find this funny. He groaned, clutching his foot.

Anzendrech knocked on the first front door facing him. A plump, motherly-looking, slightly greying lady opened. After his first breathless words she was surrounded by her three daughters, aged between seventeen and twenty two. The girls ran out of the house as soon as they grasped the gist of the boy's report.

Kleeblatt did not know what was happening. Had heaven opened and sent down three angels?

Anzendrech was not required during the rescue operation, he had time to reflect: firstly, the Boy Scout Manual needed a footnote pointing to superior alternatives when it came to the use of Scout Staffs vis-à-vis dying men on roadsides, and secondly, that his father's adage 'when a bad thing happens you never know what good might come of it' had substance.

The three sisters fussed over Kleeblatt. They bathed his cuts, dressed his wounds, and bandaged his leg. They held his hand when they removed pieces of road from his gashes, they held his head as he drank from vessels held between their sweet fingers. They stroked his hair. They told him he was brave. They vied with one another to place their cute ears to be nearest his lips when he uttered sound. In vain did Anzendrech attempt to attract attention. They took no notice of him. He was the villain, Kleeblatt the victim.

Anzendrech sat on one functioning bicycle whilst guiding a wrecked one with his right hand alongside him to Kettering station and took the train back to Birmingham. Kleeblatt, after five days convalescence in the house of the three angels returned to London.

Anzendrech added three more names to his list of missed love possibilities.

Pauli

Mrs Belfont said "Now he's married, he doesn't go on many bicycle rides anyway. We'll have it repaired. This letter came for you after you left."

Alexander took the light blue envelope. Light blue? He looked at the postmark. It was intelligible, but began with 'K'. Kettering? Peggy was the youngest, the seventeen year old. Had she, or a sister, written to him? He noticed it had been re-addressed, several times. Well, Kleeblatt had given them an old address. He had done so deliberately, he wants to keep the girls to himself. Especially Peggy, the prettiest. Well, we shall see about that.

He carefully opened the envelope. He would keep it forever. One light blue page inside, at the end, the name Lyn Jones: no address. He read:

'Dear Mr Anzendrech,

At the Dryad factory in Comberton Road, Kidderminster they have some PoW's working, and one is Paul who is your brother.'

Railway tracks led into a covered bay of the Dryad Works. Goods trucks stood haphazardly scattered about, looking forlorn and abandoned. A mountain of sugar beet spilled over a rail. A man in soiled dark green clothing, displaying POW on his back, shovelled mud from one pile onto another pile. Alexander walked up to him and asked, in German, whether he knew Paul Anzendrech, or alternatively Paul Wanzen. The reply came in what sounded like an Eastern Slavonic tongue. At the same tIme the man tapped his watch and raised two fingers, from which Alexander gathered to come back in two hours. This he did. The POW had made visible progress in his labour. He pushed his shovel into the lesser of the two piles, and disappeared into the sombre interior of the bay. Alexander waited, watched the shovel slowly keel over from its upright position to become embedded in watery mess.

The man returned, and behind him marched Pauli.

He also wore a dark green uniform. His face, a little thinner and a little older than when seen last five years ago, supported a smile stretching right across his chin.

"Xandi!" He greeted.

"Pauli."

They fell into one another.

"How did you know I was here, Xandi?"

"I had a letter from Lyn Jones."

"Yes. She works in the office."

"Father and Mother, are they all right?"

"The last news I had is seven months old. Father works on roads and in water-filled trenches. You know with a pickaxe. He's tough. Mother's all right. What's Rudi doing?"

"He's in Burma, fighting with the British Army. He volunteered. He's engaged to Greti Katherine Stubenegke, the sister of my old school friend. She's a refugee as well. You were called up?"

"They put me into forced labour. We had to repair railway lines after air attacks."

"Hey you!" The last two words, yelled from the mouth of a fast approaching British soldier displaying sergeant stripes, sounded extremely angry. "What the hell d'you think you're doing?"

"I'm talking to my brother," said Alexander.

"Get off these premises. You file proper application to the War Office for granting a permit to visit a prisoner-of-war." He turned to Pauli and said: *"Gehen Sie hinein.* Go in."

Alexander wanted to speak to the lady who had sent the letter. He located the works entrance. Lyn Jones, a young girl, sat behind a typewriter, and although indoors, wore a cute, little flat hat on top of dark brown, wavy hair. He thanked her and asked her could she pass to Pauli six chocolate bars which he had brought with him.

"You can meet your brother. Go into the bay. Someone will bring him to you."

"I've already met Pauli, and also the English sergeant who gave me the marching orders."

"Oh," said Lyn Jones, "that's bad news. The camp is only a little way behind the works. They're going back at four. I'll show you, if you wait. You can see your brother across the fence."

He was offered a chair. He sat down and had ample time to study his new acquaintance. She had an interestingly chiselled face, and when she looked up at him from time to time, her lips wanted to give him a smile, but she forced her chin forward to suppress it. He thought she was doing this to hide her slightly prominent, but otherwise beautifully white, top row of teeth.

"If you're wondering why I'm wearing a hat," she said when for the third time she raised her eyes, "I fell when doing sports, and cut my head. The doctor removed some of my hair and stuck on a plaster in place of it."

"Oh. I hope it'll heal soon."

The camp stretched over uneven waste ground. Once again Alexander stood opposite Pauli, but this time separated by eight foot high, heavy gauge wire meshing. The chocolate bars flew over, eagerly watched by one hundred and one dark-green uniformed men, and eagerly gathered up by Pauli, who pushed them into his pocket, when a bellow Alexander had heard before preceded a figure he had seen before.

"Hey you!"

The sergeant was not in a good mood. He ordered Pauli away and turned to Alexander: "If you're not out of sight in ten seconds, and if I ever see you again within a mile of this fence, I'll have you arrested."

Meeting of the Brothers

Two weeks later Rudi was on leave in England. He located Greti Stubenegke's tiny flat in Kilburn, London.

Alexander went to see them, told him he had seen Pauli.

Rudi was for setting off to Kidderminster at once. Alexander mentioned the sergeant's threats and reference to filing proper application to the War Office for granting permits to visit prisoner-of-wars.

"Bull shit," replied Rudi, and said to Greti: "I'll be away for just one day."

They took the train to Kidderminster.

The Boy Scout-like, Australian hat worn by soldiers of the Burma forgotten army instilled instant sympathy everywhere. It acted like wizardry to obtain free bus rides, free cinema visits, free fish and chips, free pints of beer, freedom to dodge rules and regulations. Alexander's fretting that his third appearance would be a vibrant stimulus to the sergeant's wrathful ego, gave way to joy as he watched from some way off Rudi's non-stop flow of words until the sergeant caved in.

So here they were, the three brothers: a British soldier, a PoW, a civilian. They talked, and talked. Pauli told the story of his capture.

His Forced Labour unit Todt was deployed in France on railway repair near the front. American bombers came flying over. The labouring men ran for cover in the goods trucks which had brought them. He and a few others stayed outside. The wagons received direct hits. Those inside perished.

The survivors heard the guns of the advancing army. Everybody in German uniform ran away eastwards. Pauli walked off westwards. He met a gang of French partisans. Knowing French from school he explained the situation and his anti-Nazi stance. They said he could go with them. They took him to a lake where there was a boat. They told him to wait for their return and left him. Getting bored, he rowed out into the lake. After a while he was hailed to come ashore. At the bank American infantry waited for him. Knowing also English from school he explained the situation and his anti-Nazi stance. The Americans wouldn't, couldn't or simply didn't want to differentiate between a German Wehrmacht soldier and a conscript to German forced labour.

"They believed I was making it up," said Pauli, "so three American soldiers jump into the boat and row out to reconnoitre. They get shot at from the opposite bank. One man got hit. The Americans throw their whole armoury at the other side. They blame me for the incident. They say I laid a trap. I told them I wasn't a soldier; I had never handled a gun in my life. Later they handed me over to the British Army."

"You came out of it alive," said Rudi.

"I had luck," said Pauli, "you need it to survive."

"When I was three years old," Rudi reminisced, "Father took me to Vienna's rubbish dump, the *Mistgstettn*, and when he wasn't looking I wandered off into an area overgrown with weeds and shrubs. I couldn't find my way out of the wilderness. I was lost in it; I thought I was the only one left in the world. It remained the most frightening experience until it happened a second time. I got separated from my unit in the Burma jungle. You force your way north, south, east or west, when you stop the new place looks just like the one where you've come from. You could be ten yards from a road or a hundred miles. By chance I stumbled into a clearing and saw people. Their village was a heap of burnt-out cinders: total devastation. We had come across similar scenes before where the villagers didn't know which aircraft had wrought the havoc, where any lone stranger in military battle dress would be a target for their anger. I wanted to tell them that I was a friend, and that I came from a far-away land, but we had no common language. In desperation I signalled by pointing at my chest, whistled, then sang the Blue Danube Waltz: *Donau so blau, so blau, so blau.* And do you know flickers of recognition and smiles crossed their thin, haggard faces. They possessed a wind-up gramophone and one record: The Blue Danube. They brought food."

Pauli continued his story: "I was shipped to Scotland. It rained, and rained and rained. We were cutting turf, soggy, wet turf, in the rain. I didn't like it there, not because of the work, but the camp held a section of Nazi soldiers. They found out I hadn't been in the German army and that I was only half Aryan. They picked on me, threw bedbugs into my bed and did all sort of things. So I asked for a transfer to another camp. So they sent me here. It's better here. I get on well with the other prisoners. And it doesn't rain here all the time."

CHAPTER SIXTEEN (1945)

The Rainbow

Slowing down, pulling away, slowing down. Anzendrech pushed his face towards the window to see whether there was anything interesting out there. The train shuddered to a halt.

"They've got to get the trucks through," explained the man sitting opposite.

"War's all but over," observed another.

Anzendrech's eyes followed the rivulets of rain water on the glass change from vertical streaks to slanting lines as the train, at last, gathered speed. One more hour to Manchester, then change to Clitheroe, then the bus to Grindleton, then walk to Riversmead for the Official Closing Day.

"Can you see a rainbow?" asked a woman passenger.

"No."

"You won't see no rainbow if there's no sun."

"The sun's still there, above the clouds. Our airmen see beautiful rainbows every time there's a downpour."

'They're flying above the clouds to finish off the Nazis,' went through Anzendrech's head, 'like I wanted to do.'

He entered the fairy tale building and mixed quickly with old Riversmead friends.

"Malig was killed in action. Mary's heartbroken."

They were dumbstruck. Presently conversation started again.

"You on leave?"

Oskar forced the ridge of his palm into the valley of his blond wave to produce assured permanence of the undulation on his head. "Embarkation Leave," he explained. "I can't stay long. Vera heard I was coming. She wants to see me. Why aren't you in uniform, Anzendrech?"

"I volunteered for the RAF. Passed A1 They wouldn't take me. They said my work was indispensable for the war effort."

"RAF! You think you're a cut above the rest of us? They'd taken you if you'd gone for the Army."

"My brother's in the Army, Nabrawovitz. They sent him to

Burma."

Eulenhaut, whose hair was still as curly as Oskar's was wavy, asked with rosy lips: "Where's Schaumberg. Didn't he start work on cars in Clitheroe?"

"He didn't get on in the garage, so I got him a job in the cement factory," said long-eared Blitz. "He asked for today off so he could be here, but gallivanted to Blackpool with Maisy instead."

"Maisy, Vera's friend?" queried Anzendrech, remembering the aborted rendezvous between the Scout troop leaders and a girl foursome on the day of the bomb. And Maisy never turned up at the Mecca Dance Hall when he went there with the express intention to nurture her acquaintance before leaving for Birmingham. Now fat Schaumberg's holding her in his arms!

"Vera wanted us to join them in Blackpool," said Oskar.

"You didn't go?"

"A typical Anzendrech question. I wouldn't be here if I'd gone, would I?"

"You'd wish you'd gone when she comes at you, hammer and nails," said Blitz.

"No, I'm only seeing her for old time's sake. There's plenty of fluff waiting for me in Birmingham. D'you remember Dot from Smith and Worship, Anzendrech? You're still at Smith and Worship?"

"Yes. No."

"What's the matter with that man? Yes, no. He doesn't even know where he's working."

"Yes, I remember Dot," said Anzendrech, blushing. "No, I don't work at Smith and Worship any more."

"When I left that place Dot gave me her address. What a hit! Have you got hooked yet, Blitz?"

"Well, we've got engaged last week. She's working in an architect's office now. You never guess who."

"Gladys?" Oskar said, naming the second girl of Vera's foursome that never was.

"Actually, it's Josie Gibson."

They congratulated Blitz, but Anzendrech's throat flipped replicating the act of swallowing a mouthful of sour lemon.

"If the Cement people find out Schaumberg's in Blackpool, they'll give him the sack," said Blitz.

Eulenhaut, who had never forgotten Schaumberg calling him a smelly Jew-boy in the early Riversmead days, ranted: "Just like that fat pig running off with his latest bit of fluff instead of meeting with old pals."

Mr Gebirge came into view. Eulenhaut ducked, and crept away.

"Eulenhaut can't talk much! Have you heard what he did?" Blank looks, so Blitz elucidated: "He's run off with Mrs Gebirge."

"Curly headed, looks-like-a Jew Eulenhaut? You're kidding!"

"They're living together."

"As man and wife?"

"As man and grandmother," Kleeblatt butted in. He supported himself on a walking stick reminiscent of Kettering, but he didn't really need it any more.

"It's true," said Blitz. "They're waiting to get married. And do you know, Eulenhaut walks up to Old Alpenstock, asks him whether he would mind if he, that is Eulenhaut, changes his name to Gebirge, as Mrs Gebirge didn't fancy changing her name to Eulenhaut. She wants to stay Mrs Gebirge."

They registered doubt as to the veracity of the tale, but Blitz swore that he be immersed in a cesspool if it weren't factual.

"And Alpenstock? How did he take it?"

"Mr Gebirge told Eulenhaut to get out of his sight and never show again. Then he went to Sister Helen and said: Sister Helen, I am all alone. My wife has left me. Can I come in?"

"And?"

"He came in."

"Good luck to him."

"The Storms will be here today."

"He married that cute little Miss Morris."

Anzendrech felt a twinge in his groin.

"Are the Sidges coming?" asked Kleeblatt.

"Mr Sidge is in the Army."

Anzendrech said: "Wasn't he a pacifist?"

"Holly gave him an ultimatum," said Oskar, "When she heard I joined up, she gave him an ultimatum. By the way, Anzendrech, my name's not Nabravowitz."

"No?"

"No. It's Oscar. If you'd joined up you'd have known that us with

German sounding handles have to change our names. So if we get captured, we'd not give our origin away. I changed my surname to Oscar."

"My brother changed his name to Arnold."

Blitz turned to Anzendrech: "You're fixed up yet?"

"How d'you mean?"

"He means have you shown Alwyn of Llwyngwryl how to open her legs?" said Oskar.

"You'll never grow up, Nabravowitz," replied Anzendrech.

"Well, have you?" insisted Blitz.

Arne charged up to Anzendrech, interrupting: "They tell me you're working in a drawing office?"

"I am."

"How long have you been working in a drawing office?"

"Two months."

"How did you get in? What do you have to do to get in?"

"I went to the Labour Exchange."

"They gave you a job in the Drawing Office just like that?"

"I told them I was swatting Engineering at Night School, and I wasn't helping the war effort to the best of my ability if I remained a tailpipe welder."

"Anybody heard from Blutwurst?"

"He can't come."

"He's got a job with solicitors in Manchester. He works in a small office with two women. They had an air raid. The women thought there was a gas attack. Blutwurst had been eating Vienna steak with Brussel sprouts."

They laughed.

"Where's Mr Foutain, the Quelle?"

"He's here. Quelled his thirst at The Crown in Grindleton drinking wine with Sister Frances."

Kleeblatt told Anzendrech that Peggy, who had two sisters and lived in the vicinity of Kettering, had been writing to him. He said she was the youngest and the prettiest, and he was going to spend his next holidays in her house.

Staff and visitors mingled in the Dining Hall. Mr Hozell's speech referred to Riversmead boys as English cricketers in the making; he dwelt proudly on the three in British uniform. When observing a minute's silence in memory of Malig, Sister Helen's cheeks were wet. Mr Gebirge stood next to her. He reached for her hand and held it for longer than the tears lasted.

Mrs Knowles brewed tea. The Sisters handed out cups and sandwiches. Several boys asked Sister Helen to say a few words. Still agitated, she was slow in responding which prompted Kleeblatt to whisper: "Quickly now."

When at last she climbed onto on the raised podium the boys went mad with cheering. Her concluding words were "… and let us all live up to the Good Samaritan."

Anzendrech wondered: 'Why do some victims lie in the path of Good Samaritans and others not? Why does injured Kleeblatt attract the attention of three such eager-to-help persons, all young and what's more of female gender, and I not? Are there Good Samaritans who go out of their way to find victims? He became aware that the Reverend W W Shimpton was standing and speaking.

"You have asked me how Riversmead came about. So let me tell you briefly what I know. Riversmead was born in the mind and heart of the Reverend Henry Carter CBE, Secretary of the Welfare Department of the Methodist Church. I was working in a North London area of Jewish population, concerned with Jewish-Christian relations. My interests and activities came to the notice of Henry Carter, and he invited me to assist him in a project he was working on with the Bishop of Chichester to set up a Christian Council for Refugees from Germany and Central Europe, of which, in fact, I became the General Secretary."

The Reverend stopped briefly. He brushed a white handkerchief across his face and went on:

"This was early 1938 when the Jewish persecution and concentration camps in Hitler's Germany were well established, and the flow of refugees to anywhere in the world was increasing. The Nuremberg Laws of 1935 were to exclude Jews from German citizenship; sexual relationships between Jews and Germans were forbidden. Anyone who had one Jewish parent or grandparent was classified non-Aryan and considered to be Jewish even though he or she was brought up as a Christian, and in no sense thought of himself or herself as Jewish. It was the persecuted non-Aryan Christian children that Henry Carter had in mind when he looked for some way of doing something to help."

The boys, now young men, listened in hushed silence.

"We began with the problem of a home. And where in Methodism could we more hopefully turn to than the Principal of the National Children's Homes. He was enthusiastically responsive to the idea. An NCH property near Clitheroe, in fact the one we find ourselves in now, had been recently vacated and was readily adaptable. I remember how the three of us travelled up to inspect this building."

Again the Reverend's pause spoke of his emotional involvement.

"We were delighted with what we saw. Thinking in terms of seventy boys in the eleven to twelve age group, the simplest solution was to look for half from Germany and half from Austria, and concentrate on the two capital cities, Berlin and Vienna where co-operation was readily available. We depended on the Refugee Children's Movement, the international organisation set up in London to take care of children's transport from the countries which were overrun by the Nazis.

And so eventually came the day when we turned up at Liverpool Street Station to meet you and see you safely en route to your new home here in Riversmead.

I have only two personal things to add apart from paying tribute to all the men and women who did so much to make the dream of Henry Carter come true. On the Opening Day, the staff, partly German and partly English, were anxious that we should hear the children sing their first English song. I sat expectantly, waiting for the performance to begin, and was virtually reduced to tears when you sang in broken English:

My bonny lies over the ocean,
My bonny lies over the sea,
My bonny lies over the ocean,
Oh bring back my bonny to me."

The boys, now young men, remembered, and many, including Alexander Anzendrech, unashamedly held their handkerchiefs against their eyes.

"It mattered not that the song was Scottish and not English, and that the bonny for whom it yearned was a prince in exile two hundred years ago. For me the immediate associations were so heart rending that I could only hope that you, who had learned the tune but could hardly have been expected to absorb the full pathos of the words, were not made feel too homesick by the performance in which you clearly took some pride.

Finally, on my way back to London, I vividly remember the train passing through a heavy thunderstorm, and as I looked up from my book and out through the carriage window, I saw a perfect rainbow shining the more brightly in the splendour of its seven blending colours because of the darkness of the storm clouds. It was a symbol of hope and promise, and it was one of the great joys of these past years to see in Riversmead, right up to this Closing Day, that the promise was being fulfilled."

(The Reverend's speech is based on Chapter 2 of the booklet 'Burgeoning Amid The Alien Corn by Audrey O'Dell.)

Anzendrech cleared his throat. One of the boys should say something. Malig would have done it. Nabravowitz, in his uniform? A few words from him would go down well. He was leaving, going to meet Vera.

Anzendrech cleared his throat: "I, on behalf of all the boys who'd come to Riversmead, would like to express gratitude, the sincerest, most heart-felt gratitude to the Reverend, the staff and everybody who had made it possible for us to be saved from the Nazis, and to the British people who are welcoming us to live and work amongst them, as equals. They were, and still are, the Good Samaritans. Thank you."

Lyn Jones

"Dear Lyn,

Remember me? A year ago you wrote to me telling me that my brother Paul was a PoW, working at the Dryan Sugar Factory. I saw you briefly in your office. I am working at Ellingham's in Birmingham, and I joined the Works Sports Club. They are organising a swimming gala for clubs in the Midlands area, and the next event takes place Thursday week at the Sports Ground of the school near the Dryan Factory. I am in Ellingham's swimming team. Although I saw you for only a short while, I have been thinking of you, and I would be greatly honoured if I could see you again. For a little longer, perhaps. I hope the cut on your head has healed, and you don't have to wear a hat all the time.

Yours thinking of you,
Alexander Anzendrech."

He addressed the letter care of Dryan Works, posted it and waited in agony for a reply. None came.

What foolish lines to have written! No wonder she didn't respond. What if he bumped into her accidentally whilst in Kidderminster; how could he show his face?

The day of the contest: he lined up in his swimming trunks behind his team. He was last in the four hundred yards relay. Crowds around the pool: swimmers, officials, onlookers. My God, there she was. Without a hat. Looking about herself.

She saw him, hustled up to him. "There you are."

"Hello. Did you...? Have you...? Are you with...? Are you alone?" Alexander stumbled over his enquiry.

"You wanted to see me. No?"

"Yes. Yes, but you didn't answer my letter."

"How could I? You didn't give me your address."

He remembered he hadn't. "You wrote to me before when you told me about Pauli."

"Well, I hadn't kept it. I couldn't ask your brother because they moved the camp. So I found out about the swimming competition, and came along."

Happiness.

"That's great. I'm sorry I didn't tell you where I live. "I've been thinking of..."

She interrupted: "They're calling for you. You got to go with the others. I'll see you afterwards. Good luck."

Bliss.

Waiting his turn he looked at her looking at him.

His third team mate touched the edge, and Alexander dived in, two yards ahead of the nearest rival. He would have to go all out to maintain the lead. He could not conceivably allow to be overtaken, not with Lyn watching.

Half way down the length he felt as if somebody was touching his backside. The sensation moved down to his upper haunches. It was beginning to impair his movements. He knew what it was. His swimming trunks were slipping down.

Fire engines flashed through his brain. The Engerthstrasse thick with people, all looking at him, naked when he was three years old. Lyn was looking at him now.

Don't think of it, carry on. The trunks were flapping around his knees. To pull them up, or down, out of the way, to interrupt his rhythm for an instant meant loosing distance he could not afford to lose. The cloth was tickling his shins, now it was like a dragnet clinging to his ankles. He must flick the garment over his heels. He saw other heads in the foaming water. He drew in one leg and kicked. One foot was free. Other heads were alongside his.

He touched the finishing rail three inches behind the grasping hand in the neighbouring lane. The race lost. Now he heard the noise.

He wanted to get out, away. All these people. The din. Lyn. Why didn't someone bring him a towel?

He saw her. She was lying on her stomach at the edge of the pool, her right arm, shoulder, neck and half her face immersed in water. She managed to fish out his trunks.

She ran up to him where he stood in the water, his hands clasped over his manhood.

"You'd be happier wearing these, Alexander Anzendrech," she said and gave him a smile without pulling her chin forward.

EPILOGUE

The Thick Black Line

On the occasion of the 50th Riversmead Anniversary Reunion, Alexander Anzendrech spoke the following words:

"My first life began when I was born, my second when a corridor-less, red-upholstered, dusty LMS carriage emptied bewildered boys beneath rain-swept Pendle Hill. The two existences are separated by a thick black line."

Alexander built an imaginary humped back bridge over the black line, so that, when standing on it and looking in both directions, he sees people of two nations. Stripping them of political prejudices and removing social upheavals, he notes small differences compared with the overwhelming similarities, but not forgetting that it is the small difference which makes all the difference.

The English goods truck on railway lines headed the parade of differences which clashed with Alexander's upbringing in Austria; its short wheelbase gave him the impression that it had run adrift from a toy set. Close behind came white bread; on first encounter he mistook it for cake. The shiny, blue packaged milk chocolate bars marched next in line, followed by double-decker trams and double-decker buses. Then there were the trees, or rather their absence in sufficient numbers to constitute a forest. Then the lack of difference between town and country: the same tarmacked surface on moorland roads as on city streets, the prevalence of two-storied dwelling houses, alike in rural valleys as in towns.

Then came many things: brown coloured tea, porridge, free entrance to museums, open fire places, too much rain, single windows, walking on grass in parks, policemen with peculiar head gear and no guns, chapels, lack of awe for men in uniforms, wine gums, the large size of newspapers, a scarcity of eating-out places other than fish and chip shops, fish and chip shops.

Two films per cinema performance, upholstered cinema seats, large cinemas, cinema organs, four traffic lights on a street corner instead of one hanging from overhead wires in the middle of the crossing, school during afternoons, totally enclosed public lavatories, hedges, dogs without muzzles, short summer school holidays, being able to pick books from shelves in free public libraries, no real candles on Christmas trees.

No bilberries, water cress, no mushrooms other than the usual white mushrooms, teachers known as misters, ditto for directors, engineers and university degree holders, fenced-off railway lines, corridor-less railway carriages, railway station platforms the same level as railway carriage floors, the last true even of remote Low Gill Junction, ice cream made with cream, ice cream with few flavours beyond that of the white ice cream which went under the name of vanilla, stone walls, wild ponies, no obsession with very-own-wee-little-places, no coffee to speak of, hot milk in the coffee there was, bicycles without back pedalling brakes.

Little chess playing, no sausages other than the English sausage, sausage rolls, milk delivered to door steps, no sour milk, the weight of steel expended on electricity pylons, the sea and everything that goes with it, Humpty Dumpty, nothing happening on Sundays, no airing of bed linen in windows, free speech, cucumber sandwiches, plates to put them on, bayonet lamp fittings, public tennis courts in parks, bowling greens, pubs opening mornings and evenings only, no food in pubs (1939), no outside letter boxes, Woolworths (pre 2010), freedom to light bonfires, absence of national costumes, absence of national dancing other than Morris Dancing, darts, Guy Fawkes, no May beetles, relatively few beds infested with bedbugs, road signs on every road junction, mince pies, no school satchels carried like rucksacks, HP sauce, no Krampus Day on December 7th, empirical weights and measures: ins, feet, yards; oz, lbs, cwts; d,s, guineas; etc, all as shown to him before his departure from Vienna in June 1939, ball games played everywhere.

Cricket.

The End